Amlin Publishing
Lightning Source Edition 2013

Printed in the United States of America

D1227752

This is a work of fiction.
Seriously. Don't do anything silly.

CHAPTER ONE

In the quiet, just before sleep, Jonathan Blake listened inwardly. The voices were always there, softly erupting in nonsensical gibberish on the far edge of his consciousness, playing a game only they could understand.

But he enjoyed listening.

"Not today I think," said one in his own voice. His voice, but not his thoughts.

"There's no way about." That was a woman's voice. The phrase became clear in the middle, as if tuned in on a radio, but then vanished again.

"Bear those glassages." The pieces of dialogue were always random and foreign, sometimes total nonsense. He couldn't force them to come; they came on their own.

He had begun the nightly ritual of emptying his mind months before in order to break the habit of replaying every horrible, wretched moment of his life while waiting for sleep to come. It wasn't enough to live his stupid life, something inside him wanted to repeat every detail and stew in the misery of it. Perhaps feeling misery was better than feeling nothing at all. He didn't know, and he didn't care. What good was self analysis, anyway? He needed a solution.

He couldn't stay up half the night, every night, browsing the Internet until he collapsed on his bed and blacked out. And no amount of heavy-metal music blaring through his headset would drown out the events of the day. It could, however, drown out the sound of his father fighting with the bartender who fancied herself to be his mom. There was some small relief in that, but Jon needed something to help him sleep.

He had tried drugs, but the horribly unfair penalty for being caught by his self-righteous father had brought that experiment to a quick end—so he had turned to meditation.

"Where is the clock tick tick ticking?" said another voice, not his own. He liked those ones the best, the ones that had a rhythm to them. They soothed him with their inviting patterns and pushed him deeper into the warm dark.

"Come on!" yelled a young child in the hollow distance, far enough away that it blended with the others in both volume and tone.

Many were like this one, recognizable colloquialisms. It seemed that each sentence was merely a snippet of a much larger conversation that some advanced race observing humanity from orbit could tap into, so it made sense that colloquial phrases would be tuned in more often than others, because they would be the most noteworthy element in the conversation, especially if the hearer were not interested in context, but merely choosing the most important phrase based on frequency of use across the spectrum of conversations taking place on the planet.

He knew that, in reality, the voices were probably caused by flashes of electricity in the language centers of his brain, but that didn't stop him from concocting the fanciful theory.

"We could, you know."

"Tell him the bottom of it."

Sometimes it sounded like the voices were communicating with him, but then the next random phrase always assured him this was not the case.

He lay still. Listening. Quieting his mind. Welcoming them.

"He's coming home and he's mad."

"Shut up and drink 'em!" That was a whisper.

"Yes. I'll take *THREE,* please!"

"On the stairs."

"It's lies guns don't."

There was a pause. Then, as clear as if someone had spoken into his ear, a voice said, "Get out of the house, Jon."

His eyes snapped open.

A loud bang came from the living room. He turned an ear to listen. There was a clanging of keys on the end table, and the television came on. His father was home. Had the voices actually predicted it? Were they warning him, or was this another fanciful coincidence made worse by his overactive imagination? He'd probably heard the muffled sound of his father's truck door slamming, and his subconscious mind had added it into his pre-dream.

He rolled out of bed, groped for his jeans and t-shirt, and started sliding them on quietly in the dark. Through the crack in the door he heard the muffled voice of his father's girlfriend, Sandra. "You coming to bed, Ross?"

He imagined her standing in the doorway of the kitchen, in her nightie, oblivious to how wrong it was to walk around scantily clothed with a teenage boy around. It irritated him how she assumed he would just accept her as a mother figure and not see her as an object to lust over. He hated her for the thoughts she made him have.

"What's going on? What's wrong?" she said.

"You tell me." His father's voice was cold and detached.

There would have been an awkward silence, but the sound of David Letterman announcing the top ten list filled the gap.

Eventually she responded. "What do you think I need to tell you?"

"I spoke with Pete," his father's voice growled.

"Pete?" she said snidely.

"Yeah, Pete."

"And he said something about me?"

"Don't give me that."

"I don't know what you think you know, but if it came from Pete..."

Jon peered through the crack into the living room. The flickering light from the television played upon the two figures. His father's face appeared grotesque as the pale light danced across his deep features. "He says the two of you have been shacking up at the motel!"

"What?! That's a lie!"

"Why would he lie about something like that?!"

"He's always wanted to see us break up!"

"And you think it helps that you act like a hooker around him?!" he roared.

"Listen." She softened her voice. "You've been drinking. We can talk about this in the morning. I'll go somewhere and give you time..."

"To where? Pete's?!"

"No! Just somewhere else so you can cool off!"

"I DON'T WANT TO *COOL OFF!*" His father's voice shook the air.

Jon's mind repeated the warning from the voices.

6

"Get out of the house." He stumbled backward toward the window. A stream of expletives poured from his father's mouth as he graphically depicted the details of Sandra's betrayal. With each word the boy's horror increased. Would he kill her? Would he kill them both? He'd never heard his father so filled with venomous rage. With trembling fingers Jon clutched at the bottom of his bedroom window.

"You have to believe me," Sandra pleaded, "I didn't..."

The living room exploded with noise, and Sandra began to scream. Jon pulled at the window, but it wouldn't move. It was locked! His hands shot to the latches, and, with a twist, the locks released. He slid the window up and scrambled out onto the lawn.

The crashing and screaming came to an abrupt stop. Did he knock her unconscious? Was she alive? A wave of guilt washed over him, guilt for being such a coward and not standing up to his father. But how could he? His father had always intimidated him. It wasn't only that he was the size of a football player, and he, himself, was a bean pole. His father had a way about him, an intensity that demanded obedience.

Jon looked through the window at the dim light of the television leaking in from the living room. He listened, but could only hear the sound of peepers coming from the woods behind him, that and the short, shivered breaths escaping his own gaping mouth.

A loud bang exploded with a brilliant flash of light. He fell backward onto the ground, and the window slammed shut. He scrambled to his feet as the neighbors' porch light flicked on, and their dog began barking wildly.

Was that a *shot?* Light from the bedroom window drew his eyes back. His heart constricted with terror as the silhouette of his father's massive body filled the entrance to his room. He dug his feet into the lawn and bolted toward the small strip of woods behind the house. There was a path leading to the school grounds, and beyond that, the city. If he could get there, his father couldn't hurt him.

Branches slapped at his face in the darkness as he searched for the dirt path with his bare feet. The sliver of a moon offered some light, but not enough.

In the distance his father's angry voice cut through the night. *"Jonny!"* He must have come out the back door.

A sharp rock stabbed into the bottom of Jon's foot, nearly dropping him to the ground, but he fought the pain and limped forward onto the path. The rocky, matted soil was better than dead branches and acorns, but still rough on his feet, and it would be slow going in the dark. If his father grabbed the flashlight, he would easily catch up. There was no way he could make it to the school in time.

He quickly picked his way through the brush on the side of the path and started up a nearby tree. Even in the dark he knew this tree. He had climbed it many times to get a view of the city. It was tall enough to escape the beam of his father's flashlight if he could get up through the branches fast enough. He climbed with reckless aggression, relying mostly on memory to find the quickest route to the top.

"JONNY!" His father's voice was louder, and angrier.

A flickering light danced through the trees, and Jon froze, suddenly grateful for choosing black as the primary color for most of the clothing he owned. His heart pounded and lungs burned as he attempted to control the sound of his rapid breathing. The beam of light groped for him, but he shifted just enough to hide most of his body behind the trunk of the tree.

"JONNY!" The rage in his father's voice sent tremors

through his ribs. *"JONNY!"* Hearing his father yell for him in anger was nothing new, but this night the sinister quality was different.

He checked his positioning. Was he high enough to escape the light? Would his father think to look up? His left arm, leg, and bare foot felt exposed as the light grew brighter. He listened to the slow approach of his father's footfalls crunching on twigs as he neared the entrance to the path; with each crunch his terror increased.

Then—a deafening silence as he entered the woods on the matted path. Jon desperately fought the urge to climb higher or shift farther behind the tree; any movement or sound would alert his father. All he could do was hope he had climbed high enough.

He quieted his heart and emptied his mind, seeking the comforting distraction of his voices. In some part of his being, he almost believed he could disappear into that place and be protected from the insanity of his father's wrath. The thought had an immediate calming effect as he hugged the chilled tree trunk. His eyelids slid shut, and his mind easily sank into that familiar place.

A voice whispered, "Did you hear that, boy?" That was the voice of Mr. Dagit, his neighbor.

Another said, "Great! Just great!" far enough away so it blended evenly with the faint volume of the first.

Another floated to the surface: "Be advised, we have a shooting on Oak Street."

His eyes flicked open, and his fingers clawed into the grooves of the tree bark. Those were definitely not random! Those were real! Random electrical misfires in the communication center of the brain don't channel the neighbor talking to his dog or a police officer calling in a shooting. What was happening?

His father passed by on the trail and started running

toward the school. The circle of light burned into the ground in front of him. He never lifted it to check the woods or the tree tops, but pushed on with singleness of purpose. Jon couldn't help but wonder what that purpose was. Could his own father kill him? Until this night he had not thought his father capable of killing anyone.

He watched the light grow smaller until it was just a slivered glow in the distance, then crawled down and ran back up the path to the house. There were things he needed, not the least of which were his shoes.

He burst through the back porch door then through the door to the kitchen as he heard the faint sound of a siren in the distance. He had maybe a minute to grab his things and get out.

His father kept a can of bills and change in the cabinet above the fridge. He grabbed it, ripped the top off, and shoved the bills in his pocket on his way to the living room. Sandra's lifeless body laid in a clump next to the coffee table. Blood flowed across the sloping floor into a pool by the corner.

He had seen enough dead bodies on the Internet and played enough First-Person Shooters to not be immediately repulsed by the sight of blood—but the smell took him by surprise. It was faint, but enough to give the scene a graphic reality no image could. He gagged, and ran to his room.

There was only enough time to grab the essentials: shoes, iPad, jacket, and hamster. He scooped Julius Caesar out of his cage with some bedding and tucked him into his jacket pocket, then zipped him snugly inside.

The sirens were loud now, and Jon could see a flashing glow in the trees beyond his neighbor's house. He ran back through the living room, leapt over the body, and looked through the kitchen window. His father was on his way back; the glow of his flashlight was flickering through the trees. Would he return to the house with the police on the way? He doubted it, but his father was still too close for him to make an exit out the back.

He crossed the living room, snatched his father's keys off the end table, and exited out the front of the house. The police had not yet crested the hill at the end of the road. There was still time. He jumped into the pitch black of his father's pickup and scratched back and forth in the key socket till the key found its mark. With a twist the engine fired. Jon pulled the headlight switch out and looked up. Standing at the corner of the house—was his father, flashlight in one hand, gun in the other. Jon snapped the truck into reverse, the engine revved, and the tires dug into the dirt driveway.

"JONNY!" his father screamed. *"STOP!"* He broke into a dead run.

Jon fumbled for the automatic lock switch as he tore out into the street. His father crashed against the passenger side door and pulled on the handle. It clicked just in time.

"What are you *doing?!* Open the door! Open it right now!"

Jon frantically wiggled the gear lever into drive.

"Open the door, Jon!" His father's frothing face contorted. *"OPEN IT!"*

Jon stabbed the gas pedal and took off, tearing the handle from his father's grip. He expected gun shots, but none came. His father's dark shadow just stood, watching from the end of the driveway, while the flicker of police lights glowed in the dark behind him.

CHAPTER TWO

Jeffery Nord was the first to arrive at the darkened Channel Seven News station. It was no surprise really; he would have set up a cot and lived there if they would have let him. The mainframe computers, to which he was allowed unrestricted access, were infinitely better than the box he had at home.

Only a few corridors were lit on the bottom floor, but there was enough light to get him to the stairwell leading down to his office. He approached the security guard and gave a meek wave.

"Morning, Nerd," said the guard with a friendly smile.

Upon hearing the nickname, his groggy brain felt a spark of life. "Salutations to you, my fine fellow," he said, lifting his coffee mug as he passed.

To anyone else, being called Nerd would have felt derogatory, but not to Jeffery Nord. He remembered fondly when the name had first been attached to him. One of the news reporters had mistakenly called him Nerd, instead of Nord, and rather than correct himself, he'd repeated it. "We need more people like you, Nerd," he said. "More people who can figure things out."

Like a blaze of fire it spread through the station, and soon everyone was calling him Nerd, but not in a mean-spirited way like so many bullies had done from the time he was old enough to carry a book bag. This was different. The cool people weren't teasing him, they were saying: we need someone smart who can figure things out for us—in much the same way Captain Kirk depended upon Spock's analytical genius. Every time they addressed him as Nerd, he was reminded that he was not a misfit or an outcast, but an integral part of the greater collective. *But not a collective like the Borg,* Nerd thought, *something cooler and less creepy.*

Nerd flicked a switch, and his basement office lit up with the green glow of fluorescent lighting. Three of the five monitors on his black desk in the middle of the room grew to full brightness, each displaying a randomly generated picture from his favorites folder.

He took in a sniff of stale air, and a feeling of nostalgia tickled him. He would miss this place. Although he was excited about transferring to New York, and giddy about the kind of equipment he would get to tinker with at a major television station, nothing would ever be quite like his lair in the bowels of Channel Seven.

He set his mug on the table and tapped the enter key on his keyboard. The screen saver disappeared and was replaced with a key code screen. He typed the password and plopped down into his office chair. The speakers beeped, and his eyes were drawn to a flashing green dot which signaled an incoming chat request. He clicked it, and a tiny box came up on the screen. In the box were the words: "It takes you long enough to get downstairs."

The message was from a user named Yellow.

"I'm sorry," he typed, "do I know you?"

The response was a single word, but it was enough. "Canary."

Nerd rolled the name around in his head. *Canary?* His hacker friend? No, friend was too liberal for the likes of Canary. He was more of an asset. In the hacker community, of which they were both a part, Canary was a ghost. Nerd knew no one who had ever spoken with him directly, and Nerd was one of only a few who had a working email for him—untraceable, of course. But Canary rarely answered it. So why was he now contacting him directly? Was it about the trigger housing he had requested information on during the bomb scare six months ago? That was old news.

"To what do I owe the pleasure?" he typed.

"Tell me about David Chance," was the response.

How interesting. Canary was perhaps the most proficient hacker he had ever met, certainly the most notorious. This was a guy who could access information on any person, living or deceased, and tell you intimate details about their dietary needs. What did he want to know about David Chance that he couldn't learn from the FBI or Homeland Security?

"What specifically?" typed Nerd, his heart rate increasing.

"Does he speak to God?"

Nerd wiped his sweaty hands on his corduroys, unsure of whether or not he would answer the question directly. He owed Canary for giving him the lead on the bomb maker; this information was singularly responsible for Karen deciding to take him to New York with her. But why did he want this information about David? It was unlikely to be simple curiosity. The currency of hackers was information, and Canary was a hacker of hackers.

He decided to play it safe and give only what he was sure Canary could find on his own. "Yeah. He gets messages from God."

"Do you think it's really God?"

Was he hoping for a boots-on-the-ground analysis? "Yeah," he typed, "I believe it is." He felt comfortable giving that much. After all, Karen had done more on network television, essentially 'outing' David to the greater Boston area.

"Why?" popped up in the window.

"Why do I believe it is God?" he typed. "Who else would it be?"

Canary ignored the question. "What evedence do you have that it is God?"

Nerd chuckled to himself. Canary was an amazing hacker, but the same could never be said about his spelling. "The messages know the future."

"Do you think only God can know the future?"

That was a good question. He had never thought about it. "I guess only God knows," he responded.

"God isn't the only one who knows."

Nerd ran a hand through his tangled orange hair and blinked at the words on the screen. What was Canary implying? Was there someone else like David?

"What do you mean?" he typed.

After a very long pause, the answer appeared. "Never mind."

"What? You can't stop now."

"I'm aldredy in trouble for helping David. I shoudn't have contacted you."

Nerd's fingers blazed on the keyboard. "Don't go! You contacted me for a reason. Whatever that reason was, it was important enough to take the risk."

After another excruciating pause, a message popped up. "I just don't want anyone to get hurt. No one was going to get hurt, but then everything changed. I couldn't let them kill the presedent."

The *president?* Was he reading that right? Was Canary connected to the people behind the terrorist plot last year? David spoke of a secret organization controlling everything from the shadows, powerful people in high places. His pulse quickened. They were the kind of people who could, at this very moment, be intercepting this communication with Canary. No—Canary was smarter than that.

"I'm going off the grid," said the next message, "but before I do, I need David Chance to know one thing."

Off the grid? What did that mean? Was he on the run? Were the powerful people after him? Nerd swallowed. What had he gotten himself involved in? His breath was labored in his chest. This was bigger than big. This was bigger than colossal. This was like, Kirk-and-Spock-pushing-the-Enterprise's-self-destruct-button big. Just reading the next line of text could put his life in danger, but he was unable to bring himself to shut it down. He waited in suspended animation, locked in a stasis of horror, till the message finally appeared, cold and silent on the screen.

His eyes ran over it several times. What did it mean? More importantly, was it worth risking his life over? It hardly seemed like it, but it obviously meant something to Canary. It was obviously something worth risking his life over.

He read it again and sounded it out in his mind. It said:

"Save Jon Blake."

CHAPTER **THREE**

David Chance twisted the key in the ignition, and the engine made a clicking noise. He tried again with the same results. Yup, it was definitely dead. *Really, car!* he thought, gripping a fistful of his wavy, brown hair. *How much money do I have to dump into you!* He climbed out and slammed the door, and was immediately aware of the scene he was creating. *Simmer down, David. It's not the end of the world.*

A click and a creak caused David to look out from under tightened brows toward his neighbor's house. As no luck would have it, his neighbor, Frank, was standing on his steps, looking in his direction.

Oh that's just perfect.

After last night's conversation with Frank, about letting go of his anger and moving on, this looked real good.

"Everything okay, David?"

"Yeah," he lied, lightening his tone. "The car's acting up again."

Frank bobbed down his steps. "You need a jump or something? I have cables in the back of my truck."

"No. It's not the battery, Frank. I just had one put in it last week. The mechanic said the alternator needed replacing, but I didn't have the money. I was kinda hoping it would last longer than a week."

Frank came up to the other side of the dead car and gave a commiserating shake of his head. "Well then, you need a lift?"

"No, Frank. I need my car to work." David didn't have to explain to Frank what was going on in his head, they had had enough conversations over the last six months about the mysterious messages that could predict the future (and about God's role in it all) to the point of nausea. David felt the price he had paid for following the messages had been too high, and things were only made worse by the fact that he hadn't received a single message since. Not one word.

"You know, God didn't break your car."

"Yeah. I know. I get it. But he hasn't done anything to get me out of this financial black hole I'm in either. Where has he been? Where are the messages now? I did my part, Frank."

"I know, David."

"I risked the lives of everyone I care about following those stupid things, and what did it get me? I know he can speak to me. There's no doubt about that anymore. I was there when he needed me, but where is he now when my car won't start?"

Frank grinned under his mustache. "He sent me."

"Look, Frank. I appreciate all you've done for me, I really do. I'm just tired of being the guy who always needs someone to come and rescue him. I thought it would be different, you know? I thought God would..."

"Would what? Make all your problems go away?"

"No," he growled, "but I expected more than this!"

A voice interrupted them. "Are you two boys fighting again?" David's wife, Sharon, stood holding the door as their daughter Emily and their son Ben filed out of the house with their backpacks on.

"Frank started it," said David, attempting to shift the mood. He didn't want Sharon to see him grumbling again. He had put her through enough.

The kids ran across the lawn and down to the sidewalk. "Bye, Dad," they sang.

"You two be good today and don't give your teachers a hard time."

"Okay," they said in unison.

Their yellow school bus was already making its turn onto the street. He watched as they ran to meet up with their friends gathered in a clump two driveways down.

"It's not that I'm ungrateful," he said to Frank while still staring at his kids. "I'm just tired of struggling."

"Then stop struggling," said Frank. "You're only getting tangled in the net."

Sharon came up behind David, and he turned to include her in the mourning of the automobile.

"I'm guessing the car is broken," she said with a light tone.

"Yeah, it's dead again. I'll need to drop you off at work and take your car."

"You sure I can't give you a lift?" said Frank. "It's no problem."

"I appreciate it Frank, but we're going to handle this one on our own."

A line of teeth appeared under his bushy 'stache. "All right. Call me on my cell if you change your mind."

"Will do," said David with a lift of his chin.

Frank practically danced over to his truck and hopped up inside. That guy was odd. Nothing ever phased him. He was happy to help and happy not to help. He was happy to give advice and happy to keep his mouth shut. David was truly grateful for Frank, but secretly convinced that he was a loon.

Sharon put her hands on David's chest and backed him against the car. "I know what you're thinking behind those gorgeous blue eyes of yours."

19

"Are you sure," he said, wrapping his arms around her, trapping her arms between them, "because I'm thinking something different now."

She slapped his chest. "I know you. You're connecting God to all this."

"And why shouldn't I?" he said.

"God isn't giving anyone else messages about which mechanic to go to or what car to buy. Why should we think he would do it for us?"

"You know it's more than that."

"I know," she said, resting her ear against his shoulder and snuggling in his arms. "But we have to move past this. If you keep waiting for messages to appear, you're going to see disappointment in everything."

He put his cheek in her curly blond hair. It smelled like strawberries. "I'm trying, honey. I'm really trying."

She slid her hands around to the small of his back. "Let's put these messages to rest and just be grateful for what we have."

What we have? he thought. *What about what we've lost?* How would he ever be grateful for that?

CHAPTER FOUR

A whisper woke Jon Blake from a shallow sleep.

"Hey, Jon. You want something to eat?"

In the darkness of the basement, he could barely see his friend Bruce peeking around the oil furnace. He rolled over on the lumpy mattress and spoke in a low voice. "Is your mom still home?"

"She's getting ready in her room, but she'll be out of here in a couple minutes."

"I'll wait. I don't want her to know I'm here."

"Okay," he whispered, "hold tight."

The door opened at the top of the stairs—as if on cue. "Bruce? Are you in the cellar?"

Bruce almost smacked his head on the maze of pipes just above his head. "Yeah!"

"You have your lunch packed?"

"Yeah, Ma. I'm all set."

"Did you brush your teeth?"

"I'm seventeen, Ma! I think I can handle it!"

The light flicked on, and Jon's heart constricted.

"Why are you down there in the dark?" The top stair creaked.

Bruce moved to the bottom of the stairs. "I was just grabbing some socks off the laundry table. I don't need a light to grab socks."

Jon could see her feet starting to come down the stairs. "You'll break your neck coming down here in the dark. It doesn't take any effort to flip a switch, for Pete's sake."

She turned and went back up into the kitchen, and Bruce jogged up after her, closing the door behind him.

Their muffled voices could be heard arguing, then the cellar door opened again. "You go down there in the dark, then you leave the light on when you leave. You want to pay the electric..." The door closed. Jon listened until finally the front door thumped and the clop of high-heels could be heard on the front wooden stairs. Jon fished around in the dark for his shoes and pulled them on.

The light flicked on and Bruce called down, "It's clear. She's gone."

He grabbed Julius from a plastic container near the edge of the mattress, gently placed him back into his jacket pocket, then picked up his iPad and climbed the stairs into the kitchen. Bruce was at the window, looking out into the driveway.

"Do you think she suspects anything?"

"Nah, she's got this thing at work today. She's been talking about it for days."

Jon's shoulders relaxed. He opened the fridge and grabbed a baby carrot from a bag on the second shelf and unzipped his pocket. Whiskers and a wiggling nose popped out. He dangled the carrot over the opening, and two little clawed hands reached up and pulled it down into the dark orifice. That would give Julius something to chew on besides his pocket liner. The little rodent had done a number on the other pocket the night before in the short time it took Jon to ditch his father's truck and get to his friend's house.

"So," said Bruce, "you never did tell me why you're hiding from your dad." He opened the bread box and pulled out a loaf. "Want some toast?"

"Yeah, thanks."

"What do you want on it?"

"Jelly, I guess."

"So what happened? Did he come home drunk and get belligerent on you again?"

"No. This was different," he said. "Worse."

"I'm sorry, man. That sucks."

Jon stared at the back of his friend's fat head, with its fine black jags, and contemplated his choice of words. He would have to tell him at some point. The proverbial Band-Aid had to be pulled off, and it was probably best to pull it quick.

Bruce turned and leaned back against the counter, waiting for the toast to be done.

"My dad murdered Sandra last night."

Bruce's mouth dropped open. "Y- You're kidding. Tell me you're kidding."

"No. He shot her. In our living room. With his Colt."

Bruce bent slightly, as though kicked in the belly. "You must be freaking out, man. Have you gone to the police?"

"No. Not yet."

"Dude, you gotta go to the police!"

"I know, but I don't know if I can face him."

"Who? Your dad?"

"Yeah. They have to be holding him in lockup, and if they think I had something to do with it, they'll probably throw me in there with him."

"Why would they think you had anything to do with it?"

"I don't know!" he said, trying to sort it out in his head. "Maybe they don't, but I don't want to take the chance." He squeezed the edge of the kitchen sink in a grip of death; his whole body tightened. "It's just so *MESSED UP*, man!"

His outburst caused them both to get quiet.

"Maybe this is your chance," said Bruce meekly. "You've been talking about getting out of there. Maybe this is your

23

chance to break free for good."

"What about school?" he said. "What about college? I was already accepted to Brown."

"You can still do that. There's only like four weeks left to the school year. Just stay here till you graduate."

"My dad had a college fund for me. He set it up when my grandfather died. I need that money." He pounded his fist on the counter. "Whatever, man! My dad is a murderer, and I'm standing here talking about college money! Who cares anyway?!"

The phone rang behind Bruce, but he ignored it. He just stood staring with the dopey expression he always had when he didn't know what to say.

Jon eyed the phone. "You gonna get that?"

Bruce's face curdled. "I'm supposed to be at school."

Riiiiinnnngg.

"Are you gonna go?"

He shrugged his round shoulders. "Not if you need me."

Riiiinnnngg.

Jon gritted his teeth. "Well press the button and dump it to the answering machine or something."

"It's done."

BEEEEEEP.

A familiar voice filled the kitchen. "Bruce. Dude, pick up. Are you there?" It was their friend Jared.

"Do you want me to answer?" Bruce hovered a hand over the receiver.

"No. I don't want anyone else pulled into this."

"Bruce," said Jared. "Come on, dude, pick up. Jon was on the news this morning. They say he killed his dad's girlfriend. The police are looking for him."

Bruce's normally yellowish skin turned ashen, and his thin eyes grew round.

"If you see him, stay clear, okay. I'll try your cell phone."

The machine went dead, and in the haunting silence, Bruce's pocket began to buzz.

Jon's eyes locked on the pocket, then lifted to meet the somewhat panicked and accusing stare of his friend. "Seriously, Bruce? Do you think I could *kill* somebody?"

"I didn't think your dad could kill anybody. He like, goes to church and stuff."

Jon pushed off the counter. "Are you *kidding* me? He's a foul-mouthed drunk who was sleeping with a bartender. I'm surprised he didn't catch on fire every time he stepped into that stupid church." He snatched his iPad off the counter. "You know what? Forget it, man. I don't need you."

Bruce's round, Samoan face drooped. "I didn't say I didn't believe you."

"You didn't exactly say you did!"

"If you say you didn't do it, I believe you, dude."

Jon shook his head. "It doesn't matter anyway. I have to get out of here. You're gonna get in trouble just being around me."

"No," said Bruce, "we're in this thing together."

They had been friends since kindergarten, and Jon recognized the look in Bruce's eyes. If he'd made up his mind, there was no talking him off the ledge.

"Are you sure about this?"

His friend pressed his lips tight and nodded. "We'll just go to the police and tell them you're innocent," he said.

"What? No way. I'm not going anywhere near that place till I find out what's going on."

"But you're innocent. The truth will come out."

"Truth," he laughed. "What truth? Their truth? My father's truth?" He placed the iPad down on the kitchen table, slid a chair out and plopped down. "I'm gonna check the local news and see what the story is. I need to

25

get a handle on this."

Within a few seconds the story was sitting on the screen in all its gruesome glory. A photographer had gotten a shot of his dad in the back of a police cruiser, and another of the body being wheeled out on a stretcher. The details were sparse, but there was no missing the fact that his father had blamed the shooting on him.

Jon gripped the tablet. "He really did! He told them *I* did it—that *I* shot Sandra? My own father!" He stared at the screen as if it were crawling with bugs. "Why would he *do* that?"

"I know, it doesn't make sense." Bruce's voice sounded distant.

Jon felt his world collapsing. It was one thing to have a father who killed his girlfriend in a fit of jealous drunken rage, but to blame it on him put into question everything he understood about his father. How could he do something so horrible? How could he betray his own son? There had to be a mistake. There had to be a reason— something he was missing.

He read the headline again and the reality of the situation began to fully sink in. "Look at this headline, Bruce. Police are searching for a young man believed to have murdered his father's girlfriend. Not suspected, *believed*, to have murdered. Not only did my father put the blame on me, the police believed him! *Why?*"

"Maybe he planted something that implicated you."

"Like what?"

"I don't know, maybe the gun."

"My prints aren't on that Colt. That was his precious. He never let anyone touch it, especially me."

"What if there aren't any prints on the gun? What if he wiped it down and wore gloves when he shot it? He could have put it in your room and said you did it."

26

"No, there would still be residue."

"Residue?" said Bruce.

"Yeah. They say when you shoot a gun it leaves residue on your hands and clothes, traces of gunpowder and other chemicals." As he spoke he looked down at the photo of his father in the back of the cruiser. "His shirt is blue," he said, eyes locked on the image. "He wasn't wearing a blue shirt. It was green. I'm sure of it."

"He changed his shirt?"

"Yeah."

"To hide the residue!" said Bruce.

"Maybe there isn't any evidence. Maybe he just covered everything up and blamed it on me."

Bruce shrugged.

"I have to find that shirt," Jon said, "if I'm going to prove I'm innocent."

Bruce scowled. "You won't get anywhere near your house with the cops there. How are you going to find that shirt?"

"I don't know," he said, rising from the table. "But we have to try."

Bruce's oriental eyes became oval again, "We? What? Do you have a rat in your pocket?" He looked down at Jon's pocket. "Okay. So you do have a rat in your pocket, but you know what I mean."

"What was all that stuff about we're in this together?"

"You know—the go-to-the-police-and-turn-yourself-in kind of together." Bruce looked sheepish.

"Whatever. Don't worry about it, man."

"I'm sorry, dude. I'm just not Bonnie and Clyde material."

"That makes two of us," Jon said, starting to pace. "But if I don't do this, they're going to Shawshank me."

"Where do you think he would hide the shirt and the

gun? Maybe we can call someone and have them go over."

"I don't know, but even if I did, I don't want to pull anyone else into this."

"Well you can't go over there and try to sneak in. You'd be better off going directly to the police and telling them your side of the story."

"Yeah. That should go well. I dress in black, paint my nails black, and listen to hard rock. They'll have me stereotyped before I get past the front door. No. I'm gonna work this out. I just need some time to think." His mind drifted back to the mysterious whispers that had warned him to get out of the house.

Maybe they would help him now.

"I'm going to use your bathroom," he said, shifting things somewhat.

"Sure," said Bruce, raising his eyebrows. "You going in there to think?"

"No. I'm going in there to take care of business!" he said with a scowl. "God only knows when I'll have another chance."

He went down the thickly carpeted hall and locked himself into the scented shrine Bruce's mother fancied a bathroom. Everything was covered with carpet, even the toilet seat.

He looked at his lean, muscular frame in the mirror. It wasn't exactly the visage of your comely, law-abiding citizen. Although, if he removed the heavy metal t-shirt, the hair gel that held his hair up fashionably on the sides, the light gauge plugs in his ears, and the black fingernail polish, he could almost pass for a handsome frat boy. But it would take the police all of one minute to see through it. Years of struggle and rebelling against authority had brought him to a place of no return. He was an outcast, and outcasts didn't get the benefit of the doubt. It was up to him to prove his own innocence. He had to make them see him for who he was, not the image in the mirror.

CHAPTER **FIVE**

David Chance scanned through the job listings and took a sip of his coffee. The list seemed to shrink daily, and almost everything was part-time work. How was he supposed to provide for his family on a part-time salary? Putting the whole God thing aside, didn't the city of Boston owe him more than a pizza delivery job? He'd saved it from a fiery death, after all, the least they could do was offer him a decent job. But the television station was downsizing, and his hopes for full-time employment were dwindling with each passing day.

"Don't let Coldfield see you job hunting," said a familiar voice. He looked up to see Karen Knight displaying a perfect set of white teeth, which seemed even more brilliant against her rich tanned skin. She always looked like she was primped for a photo shoot with her bronze hair flowing down in lightly tossed waves, swooping out at the ends as if gravity had no effect on it.

"You're still here, Karen?" he said. "Don't you have a job in New York to go to?"

"I promised I'd work till the end of the month and I'm keeping my word." Her deep chestnut eyes studied his face.

He looked down at the paper. "My job is already on the chopping block so I'm not too worried about what Jim Coldfield thinks."

"First off," Karen said with a scolding finger, "you don't know for sure they're going to can you, and second, I already put in a good word for you. When my team heads out, there'll be four jobs opening up. Jim knows you're a hero. That will play into things."

"If I'm such a hero, why has it been six months and I'm still running coffee errands and making photocopies? I would think, at the very least, they'd have me running cam like Larry, or logging hours in the edit suite."

"Boy! You wish you could run camera like me?" said a rough cowboy voice from the other side of the partition. David looked, but saw no one. Larry Turner was probably working on a computer in one of the other cubicles, no doubt proud of himself for being in the right place at the right time to make his snarky remark and give the illusion that he was ever-present.

Karen ignored him. "Look. The whole industry is taking cutbacks, David. You know that. Internet is killing us. Just be patient. The I.T. Division is growing by leaps and bounds and..."

As she spoke, David's eyes suddenly rested on the word *Tell* at the top of a poster over Karen's shoulder, then shifted to a paper taped to the side of his cubicle. The paper was an announcement that Brad and Karen Knight would be leaving the station for an assignment in New York. His eyes fixated on the word *Karen.*

His breath became shallow. Was it happening again? After six months of silence, was he getting a message? His eyes dropped down to the newspaper on his desk and landed on the word *oak,* then bounced to the word *street.*

Karen's irritated voice yanked him back to reality. "David? Are you listening to me?"

He looked up at her with large, round eyes.

It took a moment, but she was quick to catch on. "Did you see something? A message? What'd it say?"

"Tell Karen Oak Street," he said, his voice distant.

"Oak Street? What's that mean?"

"I don't know. That's it. That's the message."

"Is something going to happen to me on Oak Street? Do I get hit by a car or something?"

His eyes landed on another word at the bottom of a poster for a local court show.

"Innocent," he said, staring blankly.

She tried to see what he was looking at. "Innocent? Who's innocent?"

"I don't know. That's all it says. Tell Karen Oak Street, innocent."

Since announcing his secret to the world, Karen had become David's biggest supporter. She was quick to stand up for him when coworkers teased him, and had gone to bat for him when the FBI investigated his involvement in the bomb scare. Yet he couldn't help but detect the disappointment in her brown eyes, a disappointment that mirrored his own.

Finally the messages had returned, but not with a helpful suggestion on what direction to take with his life, or a lead on a full-time job. Instead, it was probably another cryptic task for him to accomplish—a task, no doubt, with consequences he didn't want to face. He heaved a sigh and looked up at Karen. "What did you expect? That's how they all are. They're always weird and cryptic. I told you that."

"I know." She shrugged. "I was just hoping for more."

"Yeah, me too," he said, trying not to sound too sour. "Well, I'm sure it will please you to hear that there's probably something really *nasty* coming our way—if this is anything like last time. And if we're really lucky, there will be lots of death and mayhem, and you might even get a story out of it."

"You're right," she said brightly, ignoring the

implication of his remark and the condescending nature with which he gave it. "Let's go take a look at the news feed and see if there's anything happening on Oak Street." With that, she took off down the aisle.

Karen's hips swung in rapid rhythm as her shoes thumped on the carpet and her right hand floated to the side, keeping her morning coffee in perfect equilibrium. She was a sight to behold, dressed to the hilt in tight-fitting business wear with a splash of body spray and light layer of makeup to accent her warm Spanish skin. It was her armor in the bull pen, her way of commanding the room which, in her job, was vital. No one could dispute that Karen was the queen of this newsroom, not even resident star and nightly anchor Cindy Coulter.

Karen swerved and entered the computer room. The room was dimly lit by computer screens, and Karen was already sitting in front of one of them when David entered. He watched as her manicured nails clicked furiously on the keys and her eyes scanned. "This looks promising," she said.

David stepped up behind her and leaned over her shoulder.

Breaking news in Milton: Police are on the hunt for seventeen-year-old Jonathan Blake, accused of killing his father's girlfriend, Sandra Pinkerton, at their home on 2661 Oak Street. The father, Ross Patrick Blake, is being held for questioning at the Milton Police Station. Authorities report the weapon used to kill Miss Pinkerton has not been recovered. Jonathan Blake, who goes by Jon, is considered armed and dangerous.

"Could this be the Oak Street we're looking for?"
"Well, we have a kid accused of murder, and the

messages seem to imply that someone is being wrongly accused. Sounds like it."

Karen's phone sounded in her pocket. She rolled her eyes. "This is good timing." She placed it to her ear. "Karen Watson. I mean, Knight."

After the bomb scare six months prior, Karen Watson was a name everyone recognized, even if they'd had their head under a rock. It was the bomb scare that landed her the job in New York, but being the wife of Brad Knight, her long time love interest and fellow reporter at the station, trumped all that. While most public figures would have labored over the name change or opted to keep both names (Karen Watson-Knight), Karen had decided to send a message to her new husband. The message being: we're in this together. There had been a pool set up by some of the staff members on whether or not Karen would keep her professional name. Interestingly, Brad lost $20.

Karen pulled the phone from her ear and stood up. "That was Jim," she said with a smile. "Guess which story he wants me to work on?"

"You're kidding."

"And guess who I'm bringing as my camera man?" she said, breezing past him.

"Larry?"

"No, you!"

"Whoa, slow down. I never said I wanted to follow this message."

She turned and faced him from the doorway. "Why not?"

"You saw what happened last time."

"Yeah, I did. You saved Boston from a nuclear bomb."

"Karen, I'm not... I don't know if I'm the right guy for this."

"You want a full-time position, right?"

"Yeah," he said, squirming in his skin, "but these messages have only one agenda, and that is to put my life, and everyone I care about, in danger."

She put her hands up in front of her. "Okay. Look. If things get dangerous, we'll just stop, all right?"

Would she stop? Did she even have the ability to control her reporter impulse? "Promise me you won't do what you always do and push me in over my head."

She put her hands on her hips. "Do you want a full-time job or not?"

"Yes. I want a full-time job," he said, running it together as if it were one word.

"Then go gear up. I'll start researching the story." With that, she disappeared into the hall.

CHAPTER SIX

Jon Blake sat down, closed his eyes, and attempted to push away the anxiety, the fear, and the toxic blend of flowery smells in the bathroom. He pulled in a deep breath and let it out, pulled in another, held it, and let it out. In order to hear the voices he had to set the proper environment. But his mind wasn't cooperating; it was bent on running through scenarios on how he might get to his house without being seen.

He imagined a wind blowing the thoughts away, and welcomed the quiet emptiness the voices enjoyed playing in. It seemed to take forever, but finally a sheet of familiar darkness pulled over him. He sat quietly in the emptiness. Waiting.

"It can when it's done," said a man's voice. He repeated the words in his mind reflexively, but stopped, knowing it would prevent the others from emerging.

"There's only ONE?!" screamed a voice in the far distance.

"We can help you," said another.

He resisted the urge to answer, for fear the voices would retreat. After a long time a woman's voice said, "Knock knock."

A sharp noise ripped him from his meditation.

"Did you fall in?"

They did it again! The voices predicted what would happen before it happened! Jon sat, mouth hanging open. How creepy was that?

"Jon?" said Bruce again.

"I'm not well," he snarled. "I'll be out when I'm done."

"You want me to get you some prunes?"

"I want you to leave me alone!"

"I'm sorry, dude, but I'm dying out here. This whole thing is freaking me out."

Freaking *him* out? Try hearing voices that know what's gonna happen before it happens!

"I'm just waiting for the truant officer to kick the door in and find me skipping school—and harboring a criminal."

"Please, Bruce! I need time!" As the words left his mouth a voice pushed forward from that place deep inside. "Ring ring," it said.

In the muffled distance, the phone went off. Jon froze. There was no doubt something was communicating with him. But what?

"I'll be right back," said Bruce, only slightly hysterical.

Jon released the tension in his body, took in and released a breath, then posed a question in his mind. *Who are you?*

A short pause. Then a phrase: "Down by the waterhole." It was in a bizarre, country accent. That wasn't an answer, but it felt like a response.

He posed the thought again. *Who are you?*

"Knock knock," said a raspy voice.

Bruce pounded on the door again, jumping him out of his skin. "Are you *kidding* me?!"

"That was Jared again. He's onto us!"

Jon squirmed on the toilet. "What did he say?"

"He said I better call him and tell him what's up or he's gonna rat on us."

"He's bluffing, he knows no one will listen to him."

"Yeah, but what if they *do?*"

"Look. Even if we tell him what's going on, he won't turn us in. He's just saying that because he's nosey. Call him back. Tell him you have the flu—or tell him I'm here, I don't care."

Jon could almost hear the gears turning in Bruce's head, even through the bathroom door. "All right," he said at last. "I'll call him and tell him I'm sick."

Jared could be trusted to keep a secret, but he was also a bumbling fool and prone to sticking his foot in his mouth. If Bruce did decide to confide in him, Jon was reasonably sure he would keep his lips shut. What he wasn't sure of was whether or not Jared would ditch out of school and come to where the action was. It didn't matter. He would be gone soon.

Once again he took in a breath and let it out slowly. His mind emptied almost immediately, and it felt like his consciousness expanded to fill a gymnasium. The feeling took him by surprise, but he gave into it. There was a squelch followed by a voice in static. "Be advised suspect's vehicle was found near..." It trailed off and disappeared. The voices were trying to tell him something. He was sure of it. Had the police found his father's truck? He'd parked it at a convenience store three blocks over. Did they have a list of people he might turn to? If they made the connection, it would lead them straight to Bruce's house.

"Cases and cases of it," said a voice that sounded like his.

"I'm in this thing," said a male voice.

"Bill, bill, bill, birthday surprise," said another in a sing-song rhythm.

His equilibrium shifted, and a phrase formed. It had no voice. "We will help you."

Who? Who are you? he thought.

His consciousness floated in the darkness; his body felt transparent and warm, as if he could let go and slide out into the nothingness that had enveloped him. In the distance there was a buzz, then an answer to his question came as a thought. The thought was not his own.

It said, "We are you."

CHAPTER **SEVEN**

David climbed in the passenger side of the Channel Seven News car and was immediately greeted by Karen's perfume. It had a sweet quality with a hint of spice. His eyes breezed past the slit in her skirt where her bronze leg peeked out. It was hard not to notice how beautiful Karen was, but easy to resist the temptation to gawk; she couldn't have been further from his type: demanding, self-absorbed, career-minded, and devious; the kind of woman only a man like Brad Knight could tame. David didn't care for games. He and Sharon preferred a relationship that was open and honest, they never held anything back. But Karen and Brad seemed to enjoy unraveling each other's secrets as much as they enjoyed chasing down a good story. It certainly made them exciting to watch. It was like having a daytime soap opera on twenty-four, seven. Next to them, he and Sharon probably seemed boring, but that was okay with him. He liked boring.

A loud knock jumped David out of his skin. He twisted around and looked out his window.

Nerd's exasperated face floated just outside the glass. "I need to talk to you!" he screamed.

David rolled the window down. "You scared me half to death, Nerd."

"I'm sorry," he said, gasping for breath, "but I have to talk to you. I've been waiting for you to come in, and you weren't here for very long, and I just found out you were leaving with Karen."

"Take a breath, Nerd. You caught me. I'm not going anywhere."

Nerd sucked in some air. "Do you remember Canary?"

He did. But it was not a name he cared to discuss openly. That name was connected to a secret only Nerd knew, a secret he had kept from the FBI when they had inquired about his involvement in the Boston bomb threat. "I do," he said with a fiery glare, "how about we talk about him later?"

Nerd bent his lean form over and saw Karen in the driver's seat. "Oh. Hey, Karen."

"Hi, Nerd." David heard the smile in her voice. "Don't let me stop you."

Great! David thought. Things weren't already bad enough. He flipped the latch on the door handle. "I need a second with Nerd."

Her hand snatched his forearm. "Are you keeping something from me?"

"Nothing news-worthy," he said. It was a half-truth. It was worthy of news, but only the tabloid kind. After the bomb threat, when police found the body of his best friend Alex Blackstone shot to death on the tarmac of Bangor International Airport, not two hundred yards from where Air Force One had landed, some analysts had suggested that an assassination attempt had been made, that the terrorists intended to set off a real bomb and blow up the president's plane, even though no evidence of a bomb was found. But after late-night talk shows and political humorists had finished with the talking point, no one dared to bring the subject up again for fear of ridicule. It was relegated to the conspiracy theory drawer, and David was happy to let it stay there. Only once did he consider letting the secret out, when it had come to light that he and Alex were childhood friends and the FBI investigation seemed to take on a new life. But Karen had come to his rescue, if you could call it rescue. She made an impressive case to the viewing public that David was getting guidance from supernatural messages. She got witness after witness to sit in front of the camera and make the case so well that it had even become acceptable to say that God might have been the one sending the messages.

"What are you up to, then?" she said, releasing his arm.

"Nothing I care to share."

"David, be straight with me. If Nerd is keeping a secret, you might as well tell me what it is. I can break him in two minutes with a turkey sandwich and a Yahoo."

She was right. Why had he told Nerd about Alex and the assassination attempt? It made sense to tell his wife; he was grieving, and he needed her to understand. But why Nerd? He could have been vague when the topic was brought up. He didn't have to explain where he was when he had gotten Nerd's text message tying Alex to the bomb. Why had he opened his big mouth and spilled it to the one person least able to retain a secret under duress?

"If I let you in on this," he said, pointing a finger, "you can't breathe it to another living soul. Understand? I mean it, Karen."

"I think you know by now that I would never do anything to put you at risk."

David studied her. Could he trust her? She had never betrayed his trust before, even though she'd had several opportunities to do so. And it *was* her reporting that had turned the tables for him on the bomb scare trials. If the FBI had had their way, they would have burned him at the stake like a witch. Not to mention, if there was one person capable of keeping a secret, it was Karen Knight. She bathed in secrets.

David gave her a nod and climbed out of the news car. She came around from the other side. The carport was empty, with only the sound of traffic passing by on the interstate just beyond the concrete wall.

Nerd gave a meek look at Karen, and David addressed it. "It's okay," he said. "You can talk in front of Karen."

Nerd rubbed his puffy, red hair back and made a slight attempt to correct his almost chronic slouch. "Despite what she says, I can keep a secret."

"I know, Nerd. I just think it's time she knew the whole story." God knew she'd find out anyway, at least this way, he would have some say in the matter.

She gave an expectant look at both of them.

"I've told you about everything that happened here in Boston," David began, "but what you don't know is, I travelled to Maine with Alex."

Her eyes grew. She understood the implication of where he was headed.

"Nerd sent me a text message while we were in the car on the way. His hacker friend Canary had connected Alex to one of the bombs. Alex figured out that I was on to him and left me for dead in the woods. When I woke, the messages, ones I had seen earlier, guided me to the hangar at the end of the Bangor runway. And that's where I shot him dead with his own gun."

Shock slid down Karen's face. "You? You killed him?"

As the emotion of what he had done attempted to overtake him, as it had so many times before. He fought to keep his composure. The guilt and the pain felt as fresh as if it had all just happened.

"I knew something was eating at you, but I never imagined. I'm so sorry, David."

"Anyway," he said, hoping the subject would change,

"that's what I've been keeping from you."

She spared him further questioning on the topic of shooting his best friend, and instead posed the question: "If Alex was there to assassinate the president, where's the bomb, or was there a bomb?"

"There was, but someone got to it before the authorities arrived."

"Who?"

"I don't know. They came in a mover's truck in plain clothes. They were probably the same people who employed Alex."

"Why didn't you tell the FBI about this?"

"I don't know, Karen," he said exasperated. "I was scared. I didn't know how deep their connection to the government went. I was worried about my family."

"You were worried that if you told the FBI about them, they would be mad and come after your family? You just stopped what had to be a multi-million-dollar venture. I think they were probably already mad at you."

"I know. I've thought of that every day since. The only thing that gives me any peace is something Alex said to me while we were standing in the woods. He said the bombs in Boston weren't meant to go off. This wasn't a normal terrorist attack. These people aren't necessarily killers."

"Not to burst your safety bubble, but you just said they tried to kill the president and everyone on his plane."

"Yes. But I don't think that's how it was supposed to go down. They were desperate."

Nerd raised his hand up slowly in front of him. Karen and David stopped and looked at him.

"Canary said that."

David cocked his head. "What?"

"Canary said the same thing. No one was supposed to

get hurt."

"And how does Canary know that?"

"He apparently works for them. That's what I wanted to tell you."

"What? Wait a minute, if he's on their side, why did he give you information on Alex and the detonator?"

"I think he did that behind their backs; that's why he's going into hiding."

David didn't know how to process the information. But Karen did. There was an unmistakable fire in her eyes. "You have a source connected to the organization behind the Boston Bomb Scare?"

"This isn't a story, Karen," David said.

Her face scrunched.

"Promise me you won't do anything with this without asking me first."

"Do you know how big this is?"

"Please, Karen." Had he made the wrong call? Was this too big of a scoop for her to pass up?

She bit her lip.

"Canary had a message for you, David," said Nerd, timidly.

"Me?"

"He said, 'Save Jon Blake.'"

Again, David found himself unable to process.

"He's on the news," Nerd said, "I spent the morning looking up information on him. He's..."

David stopped him. "Yeah. We know about Jon Blake. He's on the run for killing his father's girlfriend."

Nerd's forehead lifted and took his brows with it.

"You're a little late. I got a message about him this morning.

"A message? Like *a* message?"

"Yeah. Karen's trying to drag me to his house."

Her face soured.

"That's exciting," said Nerd, with childlike eyes.

"Exciting isn't the word I would use for it." There was a flash of memory. He remembered the kick of the pistol in his hand, and the hollow pop. He remembered his best friend slumped over in the seat of the luggage cart. Guilt and anger waged war inside his chest. Was there no other possible outcome? Did Alex have to die? He squeezed his eyes shut and pushed the images back. "Anyway," he said, "what do you suppose Canary has to do with Jon Blake?"

"He didn't say. He just said save him."

"That was his whole message?"

"Well, he was also curious if your messages really come from God."

"Hmm. That's odd."

"Yeah."

"Did he have anything else helpful?"

"No. We didn't talk long. He said he was going off the grid. I don't think I'll hear from him again for a while. Maybe never."

Karen spoke up. "So, you have no way of contacting him for follow up questions?"

David grimaced. "Karen, please."

She heaved a sigh. "Okay. Then let's all go see what we can dig up at the Blake residence." She gestured to Nerd. "There has to be some story I can use in all this."

Nerd's shoulders sank. "I can't come. Coldfield wants me to train my replacement today."

Karen started around the vehicle. "Then hop on the computer and see if you can learn more about Canary. There's a good chance all this is tied together."

Nerd gave a nod like a bobble head.

David slapped him on the shoulder. "We'll keep you up to speed, okay, bud?"

Nerd's head continued to bob.

David and Karen hopped in the news car, and Karen set the GPS for the home of Jon Blake.

CHAPTER **EIGHT**

Jon looked around the lavishly knickknacked living room. Where had Bruce gone off to? "Bruce?"

"In the kitchen, dude."

Jon passed through into the kitchen and found Bruce sitting at the table with the phone next to him.

"What'd you tell him?" he said, peering out the window at the street.

"I said I was sick, and coughed some."

Jon's brows rose. "Did he buy it?"

"Seriously? I'm like the worst liar in the world."

Jon sat down across from him. "He didn't buy it."

"He said my fake cough was as believable as a kung-fu voice over."

"Great."

"He's coming over." Bruce had an expectant look.

"It doesn't matter," said Jon with a shrug, "I won't be here."

"What? Where you going?"

"I don't know, but I can't stay here."

"Do you have a plan?"

"Not yet, but I'm working on one." His eyes fell on a stack of letters on the kitchen table and his mind whispered, "Bill, bill, bill, birthday surprise." *No,* he thought. *No way.* He picked the stack up and noted the return address for the top envelope. It was from the cable company, definitely a bill.

He slowly lifted his eyes to Bruce. The expression

on his face must have had a mix of crazy in it, because Bruce gave him a double take. "You finally snap from the pressure, or have you come up with a crazy plan I'm going to hate?"

Jon tossed the stack down in front of Bruce. "Pick those up."

Bruce flinched. "O-kay."

"The top one is a bill, right?"

Bruce looked at the address. "Yeah."

"Check the second one. Is that a bill too?"

Bruce slid the top one aside. "Yeah. You're point?"

"The third one is a bill."

Bruce slid the second one aside. "Wow. You're amazing, Jon. What are the chances we would get lots of bills in the mail?"

"Fourth one: birthday surprise."

The third letter fell to the table, revealing the fourth. Bruce gave an incredulous look. "Birthday surprise?"

"Birthday surprise," said Jon with false conviction.

"Sorry, man. It's something from the Army, and it's addressed to my mom. Nice try."

"Open it."

"It's to my mom. She'd kill me."

Jon gritted his teeth. "Open. It."

His friend's lips twisted. "Fine." Bruce ripped the edge off the envelope and pulled the letter out. His eyes scanned down the page; a thick silence filled the room.

Were the voices right? Had they predicted this event? Jon struggled for a breath as he leaned forward on the table. "Well?"

Bruce looked over the top of the letter and his expression said it all.

The voices were right.

Jon's gaze grew intense.

"Okay. Seriously," said Bruce, dropping his hands down on the table and crushing the letter in his grip. "Was this day not weird enough for you?"

"What does it say?"

"It's from the army. It says my dad is coming home three weeks early."

"In time for your birthday."

"Yeah. Just in time." Bruce stared at his friend. "Dude, that's not funny. How did you do that? Did my mom tell you about this? My mom told you, didn't she?"

What was he going to tell him, that voices in his head were predicting the future? Not likely. If he had any credibility with Bruce at the moment, it would all go out the window with one word of voices and predictions. "Yeah," said Jon with a forced laugh, "your mom told me."

Bruce's expression remained the same. "How'd you know this was about my dad coming home? It could have been anything."

Way to go, Jon, he thought. *They probably get letters from the army all the time.* "I guessed," he said with a shrug.

Bruce's eyes narrowed farther. He was obviously not buying it.

"I'm just messing with you, man. Your mom and dad were talking on Facebook the other night and he..." Jon stopped in mid sentence. He ducked down as a police cruiser came to a stop in front of the house.

A distant voice echoed inside his head. "Don't run."

CHAPTER **NINE**

Oak Street was long and straight, with dense pine and poplar trees on both sides. The only sign of habitation was the occasional mailbox. If David tried, he could almost imagine himself somewhere in the back woods of New Hampshire or Maine, but the illusion was broken now and then by a thin or open patch in the trees where he could see the Interstate and suburban sprawl just beyond.

He and Karen didn't speak of Canary or Alex. She left him to his brooding, and he left her to scheme about how she might turn this new information into another national news story.

"Here we go," said Karen. The police roadblock came into view as they rounded the corner. Karen slowed and rolled her window down.

The officer stood stiff on the side of the road. "The road's closed off, ma' am, except for local traffic. You can turn around in that driveway right there," he said, pointing.

"I'm with Channel Seven," she said.

He gave an incredulous look as if to say, *Duh,* I can read the logo on your car. "Ah, yeah. No media is being allowed in at this time."

"I'm Karen Watson," she said strategically. "Captain Jackson said we could get a shot of the outside of the home."

His rigid formality seemed to melt off. "Oh, hey, I didn't

recognize you. I saw you get shot during the story on the dirty bomb! We had the television at the station set to Channel Seven through the entire thing. Good coverage."

Karen shrugged. "We were just doing our job. So do you mind if we grab a quick shot? We won't get in the way."

"Captain Jackson didn't mention you were coming," he said, furrowing his brow.

"I can get him if you like," she said, holding up her phone.

He looked down the road, then back at Karen. "Nah. I believe you. I bet you got lots of friends in high places after covering that nuclear scare."

"A couple," she said, with a sheepish smile.

"Go ahead." He waved to the officer behind the wooden blockade. "Hey! Let them through."

"Thank you, officer, we appreciate the help."

He tipped his hat and resumed his rigid stance as they crept past the roadblock and continued on toward the house.

David looked back over his shoulder. "Good thing you have friends in high places."

"Good thing," she said, looking ahead at the house on the hill.

Off to the right, the trees gave way to an open field. Official vehicles lined the road leading up to the house which, unlike the rest of the houses on the street, sat right on the edge of the road. As they approached they saw activity in the front yard. Karen slowed the car and found a place to park on the left bank. "Grab the camera," she said, hopping out.

As Karen stood on the road surveying the situation, David went to the back of the car and flipped up the hatchback. He slung the camera strap over his head and grabbed the remote mic.

"What are you *doing?!*" shouted a male voice behind him. David craned his neck to see a man, with a large, bushy mustache, wearing brown suit pants and a light green dress shirt, break free of the group that was mulling in front of the house. "Who let you in? Get that camera out of here!" The temperature in his face was clearly visible all the way across the road.

Karen straightened her posture. "We'd like to ask a few questions."

"This is a closed crime scene!" He strutted across the road. A uniformed police officer followed.

"I'm Karen Wat..."

"I know who you are!" He shoved a finger of warning at David. "Put that camera back in the car, son."

Karen stepped in front of him. "Do you mind if I ask who you are?"

"I'm Captain Jackson, and this is my crime scene."

Friends in high places, huh, Karen? David thought to himself as he moved toward the back of the car to put the camera away. She was going to get them both thrown in jail.

"We have a source who says the young man is innocent, could you make a comment on that?"

Captain Jackson looked as though he might pop a vessel in his neck. "Who let you in here?" he growled.

"Please, just a few quick questions. A young man's life is at stake."

Jackson looked at the officer who had taken a position on his right side. "Escort this young lady back to the perimeter and find out who let her in."

The officer gave a nod. "Yes, sir."

"And," he said, looking at Karen, "if I see you on my crime scene again, you'll be doing your next broadcast from county lockup. Do you understand me?" His bushy mustache twitched. David assumed it was in response to a snarl of his lip, but it was impossible to know for sure. The Captain reminded him of his neighbor Frank, only thinner and more angry.

"Captain?!" A man in a blue jacket called out from the group on the lawn. He strode toward them.

The police officer directed Karen and David to get back in the news car.

"Please," said Karen, "we have information that can help you." Her plea fell on deaf ears.

"May I speak with you a moment, Captain?" said the man. He was tall, clean cut, had thick brown hair and striking blue eyes. From the no-nonsense look on his face, David would have guessed he was from the FBI, even if it hadn't said FBI on his jacket.

The police officer held his arms out, blocking Karen. She swatted at him.

David grabbed her arm. "C'mon. We're in enough trouble." This was the side of Karen he didn't care for, the side that felt the world owed her free and uninhibited access. Apparently because she had the title of Reporter, she figured the whole world owed her an explanation. If they weren't willing to give one, well then, they were hiding something from the American public, and in her mind, that was an unpardonable sin.

The FBI agent whispered something to the captain, and the captain's hand rose into the air. "Wait."

Everyone froze.

The agent looked at David. "You're David Chance, right?"

"Yes?" he said.

"I'm Special Agent Collins."

David recognized the name. He'd spent hours at FBI headquarters in Boston in the aftermath of the bomb threats. Agent Collins had been mentioned many times.

"I'm here with Agent Cooper. I believe you two are acquainted."

That was an understatement. Agent Cooper had made several visits to his house, not all friendly, as he tried to piece together David's involvement in the terrorist threat on Boston.

"Yeah," he said, "we're acquainted."

"Are you here because of those messages you claim you see?"

David's pulse quickened. The FBI had made it abundantly clear what their position was regarding his so-called ability. As far as they were concerned, he was in need of psychiatric treatment, treatments they would be more than happy to arrange. In fact, admittance to a psychiatric hospital had been suggested on more than one occasion.

"I'm here," said David, with a glance at Karen, "because my associate likes to stick her nose in places it doesn't belong."

She looked aghast. "You're throwing me under the bus?"

"For lack of something larger," he said, matter of factly.

"Look," she said with wild eyes, wagging a finger at him. "If you want to be a coward and hide your little head in the sand..."

"Enough!" barked the captain. He turned to the agent. "You want 'em, you got 'em, but they're your responsibility! And," he added, "when you're done with them, I want 'em turned over to Officer Shaw so we can figure out where our breach in security is." With that, he turned and stomped back over to the group on the lawn. The uniformed officer followed.

Agent Collins put his hands on his hips and slid his coat

back, revealing his gun and credentials. "What are you doing, David? Aren't you in enough trouble?"

"Apparently not," David muttered.

He came in closer. "I can't say I'm surprised, though. From everything I read, you can't resist these things, can you?" His blue eyes were intense.

He didn't bother to reply.

"Well, you can relax," he said. "You don't know it, but I fought for you at the Bureau."

He remembered hearing something to that effect. Collins had come up from D.C. to debrief the agents involved in the bomb threat, and the day he left, the investigation had simply ceased.

"I looked at the same evidence Coop looked at, and I believe you. Truth be told, Cooper believes you too, but he has to do everything by the book or his superiors will roast him over a fire."

"I thought you were his superior," David said. He certainly looked the part. Under the jacket was a grey three piece suit with stylish striped tie, and his height and posture gave the impression that he was someone in charge.

"No. I work in a specialized agency, slightly higher on the food chain, that's all."

"What agency is that?"

"You wouldn't have heard of it," he said, shifting the topic. "Look. I don't think it's a coincidence that you're here. Weird and paranormal seem to be your thing."

David's mind locked onto the words 'weird and paranormal.'

"I'm just curious what your messages are telling you."

Karen sensed an opportunity and seized it. "Do you need David's help?"

Collins gave a half shrug. "If it will give us some insight

into this case, yes, I would be interested to hear what he has to say."

"How about a trade? David gives you the message, and you let us take a peek inside the house."

David had to give her credit, she knew how to play the game. She never missed an opportunity to leverage her position.

"I'm afraid that's not going to happen. Local law enforcement have jurisdiction here. Even if I wanted to, my hands are tied."

"Then can you at least tell us what's going on?" she said.

Collins acquiesced. "All right. I'll tell you what we know so far, if you'll tell me what you know. Deal?"

They both nodded.

"As you know, this is a murder investigation. The suspect, Ross Blake, came home drunk last night. During an altercation with his girlfriend, he claims to have blacked out. When he came to, his son was exiting out the side window of his bedroom." He pointed toward the right side of the house. "And Mr. Blake's live-in girlfriend, Sandra, was lying dead on the living room floor. Mr. Blake claims to have checked for a pulse and breathing when he heard his son exiting his room. That's when he gave pursuit. He chased his son through the woods. The boy circled back and made his escape in his father's truck. Mr. Blake claims to have reentered the house and, in the shock of the moment, realized his girlfriend's blood was all over him. He began washing his hands in the kitchen sink and that's when authorities arrived on the scene."

Karen said, "Why was the FBI called in?"

"We are here to observe. It is part of a Homeland Security initiative." He put his hand up to stop what was sure to be a flurry of questions. "I told you what I know,

now I want to hear what David knows."

David's eyes flicked between them. "Ah, Karen made more of it than it actually is. I only have one sentence, and it doesn't offer much. The message said, 'Tell Karen Oak Street, innocent.'"

He saw the same disappointed look on Collins that he had seen on Karen.

"I wish I had more to give you."

Collins' response was contemplative. "That's the entire message?"

"Yup," said David, happy to receive his rejection and get going.

"And on that, you came here?"

"Karen looked at the news wire, and this was the only Oak Street she found. When we saw that a young man had been accused of something, we figured this was the place."

"Well, I appreciate your honesty, but as I'm sure you know, we'll need more than that. We need evidence." He shifted his weight backward, as though he intended to move on.

Karen wasn't ready to give up. "There's more to the message," she said.

That pulled Collins back in.

"There's always more. But David needs to get in there to find it. If you can pull some strings and get us in, it's likely you'll get the rest of it."

David started to object, but Collins spoke first. "Do you believe you'll get more if I can get you inside the house?"

The fact that Agent Collins was curious at all about the messages surprised him—but this bordered on bizarre. Was Collins actually willing to put his own reputation on the line to hear the next message?

David let out a nervous breath. "I don't know, maybe. I

don't have any control over it. They come when they want to."

There was a subtle pause as Collins processed the situation. Then, as though a hypnotist had snapped his fingers, he looked at David with a detached professionalism, and said, "I'll see what I can do."

CHAPTER TEN

Bruce cowered in the corner next to the sink, repeating one phrase over and over. "I can't do it. I can't do it. I can't do it..."

Jon crouched in front of him. "Pull yourself together, man!"

"I can't. I'm transparent, like glass. They'll see right through me." Perspiration was forming on his brow.

There was no way he was going to gain his composure before the police came to the door; they had to be halfway up the front walk by now.

Jon clutched his friend by the t-shirt and dragged him across the floor, struggling and crying, around the corner and into the living room. "Just shut up!"

"I don't want to go to jail," he whimpered.

"You won't! Just shut your mouth."

"I don't look good in stripes."

"Bruce!"

He cowered down.

Jon looked at the front door in the kitchen. If the police peeked in they would easily see them. He grabbed Bruce by the legs and pulled him farther into the living room.

"What if they come in?" whispered Bruce.

"Then I'll meet them at the door and turn myself in." It was more likely he would make a run for the back door, but he kept that fact to himself as he lay on the rug next to his shivering friend.

"Why haven't they knocked?" whispered Bruce,

his erratic eyes surveying the room. "Maybe they're surrounding the house."

"Maybe you should keep your mouth shut." Jon spoke low through clenched teeth.

"I'm not good under pressure. I'll probably pass out."

"Be quiet, Bruce, or I'll knock you out myself!"

A muffled squeak caught their attention.

"That's the porch door!" said Bruce in an exasperated breath.

Jon felt something move underneath him and jerked away from it.

"What?! What's the matter?" said Bruce.

Jon let out a breath. "Nothing, it's just Julius," he whispered.

"Not the back porch?" said Bruce in a daze.

"No, ya big baby. I was crushing my hamster."

Bruce looked down at Jon's pocket, and a light came on in his eyes. "Oh thank God!"

They both slipped into a quiet apprehension, listening for the police on the front steps. Jon wanted to peek around the partition and look at the kitchen window, but he didn't dare. "They should have knocked by now," he whispered. "What are they doing?" He got on his hands and knees and crawled through the living room to poke his head up and look out the side window. Through the thin, white curtain he saw the police officers standing on the neighbor's porch. They weren't coming to Bruce's house, they were talking with his neighbor! A wave of relief washed over him, but more than that, a wave of gratitude. If he had made a run for it, they would have seen him and given chase. The voices had saved him again. Whoever, or whatever, they were, it seemed he could trust them.

"Are they circling the house?" said Bruce in quiet

hysteria.

"They're next door. They're not even coming here."

"They're not? Oh thank God!"

Jon twisted around and sat back against the wall. "When they go, I'm outta here. I don't want you in any trouble."

Bruce offered no argument, though the expression on his face gave hint of his inner conflict. He wanted to rise to the occasion and be there for his friend, but there was no denying the stark reality that he was a coward. When it came to matters of espionage or deception, he was perhaps the worst choice ever. To use a playground kickball metaphor: if the CIA lined everyone up against the wall and picked teams, Bruce would be the last chosen, and grudgingly at that. But this wasn't kickball; the stakes were much higher.

For both of them, Jon needed to cut the cord and leave his friend behind.

CHAPTER ELEVEN

Karen leaned against the news car, studying the men scouring the yard and woods across the street. Her thin, tanned fingers slid repetitively down a tuft of silky brown hair she had pulled to the front.

David's brows lifted. "You still with me, Karen?"

She continued to stare absently. "What do you think he meant by paranormal?"

"I don't know." David crossed his arms. "I was wondering that myself."

"I should have asked him when he brought it up."

"Yeah. Why didn't you? I'd think you would jump all over that."

"Do you know what an elevator pitch is, David?"

"Uh—no."

"When you jump in an elevator and realize there is someone in there who can make or break your career. You only have a minute and you don't have the luxury of following every rabbit trail. You get right to the point, make every word count."

"Okay."

"When I realized he had an interest in the message, however small, I knew I had to jump on it."

"Well, it worked."

"It hasn't worked yet."

Agent Collins started back toward them.

"Are you going to ask him about the paranormal thing now?"

"If the opportunity presents itself."

Collins crossed the road and came up to them. "Okay, here's the deal. You have ten minutes but you can't touch anything and you can't report anything. And," he said, looking at Karen apologetically, "you have to stay out here, Miss Watson."

Karen's mouth gaped open.

"I'm sorry," said Collins, "it's the best I could do."

Her mouth snapped shut. "Fine," she said, straightening. "I'll make some calls and see what I can find." She slid her phone out, and it was as if a shield came up. Instead of being left out she turned the tables, and, in an odd sort of way, David felt as if he and Collins were the ones being excluded.

Collins turned and headed toward the house, and David tagged along behind. They passed under the yellow crime-scene tape and entered into the living room. Yellow cards with thick, black letters were placed around the room marking points of interest. An outline where the body had lain was at the entrance to the kitchen. Two men and a woman, probably part of the forensics unit, crouched in various spots examining evidence. Another man was searching the kitchen. What David noticed most, however, was the smell of decomposing blood which was pooled in the corner.

He covered his nose. "How do you get used to that?"

"When you've been to a scene with a cadaver that's been rotting for more than three days, everything smells better," said Collins, stiff faced.

David fought back a dry heave.

The agent stepped to the side. "All right. Do your magic."

Magic? It was hardly magic. With magic, at least David would have some control over the outcome. He scanned the room. Someone in the house had a comic book addiction; mint-condition comics in plastic sheets were displayed on the wall near the ceiling and over the front door. There were plenty of words to choose from. Next to the door was a sign that read: **A Happy Home** *A house is built with walls and beams. A home is build with love and dreams.* On top of the television sat a religious plaque that read: Love is patient. Love is kind. Love never ends.

David watched his step and positioned himself to see all the words at once. His eyes began bouncing from one to the next. Being fairly confident that the message wasn't, "Happy Aquaman dreams kind beams," he gave it a second shot. Word after word strung together in his mind, but he stopped before he got to the end. There were so many pertinent words to chose from: Detective in Detective Comics; Identity, in Identity Crisis; or his favorite, Captain, in Captain Marvel. But nothing made sense. And the familiar confirmation that always accompanied the messages was absent.

He sighed. It was a waste of time to force it. If there was a message here, it would come. He needed to shake off the pressure of Agent Collins' prying eyes (and the noxious smell of the rotting blood), and simply let events unfold as they were meant to. He walked gingerly around the room and found his way back to the front door.

"What do you see?" said Collins, more respectfully than David felt he deserved.

"Nothing, yet. I'm sorry."

"Do you want to try another room?"

David scanned one last time, expecting the same results, but this time his eyes fell on a yellow card with the letter *U* in bold black. His eyes bounced to the next card with an *R*, and to a comic book above the door. The title said: "Close Encounters." David's mind grabbed the word *Close.*

U R Close.

"You getting something?" Collins must have noticed the expression on his face.

David gave an optimistic smile. "It says I'm close."

"To what? The murder weapon?"

David continued to scan the room. His eyes fell on the letter *B* on another yellow card, then bounced to the religious plaque on top of the television, drawing the word *patient.*

"They're saying, 'Be patient.'"

A loud male voice filled the room. "What's he doing here!"

David stumbled backward.

The voice came from a very tall, very muscular uniformed officer standing in the doorway to the kitchen. He held a clipboard in his hand, and had bright sergeant stripes above both biceps.

Collins postured. "I advise you to change your tone, Sergeant."

"This is that nut job who says he's getting messages from God. We're letting terrorists into our crime scenes now?"

"Sergeant, your behavior is inappropriate. This man is authorized to be here. Stand down."

"You don't believe this guy, do you?! He's a con artist."

Collins stepped forward and faced off with the hulk of a man. "Look, Sergeant," he leaned in and read the man's name patch, "Gram. If you have a grievance, bring it to your captain. We're trying to conduct an investigation here."

The sergeant looked down at Collins, his face twisted in disgust. "You believe this nut job, don't you? You know what, I have some advice for you, Agent. You Feds need to keep your nose out of real police work and go chase some flying saucers." He backed away, chest out, eyes on David. "We're not done."

David knew better than to offer a response. It would only inflame the situation, a situation he didn't want to be a part of in the first place.

The man turned and exited out the back of the kitchen. David's body loosened. "Do you ever get the feeling you're not wanted?"

"Don't let him get under your skin. We only have a couple minutes left. Do you see anything else?"

David attempted to scan the room again, but all he could think about was the run-in with the officer—and a possible rematch outside. It felt like high school all over again, only this time the bully had the authority to throw him in jail.

"I'm sorry," he said at last, "nothing is coming to me."

Collins did a less-than-subtle peek out the window, no doubt searching for the belligerent sergeant and calculating their remaining time. "Let's try the kitchen," he said.

The kitchen was small and cluttered, with dishes stacked in the sink. A few cereal boxes sat on the table, and an open bag of bread was in front of the bread box.

David's eyes rested on the word *Wonder,* emblazoned in red across the side of the package, then bounced to the cutting board and pulled the word *wear* from the logo, Stonewear, etched on its surface. The message formed. *Wonder wear?*

"Wonder where?" said David, mostly to himself.

Collins tried to see what he was seeing. "Are you getting something?"

David looked at the table. His eyes jumped from the *Chex* cereal box to a headline on a newspaper sitting in a bin next to a wood stove which read *"Behind* in the Polls" then jumped back to the word *Cap'n,* in Cap'n Crunch.

"Chex behind Cap'n?" he whispered.

"Check behind the captain?" said Collins, already heading toward the back door.

They found the captain standing in the garage, arguing with Sergeant Gram about David's involvement in the Boston Bomb Scare. Judging by the captain's tone, the sergeant was getting his way.

"Get him out of here!" said the sergeant when he saw them enter the garage. "We don't need the assistance of terrorists."

"Is this kind of undisciplined behavior allowed in your department, Captain?" said Collins, facing off with the sergeant again.

"Back down, Sergeant," said the captain.

The sergeant puffed up. "They have no business..."

"Back down!" The captain's shout reverberated off the tools hanging from the walls of the garage. The sergeant slowly moved his bulk away from Collins.

"Look," spat the captain, "you've had your time, now get him out of here."

"We need a couple more minutes, if you don't mind."

"I do mind," he said.

"We have an agreement. Don't forget why you allowed me to bring him in here in the first place."

David didn't think it possible, but the captain's face grew even redder. "I know why I allowed you in here! But you're on borrowed time, Agent. I won't let you undermine this investigation for a little political posturing."

Collins took a step toward the captain. "We all want to get to the bottom of this murder. All I'm asking is for an additional minute of your time."

"Don't trust them, Captain," the sergeant blurted.

The Captain raised his hand. "Not one more word out of you."

Collins passed by the captain and examined the wall behind him. It was covered with metal tools, more than adequate to conceal a handgun from metal detectors. He tapped the paneling behind the tools. It wobbled.

David noticed the sergeant squirming as the agent examined the tool wall. "Collins?" David said under his breath, "I don't mean to stir things up, but the sergeant seems agitated by your actions."

Collins looked at the sergeant. "Really? Is there something you're not telling us, Sergeant?"

His face contorted. "Don't spin this around on me. You know why I'm agitated."

"Are we going to find something hidden behind this paneling?"

"Why? Is that what the terrorist told you? Go ahead, rip it down."

Collins stepped back. "Have you brought the dogs in here, Captain?"

"Not yet. Why?"

"Could we have them check this back wall and see if they smell gunpowder residue. That is, of course, if the sergeant doesn't have a problem with that." He looked over at the sergeant who was clearly beginning to worry about the direction the argument was taking.

"Captain, I'm not hiding anything about this case. If that gun is there, I want to find it just as much as anyone. They're trying to paint this..."

"Go get a dog, Sergeant, and let's start working together on this. If Agent Collins is wasting our time, we'll give him enough rope to hang himself."

The sergeant glared at David. "I hope it's enough rope

to hang them both."

They all cleared out of the garage and in short order Sergeant Gram returned with a police dog and handler. His disposition had not changed. The way he was acting earlier, David would have expected more nervousness in his countenance, but all he could detect was resolve. This officer was bent on proving him to be a fraud, and David was beginning to wonder if he would succeed. He didn't have much to go on; *Chex behind Cap'n* wasn't the clearest of messages.

The K-9 officer guided his German Shepherd through the garage while the rest of the growing assembly of officers watched from the driveway, which now included a grumpy-looking Agent Cooper who had returned from searching the woods in back of the house.

"Why is Chance here?" said Cooper, discretely, to Collins but still loud enough for David to catch.

"I invited him," said Collins, his eyes tracking the dog's behavior.

"He's still under investigation, last time I checked."

"Now is not a good time, Agent Cooper," he said, stiffening his posture.

Cooper backed off.

The officer guided the dog around the wall of the garage and stopped at the back. A command was given and the dog began to sniff around paint cans under the tool bench. He moved to a set of rakes on the side wall, then to a stack of old tires.

David watched the dog's every movement, acutely aware that if the dog failed to detect the murder weapon, the crowd of official men standing around him would quickly become ravenous wolves. There would be no refuge from their wrath.

The dog put his paws up on the tool bench and began

sniffing the top, but nothing caught his attention. He shifted his attention to a pile of junk in the far left corner.

Collins looked at David, and David looked away. When he did, his eyes landed on the name tag of the man next to him. It said, Quick. Recognizing the familiar feeling washing over him, he bounced to another name tag, a man with the last name Kitchen. Quick Kitchen?

Every eye was on the dog, so David took a slow step away from the garage. Collins snapped a look at him.

"I'll be back here," David said, sheepishly.

Collins' eyes squinted, and his lips tightened. "If you make a run for it, I swear I'll shoot you."

"I just need air," said David.

Collins turned back to the garage, and David bolted for the kitchen.

"Hey!" shouted Collins, giving pursuit.

David ran down the stone path behind the house, up the back stairs, through the porch, and into the kitchen. A man in a blue blazer stood frozen in the middle of the room. David's eyes brushed for words even as the pounding of feet stomped through the porch behind him.

He looked at a magazine laying on the table; his eyes landed on the word *Shirt* in the headline. He bounced to the word *in* and finally to the word *Fire* in Fire Sale.

Men filed into the kitchen, and David twisted around. "THE SHIRT'S IN THE FIRE!"

Collins held his arm out. "What?"

David caught his breath. "The shirt's in the fire. I don't know what it means. It's just what I know."

"He threw his shirt in the fire?" Collins looked at the forensic man in the blue blazer. "Did you check the wood stove?"

The man looked shell shocked.

"Did you check it?"

"No," he said, "not yet."

More men pushed into the kitchen behind Collins.

"Well check it!" shouted Collins.

The man opened the door on the wood stove and used the poker to drag through the ashes. He pulled a penlight out and shined it in the center of the ash pile. He stabbed at it again.

David could feel the presence of Agent Cooper moving in behind him. This was a man he had spent the last six months trying to prove his innocence to, a man interested only in facts and evidence. Sadly, when pressured to prove his ability, the messages had been frustratingly sketchy. If this went south, it would make what was already a fragile situation much worse. That was the last thing he needed right now. David lifted a silent prayer. *Please, God, I need this.*

The man from forensics took some large tweezers and reached into the belly of the stove. "Well, what do we have here?" he grunted, slowly pulling a burnt clump from the ashes. "Definitely burnt fabric, most likely cotton, but we'll have to bring it back to the lab to figure out if it came from a shirt."

"All right," said the captain, appearing in the doorway to the living room, "that's enough parlor games for one day. Let's get back to real police work. Agent Collins, Mr. Chance, why don't you accompany me to the front of the house. The rest of you get back to what you were doing before the show began."

There were some groans and a couple grumbles as the group filtered back out onto the porch. More than a few men paused to look in through the window at David as they herded through to the back door. He had not produced the murder weapon, but at least a portion of his integrity was still intact.

Once they reached the front of the house, the captain turned around and addressed Collins. "You got your ten minutes. I expect you to keep your word."

Collins straightened his suit coat. "You've been more than fair. I don't see any reason why we shouldn't proceed with our original agreement."

"As for you," said the captain, turning to David, "good guess on the burned shirt. I'm sure that piece of evidence will prove helpful in the case. But I don't want you anywhere near this case again. You got it? Our job is hard enough without a three-ring circus."

David nodded.

"And, as you could tell from the sergeant's behavior, some of our guys don't exactly like you. They think you had something to do with that dirty bomb scare. A lot of people were put in danger during that whole thing."

"I know," said David.

"They're not exactly happy to have you around. Even if you do have some kind of weird psychic thing, you'll have a hard time changing their opinion about you. So why don't you just go home and keep your nose clean and leave the crime fighting to the men in blue." He adjusted his belt and pointed at Collins. "And I would advise you, Agent, don't get caught up in this man's delusions or you might find your reputation permanently marred." The Captain didn't wait for a reply, but turned and headed toward a group of waiting officers, and one steely-eyed sergeant.

Collins leaned in toward David. "I'd say that went well."

"If being run over by all sixteen wheels of a tractor trailer is considered well, then I'd say it went well too."

He held his hand out. "Thanks for the help."

David shook it. "I wasn't much help, but you're welcome."

Collins gripped David's hand and drew him in slightly. "I'm not authorized to explain, but I want you to know that what you did here today was a great help to our case. I owe you. If you ever need anything, call me at this number." He held out a business card.

"Okay, and anytime you need me to find a small fragment of barely distinguishable cloth, give me a ring."

Collins laughed. "I just might take you up on that."

CHAPTER **TWELVE**

"Hello?" said the gravelly voice on the other side of the line.

Jon Blake gripped the phone in his hand, and cleared his throat. "Pete?"

"Jonny?"

Jon struggled to contain his anger. Pete had been like an uncle to him. He had been to every one of his birthday parties and many other important events of his life. In some ways, he was more of a father to him than his own dad. That made the betrayal worse. Jon hadn't fully realized how deep the wound was until he heard his voice.

"Wow. I don't know what to say, Jonny."

"How *could* you?!" spat Jon. "How could you *do* this to us?"

"Whoa, slow down there, kid, things aren't what they look like."

"Don't lie to me, Pete!"

"You've known me for years, Jonny. Think about it. Have I ever hurt you or your dad?"

Jon was silent.

"Jonny?"

"What are you saying? You didn't do it? You didn't sleep with Sandra and drive my dad to kill her?"

There was a rumble in the phone, then Pete was talking to someone else. "Yeah! Hold on. Just take this one. I have to go out back." Pete worked at a local gas station and it sounded as though he didn't want news of his exploits circulating around the garage. Jon heard the sound of a door slamming, and the background sound became muffled. "Listen, Jonny, this is not what you think. I didn't sleep with Sandra."

"My dad came in screaming you did!"

There was a short silence, then, "Are you alone?"

"I'm at Bruce's house. It's just us."

"What I'm about to tell you, you can't tell anyone. If you do, I'm a dead man. Do you understand me?"

Jon's head was spinning. He expected to give Pete a piece of his mind while he was still in a place where he could make a decent phone call. He didn't see this coming. Could he trust Pete? Was this all a twisted attempt to avoid confrontation?

"Jonny?"

"Yes," he blurted. "I'll keep it a secret. Just tell me what's going on."

"Someone came to me with an envelope full of money and said they wanted your dad and Sandra to break up. When I asked him why, he told me Sandra's a grifter. She rolls men for money."

"Are you *kidding* me? My dad doesn't have any *money!*"

"She was after your grandfather's money, you know, what your dad put into your college fund."

"How would she even know about that?"

"I don't know, Jonny. All I know is, I was holding an envelope full of hundred dollar bills and I thought I would do your dad a favor. I figured he'd go home, they'd have a big fight, and he would kick her out. Then later, after the dust cleared, I would explain what happened and give your dad half the money. I didn't think he'd *kill* her! That's nuts! He's not a murderer! Now I'm freaking out! It just doesn't make any..." Pete was quiet for a moment, then spoke as if to himself. "I think he wanted her murdered."

"Who? My dad?"

"No, the man who paid me. I asked him why he cared if Sandra grifted your dad. You know, because it was a lot of money he was handing me. He said all he was allowed to say was that his client was very wealthy, and that he needed Sandra to think what was happening was real. I asked a few more questions, but he just kept saying his client didn't want to reveal any more; that was why he was paying such a large amount."

Jon let out an exasperated breath. Wh- why did you do it? You know Dad gets crazy when he drinks."

"It's easy to be judgmental after the fact! I didn't know he would kill her!"

Jon couldn't believe what he was hearing.

"I could have turned the money away and gone to your father and told him, but what if it was true? What if she was grifting him? He wouldn't have changed his opinion about her because some stranger was making accusations. She would have taken him for everything and your college fund would be gone."

"You should have given him that option."

"You're right, Jonny. I should have, but I can't change what happened. I'm sorry."

"Are you going to tell the police?"

"They already came and questioned me."

There was a short silence.

"And?"

"I told them I slept with Sandra."

"You what?!" Jon gripped the phone.

"I told them I slept with her but that I never meant for any of this to happen."

"You *lied* to the police?"

"I needed to buy some time and think!"

77

Jon gripped his head in his hands. "Pete, they don't think my dad killed Sandra. They think I did it."

"I know. The police told me, but I knew it wasn't true."

"My own *father* betrayed me."

"I guess neither one of us knew him as well as we thought."

Jon's face tightened—then he shook off the emotion.

"I'm sorry, Jonny, I never meant for it to go down like this."

"Look," Jon spoke low, "if you're asking for forgiveness, you're barking up the wrong tree."

"Well hate me if you want, but we have to work together on this. Someone is behind this, and we need to figure out who."

"You want me to work with *you?* That ain't gonna happen."

"Whether you like it or not, we're in this together."

Jon dug his fingers through his hair and ground his forehead into his palm.

Pete pleaded. "Jonny, we go way back. I know I have my issues, but I've always been a good friend to your father and you. I never should have lied, but we're in this thing now. You have to trust me."

"I can't trust you. You're a liar."

"We're all liars, Jon. I just said the wrong lie for the wrong people."

He had no answer for that.

"I have the money in my pocket. Let me come get you. I don't want the police grabbing you until we have evidence to prove you're innocent."

The pieces swam in Jon's head: his father changing his shirt and hiding the gun; the mysterious rich man and his intentions for Sandra; and Pete, a guy who, up until last night, was a familiar face and a trusted friend. His whole world had been flipped on its ear. But Pete was probably right, maybe they were all being played somehow. Maybe he was as much a victim as his father and himself. If someone with power was behind all this, Jon needed the resources to find out who that was—and at the moment, he didn't even have a vehicle. "I just want to find out who is doing this," he said through clenched teeth. "I'm not okay with what you did."

"Fair enough."

"Can you pick me up at the 7-Eleven on Center?"

"What time?"

"Thirty minutes."

"Okay. I'll tell Ralph I need to take the day off. I'll see you there in thirty."

"All right."

Jon stabbed cancel on the phone and laid it on the counter.

Bruce stood in the corner of the kitchen, peeking out at the road. He looked over his shoulder at Jon. "That sounded heavy."

"Yeah," said Jon, putting his hand in his pocket.

"I only caught pieces, but it sounds like you were expecting the call to go different."

"Yeah."

"You want to talk about it?"

"No," he said, pulling Julius from his pocket. "Can you do something for me?"

Bruce looked at the hamster, taking note of his its matted fur. It was probably urine.

"Can you watch Julius? He's making a mess of my pocket. I need a place for him while I figure this stuff out."

The look on Bruce's face left no doubt that, although he detested the idea, he would do it.

"Thanks, man." Jon cradled the hamster into his friend's

hands. "I won't forget this."

Bruce frowned and held the hamster at arm's length. "The amount you owe me cannot be contained in all the vaults in the world."

Jon gripped his friend's shoulder. "He likes carrots."

CHAPTER **THIRTEEN**

"Good morning, sir," said a stout, female officer standing near the elevator.

"Morning, Captain," said a detective from his desk.

"I put the Grabowski case on your desk," said a suited man passing by.

Captain Jackson addressed each with a nod as he strode down the long aisle to his office. Everything was moving like a well-oiled machine. The worker bees had their assignments, and the pressure to perform was keeping them sufficiently distracted. He watched them all scurrying about their tasks, most of them unaware of their role in the grand scheme, the rest playing the game to climb the ladder. They were all just grease. The wheel bearings of bureaucracy required ample grease—dirty filthy grease. Fortunately, grease was also a lubricant, and, when necessary, quick to allow things to slip through the cracks.

He looked at his secretary, typing furiously on her computer. "I'll be on a private call, Stacy. I don't want to be disturbed."

"Yes, sir." Her eyes held on him for only a moment before returning to the screen.

Captain Jackson stepped into his office, closed the doors, and closed the shades. From his pocket he drew a pair of medical gloves and slid them on his hands. He took the phone receiver and set it on the desk, a button lit red on the phone panel. With his other hand he swooped his dress coat aside, reached back, and pulled a .22 revolver from his waistline. He smiled.

Gunpowder residue, he mused to himself, clings to everything, the hands, the weapon, a shirt, a pair of trousers. There is hardly a place in a police cruiser where residue couldn't be detected by a police dog.

Police dogs have an acute and discriminate sense of smell. If a drug dealer were to hide a pound of weed in a pool of pudding, a police dog would not shrug his shoulders and say, all I smell is pudding. If the dog could speak, he would say, I smell marijuana pudding, and mmm, do I detect a hint of cinnamon?

But police dogs are at the mercy of their training. Though they can detect the smell of gunpowder from a handgun buried in a pile of dung, they must be discriminate. When there are twenty officers standing around with microscopic particles in their clothing, on their hands, and in their hair, the dog and its handler must choose to rule out what are considered known sources of the smell, and seek out the unknown.

He slid his drawer out and twisted the combination lock on the safe inside. It opened with a click. He carefully slid the handgun inside and sealed it in.

The gun and its fingerprints would be found, eventually, but not yet. For now, the boy was on the run, alone, and scared. Besides the mistake of allowing David Chance to poke around, everything was moving forward according to plan. The pieces were in position. It was time to strike.

CHAPTER FOURTEEN

Jon watched the 7-Eleven from the bakery across the street. He tapped the home button on his iPad and checked the time. Pete would be rolling in soon. The thought was both comforting and disconcerting. They had known each other his whole life, and there was a familiarity, even a closeness, but recent events had so distorted Jon's perception that he didn't know what to think. Everything felt strange and unfamiliar. There was no longer anyone in his life he could truly trust. He had always felt alone, but now he felt even more alone, if that were even possible.

Cars came and went, some for fuel, some parking in the spaces in front of the store, some parking along the road. In all cases, the driver of each vehicle got out. All except one, in a dark blue sedan. There was no plate on the front of the car, and the glare on the windshield and the darkened side window prevented Jon from making out the driver. *Probably an unmarked police car,* he thought. He had wondered why they questioned Pete and then left him alone. Now it made sense. They weren't ready to take him in just yet. They needed him—for bait.

There were any number of reasons why he would try to get in contact with Pete. The police must have known that and decided to play a little catch and release. Throw the little fish back to catch the big fish.

Pete's truck came into view. It rolled down the street, passed the blue sedan, then slowly turned into the parking lot of the 7-Eleven and stopped. Pete hopped out and looked around, but did not look in the direction of the blue sedan. Either he didn't know they were watching, or he was purposely avoiding them because he didn't want Jon to realize he knew. It didn't matter. Jon had no intention of meeting Pete with that car there, whether Pete knew about it or not.

He slid his earphones out of his pocket, plugged them into his iPad, and called up his phone app. Time for plan B. Pete's name and number were already cued; he figured something like this might happen. That's why he had come into the bakery. It had free WiFi. With his iPad connected to the Internet, he could call anyone in the country, free of charge. It wasn't as convenient as having a cell phone, but it would get the job done. He tapped the screen and listened for the rings.

Pete stopped and pulled his phone out of his pocket. "Hello?"

"Pete."

"Yeah, where are you?"

Jon spoke discreetly into the microphone hidden in the earbud wire. "You're being watched."

"No, I'm not, I made sure I wasn't followed."

"They arrived before you did."

Pete looked around. "You're kidding. How could they know?"

Jon stared at the car. "I don't know, but there's no way I'm coming over there while they're watching."

Pete continued to look around. He turned toward the bakery. Jon leaned back behind the posters on the window in front of him.

"Well," he said, "maybe we can meet somewhere else."

"What if they have your phone bugged?"

"How would they bug my phone? It's been in my pocket

84

all morning."

"I'm not taking any chances. I'm not going to jail."

"Look, how about you pick a place, and then tell me what it is by telling me when we were there last, or what we did there."

That would require coming up with another location where he could observe from a place with WiFi—but he couldn't think of anything off the top of his head. "I don't know, Pete, I can't..." He stopped.

The sedan was pulling out of it spot, creeping into traffic. Jon hid even farther behind the posters. As it passed, he could see the dark silhouette of the driver, but no features. Had he been wrong? Was it just a random vehicle? The car took a right and pulled around into the side entrance to the 7-Eleven. Jon's stare intensified. "I think the police are coming for you." His voice grew intense. "They probably know it's me on the phone."

"What? Where? The blue car?" said Pete, turning toward it.

"Run, Pete! If they bugged your phone they know all about the money and how you lied to them. Run through the store and out the back!"

The sedan slowed to a stop in front of Pete, and he stepped up to the driver's window. Jon could hear him talking. "I told you fella's everything you wanted to know. Give me a break, will ya?"

Two loud cracks exploded inside the earbuds, and Jon ripped them from his ears. He heard muffled screams as people ran for cover—and immediately their terror became his. Those were not police officers.

He ran to the door of the bakery, but fear kept him from bursting through it. Fear kept him from running across the street. And fear made him crumble into a squat, paralyzed, as the blue sedan peeled out of the parking lot.

Pete's lifeless body lay in a lump. Unable to even look at the rear plates, Jon's body shook with terror, locked in a tight knot.

The old woman who worked the counter called out to him," Are you okay, young man?" She must have been hard of hearing to not have heard the gun shots. Jon's eyes stayed locked on the scene unfolding across the street.

People slowly returned from the cracks they had hidden themselves in, but judging from their expressions, it was too late to help Pete. Whatever wound he had taken was clearly fatal. Those who dared to approach the body were instantly repelled, their faces showing a strange mixture of revulsion and pity. Jon stared in numb disbelief. What was happening to him? His life was shattering into a million tiny shards. Something was going on here, something far bigger than his dad and Sandra.

Behind him, the squeak of the bakery woman's shoes could be heard on the ceramic tiles. "What's going on?" she said.

"Someone shot that man," he said, trying to keep his voice even. He kept the back of his head toward her. He had not seen any television all morning, and for all he knew, his face could have been plastered all over the news.

"Oh God," she said, her voice shaky. "Is he gone? The one who shot him?"

"Yeah," he said. "They drove up the road." Jon rose to his feet slowly, keeping his back to the woman.

"Should we call the police?" she said.

"Um, probably someone already called." He walked briskly to his table and grabbed the iPad, still not turning.

"Are you all right, son?"

Jon looked down at the tablet. "Yeah, I'm okay."

He could feel her eyes boring into the back of his neck.

Did she recognize him? Was she waiting for him to turn around so she could identify him? No. She would have recognized him when he bought the donut. *Get a grip, Jon!*

He lifted the tablet off the table and turned, expecting her suspicious eyes to scan him up and down, but she wasn't even looking at him. Her attention was on the crowd across the street. Her frozen expression and the sirens wailing in the distance hit him like a bucket of water. He had to get out of there! His fear of the assassins was momentarily trumped by the fear of being caught by the police. He pushed past the woman, squeezed out the door, and ran up the sidewalk. As police rounded the corner at the base of the hill, he dropped to a walk and moved toward the alley.

Once in the alley and out of sight, he broke into a sprint. His sneakers slapped on the tar, and his heart burned in his chest and neck. He didn't know where he was running to, or why he was running at all. No one was pursuing him, but he felt pursued. He had to get away. Far away. But where could he go? Who would he turn to? How would he ever claw his way out of this nightmare?

A faint voice spoke through the noise of his heavy breathing. It was a small section of a longer sentence. "...buried by Hunter Brook," it said.

He caught the phrase and repeated it over and over as he ran. He clung to it as though life itself depended on his remembering the cryptic message.

Because, for all he knew, it was quite possible it did.

CHAPTER FIFTEEN

Karen chewed the end of her pen, and stared across the barren surface of her desk at David who was staring at the station's cluttered bulletin board. He started at one end, then walked his way down and back again, for the fourth time. After each pass he paced with the same look of disgust on his face.

"What are you doing?" she said.

"There has to be something here, something I'm missing."

She squinted. "You really are a junkie, aren't you?"

That got his attention. He gave her an irritated look.

"All the way back to the station, you complained about how the messages always leave you hanging, and how you're sick of being a puppet. Yet the first thing you do when you get back is stare at that board looking for more messages."

"What else am I supposed to do?"

"I don't know. It's just funny."

"I'm glad my misery makes you happy."

"Why don't you just do what you can, and let the messages sort themselves out?"

David drove his fist into the bulletin board, sending index cards and tacks flying. He stormed off down the aisle. She watched him depart and chewed a little harder on the end of her pen.

"Are you terrorizing the interns again?"

She smiled when she heard the voice. It was the sound

of her husband, Brad Knight. She could already smell his cologne enveloping her. She looked back over her shoulder and was immediately greeted by the tight fibers of his light-blue dress shirt. She followed the marble-white buttons up to his strong chin, to his beautiful, blue eyes.

"What are you doing here? I thought you'd be home packing for your trip."

"I had a couple of things I wanted to wrap up here before I go, besides, my flight's not till later." He looked across the room. "What's gotten David's undies in a bunch?"

"He's getting messages again and having some post traumatic stress."

He came around and stood in the aisle, sipping on his coffee. "Messages? You still believe all that?"

"You still don't?"

He gave a mischievous smirk. "I never said I didn't believe. I said I was surprised you did. I was also surprised when the rest of the city went right along with you."

"Not everyone."

He took note of the grit in her tone. "Someone giving you flak?"

"Not me. David. You know that man who killed his girlfriend in Milton and blamed it on his son? We were at the crime scene this morning, and there were some serious bad feelings coming from our boys in blue."

"They gave him a hard time?"

"Some of them still believe he's behind the terrorist bomb plot."

"Hmm, so that's why he's frustrated. Should I talk to him?"

"No. I think he just needs some time to work it through.

He has a lot on his mind, you know, with his job here stagnating, and dealing with the loss of his best friend." Her mouth snapped shut.

Her slip of the tongue did not go unnoticed, however. If it had, in a weird way, she would have been disappointed, disappointed in Brad.

He looked at her casually. "Lost his best friend, huh?"

"Yeah. It's been real tough on him," she said, hoping he wouldn't press the issue, but knowing full well he would.

"So—why did he share this best-friend thing with you and no one else? He could have gotten time off from work for that."

She slid her chair back, and stood. "Not everything is a network of secrets and lies, Brad," There was a smolder in her eyes and a pucker in her lips.

They faced off. "Are you withholding information from me?" he said, warming his words to let her know that, in no uncertain terms, he was onto her and looking forward to the game he would have to play to extract the information.

She dragged her nails lightly across the fabric covering his arm as she passed by. "Maybe," she said with a playful tone.

The adversarial reporter relationship was one of the spices of their marriage. Though it was safe to tell Brad that David's best friend was the notorious Alex Blackstone, she would enjoy fending off his attempts to extract the information well into the foreseeable future.

CHAPTER SIXTEEN

When Jon finally stopped running, he was several blocks away from the 7-Eleven in a quiet neighborhood, with no pedestrians and hardly any cars. He leaned his forehead against a black, iron fence, in the covering of a line of bushes, to catch his breath. Sweat ran off his brow and dripped on his forearm. He moved the iPad to the side to protect it and wiped the sweat from his upper lip on his black sleeve.

Now what? he thought. He had no car, not much money, and if it wasn't enough that the police were hunting him, now there were assassins too. Could it be any worse? Jail was starting to look like the only option because he couldn't live in hiding forever. He kicked the dirt and gripped a rung of the fence and shook it violently. "WAS MY LIFE NOT BAD ENOUGH FOR YOU!"

He wasn't sure who he was yelling at, if anyone at all. He might have been yelling at himself. There were so many bad choices he had made. If he had been a different person, a better son, maybe his dad wouldn't have turned into a drunk, maybe his mom would have stayed. If he hadn't been so shy, maybe he wouldn't have isolated himself from almost everyone at school, except two social rejects he could barely call friends. If he was not so weak, he could have run away from it all a year ago and avoided all this. Any life was better than this life. Anywhere was better than here. But now there was nowhere to run. The police in every state would be looking for him. His future had four cement walls and bars for windows, or a bullet.

He slid down to a squat, and his mind slid into a numb empty void where only the word bullet existed. It floated like fog in the midst, as only a word. There was no longer any meaning attached to it. It was a mystery, begging for him to look inside and have its secret revealed. He let it float there, just out of reach. This was an exercise he had perfected, a form of psychological detachment that helped him to relax. With ease he slipped into his bubble of protection, his peaceful void of darkness, quietly panting in the shade of the bushes. But he was not alone.

A phrase materialized in his mind. "Move over a little," it said.

Was it talking to him?

"About ten or so," said another voice.

"It came to telling fifteen," said a third.

These were random; he was sure of it; they had a different feeling to them.

Then a deeper voice said, "We are many."

Jon let the voices play. Each phrase offered hope. Perhaps one might even offer a solution.

"Don took it."

"I left it."

"But you took it."

"Show him."

"Under the sun."

"In plain view."

"Finch, finch, and finch."

"Under the stone of the sun."

"He's coming."

The last phrase made Jon's eyes flick open. *Who's coming?* He pressed his back against the hard rungs of the iron fence and peered through the bushes. A car was approaching. He could hear it but couldn't see the road clear enough to get a glimpse of it. Was it the blue car? Were the voices warning him to run? He gripped the fence and shifted his weight to see out a larger opening. The blue car came into view. Instantly, he felt exposed, as though he had stepped out into a spot light. He recoiled and burrowed farther into the bushes.

Please, please, please, don't see me.

He listened as the engine grew louder. With each passing second his urge to bolt grew. There was no way they could miss him. It was broad daylight, and the bush offered hardly any cover. He had to run. This wasn't like being in the tree at night with his father searching through the darkness. He was a sitting target, in plain view.

The sound of the engine was almost upon him, and his terror escalated to a frenzy. If it reached him, there would be no chance of escape. He had to leap the fence. He had to do it now! But there were spikes on top. Would he make it? It was too late, the car was upon him.

Was it slowing? Did they even have to slow? They could shoot him from the car at that speed. He gritted his teeth and shut his eyes. His only hope was that one shot would hit its mark and end his life instantly. He didn't want to suffer in agony.

Please make it clean!

Jon's eye opened a slit, and he watched the car pass by, almost in slow motion. For the briefest of moments, he was fully visible to the car and its occupants, but it was not the blue sedan from the 7-Eleven. This car did not have the tinted side windows—and he was fairly confident that the other car didn't have a window sign reading, "Baby on Board."

He let out a long breath of relief, but then his mind replayed the phrase that had caused him to leap to the conclusion that his life was in danger. "He's coming." Now it felt flat and hollow. Why would the assassin be coming for him? The police were scouring the area for the blue sedan. It wouldn't be casually trolling the neighborhoods looking for him.

He got to his feet and brushed himself off. Although the last phrase had been random, did that mean the rest of the phrases were random? The voices were telling him to find Hunter Brook; something was buried there, maybe something that could help him. But he had never heard of Hunter Brook.

He grabbed his iPad and slid a finger to unlock it. In the upper left corner a little white dot indicated that the tablet had found a Wifi signal. It was weak, and possibly password protected, but it was worth a try. He activated the maps program, and slowly the map appeared on the screen in chunks.

The signal was enough to get the job done. He typed Hunter Brook into the search—and waited. Finally, a little red pin marked it on the map. It wasn't a brook. It was a street, Hunterbrook Street, and according to the map, it was one street over. If he followed the street he was on, it would bring him to French, which connected to Hunterbrook.

A straighter route, however, would be to climb over the black, iron fence and cross through the Plainview Cemetery that was marked in dark grey on the map. His eyes brushed over the name of the cemetery again. Plainview. The item that was buried wasn't buried in plain view, it was buried in Plainview. He didn't have to go around, he needed to go inside. The thought produced an immediate reaction.

I'm not digging anything up in a cemetery! You gotta be out of your mind! He was desperate, but he would never

94

be that desperate. Besides, he didn't have a shovel. Maybe he didn't need one. Maybe whatever he was meant to dig up was not buried deep.

He followed the black, iron fence and made his way to the entrance to the cemetery. If it did come to the point where the voices led him to dig up a dead body, he would simply refuse and move on from there.

The sign with its curly, metal border and gothic shape had an air of mystery, as though ancient secrets were held in this place of stone, marble, and gently rolling hills. In the daytime it was friendly and inviting, with its oak trees and network of babbling brooks which emptied into a duck pond with lilies, reeds, and grass.

He walked along the meandering, tar path until a large, marble stone with the name FINCH caught his eye. Next to it was a smaller stone that also had the name FINCH, and beside that one was a small, flat stone that said Finch. "Finch, finch, and finch," he said in his mind.

He read the names: Charles, Martha, and Thomas. Father, mother, and son. It was buried under the son!

He crouched down and looked at the small, thin stone. Was there something buried under it? He could probably lift it easily enough. His eyes snapped up and looked around as the thought hit him. There was a family several rows over, and a women taking flowers from her car six rows back. He'd seen the groundskeeper drive his electric cart to the main building a few minutes ago so he was probably still inside.

He slid his fingers behind the back edge of the stone and pulled. It was heavier than it looked, but it lifted. He checked again to see if anyone was looking in his direction, then pulled as hard as he could and flipped the stone onto its face, revealing a dark patch of moist earth and a long brown worm.

He scraped at the earth and felt something hard just below the surface. A few more swipes revealed metal with patches of rust. Was it a box? Was it treasure? He looked up again. No one appeared to take note of his activities, so he dug at the light covering of dark dirt until the entire dimension of the object was visible. Whatever it was, it was solid metal and there was a round eagle stamp on the top, partly obscured by the soil caked to the metal.

It wasn't large enough to hold a body, even a baby's body. And he had never heard of someone having ashes buried in a metal box—though he guessed it was possible. He tilted it on its side and brushed the dirt away. On the front of the rectangular container was a metal handle, and in the lower right corner was an inscription on a raised copper plate. It said Norfolk County Savings and Loan. It was a safe deposit box. Excitement and paranoia hit him simultaneously. Again his eyes scanned the cemetery grounds.

A young girl in a flowered dress with the family was watching him, but she had not raised an alarm. She only stared, like a quiet specter, observing his actions with detached interest.

He set the box to the side, out of view of the little girl, and brushed the excess dirt back into the hole. Eventually the girl looked away, and he took the opportunity to flip the stone back onto its spot. It balanced on the rim around the hole, covering the hole completely.

Across the sea of tombstones, he caught a glimpse of the groundskeeper on the move again. How would he ever get this box out of the cemetery without being seen? The closest covering was a group of trees back toward the entrance. Could he make it there before the groundskeeper came back around?

A voice spoke. "Should we tell him to run?" It sounded less like a voice and more like a thought. But the thought was not his own.

"Run, now," said another.

He snatched the box up and ran toward the tarred path and the patch of trees beyond. The woman with the flowers had gotten into her vehicle and was slowly creeping down the access road. The family had all turned to watch him, but no one said a word as he jogged through the stones, holding the box in a football carry. It might have been partly due to the smile he forced onto his face. He imagined a smiling man jogging with a box would be less suspicious than a scared man jogging with a box. His theory appeared to be working. There was no attempt to stop him.

He made it to the trees and gave a look back, half expecting the groundskeeper to be racing toward him in his cart, but there was no pursuit. All but one of the family by the gravestone had gone back to their ceremony. The tall father figure had left them and was walking toward the main building, possibly interested in knowing why a young man with a dirty, metal box was jogging around the cemetery—but by the time they investigated, he would be long gone.

He took off through the woods, home free—until he ran into the spiked, black fence.

CHAPTER **SEVENTEEN**

David typed in a search for Special Agent Collins, but only gibberish came up in the search list. He typed in Agent Cooper. There were a couple of hits regarding the recent bomb threat in Boston, but nothing of any value. Their involvement in this murder case had weighed on his mind all the way back from the crime scene. Why would the FBI be involved with a local homicide? And what did Collins mean by supernatural? If David called and asked, would he get a straight answer? He slid the card from his pants pocket and pulled his cell phone out. There was one way to find out.

In short order the phone was ringing. "Hello, you've reached the Federal Bureau of Investigations. If you know the extension of the party you are trying..." He stabbed the numbers for Collins' extension and after a long pause there was a click. "Agent Collins."

"Yeah," stammered David, "this is David Chance."

"Hello, David. Did you get another message?"

"No. But I was wondering if I could ask you a couple questions."

"You can give it a shot," he said.

"Why don't you think I'm a nut case like everyone else?"

"Direct and to the point, I like that. It's a fair question."

There was a subtle pause, and David filled the gap. "You risked a lot trusting that I would come up with something on that crime scene. Weren't you worried about your credibility?"

"David, the department I work for at the Bureau is pretty much the laughing stock of all law enforcement. I'm used to the ridicule. It comes with the job."

"What do you do?"

"Well, a little of this and a little of that, but mostly we hunt aliens—at least, that was our original mandate. It's broadened since 1947."

"To include what?"

"Everything weird."

"Like me," he said.

Collins laughed. "I've seen weirder than the likes of you, Mr. Chance."

"Are there others like me?"

"Sorry, that's classified."

"So you're saying there are."

"No. I'm saying it's classified. I'm not allowed to discuss any case currently under investigation by my department unless the individual I am speaking with is directly connected, and even then it is on a need-to-know basis."

"Are you at least allowed to tell me how you think this Blake murder is connected to the supernatural?"

"I wish I was. The last thing I want to do is alienate the one person who can possibly help me the most, but the nature of this situation is volatile; it's best if you don't know the details, for your protection as well as your family's. But if it'll make you feel better, I've told you more than I tell most people. Usually I just pretend that I have a boring job chasing down things that don't exist and let people have their laugh, but I didn't imagine you'd buy that."

"Well..." David paused a moment.

"Yes?"

"If you want my help, you need to let me know what I'm

getting myself into."

"I wish I could, but my hands are tied."

"C'mon. You have to give me something. I could be putting my life in danger, and who knows who else's. Last time my family was kidnapped."

"For now, David, just wait for the messages to come. If you need backup, give me a call. I can't do anything else for you at this time. If you get anything else, you have my number, otherwise, I'll be in touch. Okay?"

"Yeah, okay. Thanks." The line disconnected.

David dropped his hand to his lap. *Great!* That helped a lot. How easy it was for everyone to tell him to wait. They weren't the ones whose already-fragile life could be thrown into life-threatening turmoil at any moment. They weren't the ones who had to deal with the repercussions of obeying the messages. As he sat fuming, his eyes rested on a yellow pad someone had left next to the computer. It was covered with scribbled words. David's eyes bounced from the bottom to the top, and a message formed. *Care package 25 Main.*

25 Main? Was that a street address? He called up Google Maps and typed Massachusetts 25 Main; a list appeared. *Yeah, this is helpful,* he thought, *every town in Mass has a 25 Main Street!* He started scrolling, until one caught his eye: 25 Main Street, Milton, MA. That was the town where the murder took place. He zoomed in to the street view and pivoted the camera. It looked like a residential neighborhood, but there was a sign on a corner house that said Helping Hands Food Kitchen.

"Did you find something?" said Karen, over his shoulder. His heart surged with adrenaline, but he didn't let on. She leaned in. "What's going on at the food kitchen?"

"I don't know," he grumbled. "I think I'm supposed to

go there."

"You think we'll find some clue about the murder?"

"I don't know. I got a message that said, 'Care package 25 main.' That's all I know."

Her lips pressed. "Well—let's go check it out."

"Check what out?" said Brad from the doorway.

She twirled around. "We have a lead on the Blake case."

"Really? What do you have?"

"Wouldn't you like to know?"

"Marriage has made you feisty, little Karen."

"You know what they say, keep your friends close, and your enemies—well, you marry them."

He expressed mock surprise. "Is that what they say?"

She smiled.

"Well, if you hold your enemies close," he said, "I'll see if I can be the worst enemy you've ever had."

David scowled. *"Really?* This doesn't make you sick? Am I the only one?"

They laughed.

Karen nudged him. "Come on, let's go see if we can dig something up. My enemy has a plane to catch."

CHAPTER EIGHTEEN

Jon looked back through the pine and oak trunks of the cemetery woods. The tombstones and network of tarred paths were no longer in sight, and there was no sign of pursuit. It was quiet, except for the chirping of birds and the occasional sound of a car passing by just beyond the black, iron fence and eight-foot hedge beyond. The hedge provided reasonable cover and gave the wooded area an air of seclusion.

Jon sat down on a thick tree root, set his iPad against the tree, and looked down at the dirty, metal box. What riches might it hold? He couldn't help but allow a smirk to bend his lips. If this box contained a chuck of cash, he would happily relive the last several hours. The only downside was running from the police—but with a wad of cash, he might be able to do it effectively. He had always intended on leaving anyway. What difference did it make if people were dead or in jail? What difference did it make if his father had pinned the blame on him? It didn't matter what these people thought of him; this entire state could be wiped out by a plague for all he cared. He never intended to come back. There was nothing here for him. All he'd ever cared about left when his mother couldn't stand to be around his dad anymore.

He gripped the lid and paused. The apprehension of having his hopes dashed upon the rocks caused him to hold onto the moment, as one might do before scratching off a lottery ticket. On this side of opening the box, all of his dreams could come true. On the other side, could be crushing disappointment. After all, who would bury money in a cemetery? And if they did, who would bury any amount of significance? The box could be like the police scanner box he opened two Christmases ago. For the briefest of moments, he thought someone had given him a police scanner, but instead the box contained a pair of knitted winter gloves.

In this moment, he chose to allow himself to believe the voices had led him to salvation; he chose to believe the box contained his ticket out of this nightmare. Despite the danger, he allowed hope to creep in.

Here goes nothing.

He pulled the lid up, and saw a single envelope. He fought the urge to throw the box at the tree, ripped the envelope out, and slammed the cover shut. The envelope was heavy in his hand and upon its face were the words: "I'm sorry," in faded ink. It felt like an apology from the voices—an apology that was sorely rejected. He opened the letter and slid its contents onto the top of the box. There was a stained letter and a key with the number 2362 on it. He put the key in his pocket and unfolded the letter.

Dear Donnie,

I never meant for this to happen. I never meant for no one to get hurt, especially Tommy. He was supposed to be alone at that bank, Donnie. That was the deal. You know that.

Well I wanted to say sorry, but I didn't dare to go

nowhere near that prison you was in. I know I should have been the one to take the fall. And I have had to live with that my whole life.

It wasn't so hot for me you know. I never spent none of that money. I was too scared. But I'm old now, and I ain't got much time left. There's no one to leave it to. No woman could ever stand a week with me. So I put it all back in that bank, in the same place we got it. I think in some way I'm hoping it will feel like it never happened, so I can go to heaven, but I doubt it. What's done is done. Now alls I have to look forward to is coming face to face with you, and nothing scares me more than that. So here's the key. I'm just hoping you forgive me.

Charlie

There *was* money! All the money he needed! He pulled the key from his pocket and looked at it. All he had to do was get into the Norfolk County Bank and get it from the safe deposit box! The thought immediately dowsed his enthusiasm. *How* would he ever get into a bank when his face was on every television in the state?! The money would be easier to get from Fort Knox. Unless—unless someone did it for him—someone like Bruce or Jared.

"Hey!" shouted a voice through the trees.

The groundskeeper and two other men were walking toward him. He crammed the letter and the key into his pocket and stood. The three men were a good twenty yards away, but there was nowhere to run, and no way to get over that spiked, iron fence.

He stood, frozen, watching the men approach through the trees, afraid to make any move that would cause them to break into a jog or a run which would decrease his time to come up with a plan of escape. He considered running along the fence and dodging through the trees, but he was no match for three grown men. He could place the box at the bottom of the fence and try to spring over the top, but even with the box, there was little chance he would clear it without taking considerable damage. *But,* he thought, *if I put the box on the spikes, maybe I can slide over.* He grabbed his iPad and slid it through to the other side, then grabbed the box and jammed it on top of the spikes and stepped back.

"Hey," shouted the man. "Stop!"

He ran forward, braced his foot on the horizontal holding bar that held the fence poles in place, and launched himself up onto the box. It felt almost as painful as he imaged the spikes would feel. The edge of the box cut into his abdomen as he wiggled forward. His legs eventually rose into the air, and his body crashed down on the other side.

The men had bridged the distance and were within a few feet of the fence. Jon scrambled onto shaky legs. He couldn't allow them to get the box; they might see the plaque for Norfolk Country Savings and Loan, then he'd never get into that bank.

He lunged upward, gripped the box with both hands and pushed with all his might. It lifted off the spikes and he came down hard. A hand shot through the rungs of the fence and snatched him by the shirt. No words were exchanged. The man had a look of determination on his face, and a strong grip. Jon panicked and brought the metal box down onto the man's forearm. The man screamed in agony and lost his grip.

"I'm sorry," yelled Jon, over the man's lamenting groans.

"That box is cemetery property!" said the groundskeeper. "If you take it, you're breaking the law."

Jon scurried backward with the dirt-covered box and said the only thing that came into his head. "My box!" It was neither articulate nor intelligent, but it conveyed the most important point. It was his, and he had no intention of letting them have it.

"If it's your box then we don't have a problem," said the groundskeeper, panting.

Jon's eyes brushed over his iPad which was laying within arm's reach of the fence. He lunged forward and slammed the box hard against the fence. A horrendous clank caused all three men to shift backward. Quickly he squatted down and picked up the iPad without taking his eyes off the men. He rose slowly. "You can have my box when you take it from my cold, dead hands. That's what you do anyway, right?"

The groundskeeper pulled his phone out. "You won't get three blocks with that box in your hand. You sure you want to do this?"

Jon began pacing like a caged lion. Was it true? Would the police get him before he could find a place to hide the box? Even if he did find a safe hiding place, they would have a description of him. No matter how this played out, if the police were called, he was in trouble. They would come looking for a vandal, and find an accused murderer instead. "What if I give it back. Will you let me go?" he said, not looking at them.

The man pulled his phone away from his cheek. "We might be able to work something out. Just give us the box and tell us where you got it from so we can return it to its resting place."

A convincing lie began to piece together in his mind. "There's nothing in it, anyway." He opened the box and showed them. "I just took it to show my mom. She said my cousin buried my baseball cards under his brother's gravestone, but they're not here."

"Which stone?"

He continued on, imagining how he should act and playing it out. "Those cards were worth a lot of money. I had old, old ones in those decks. I was gonna sell 'em."

The man with the damaged arm said, "You should have come talked with us. We have policies. You can't just come in and dig things up."

"There wasn't much digging," he said, it was right under the stone.

"It doesn't matter. It's against the law. Give us back the box."

He looked down at it with its eagle marking and copper plaque. How would he ever get them to believe his cousin had a safe deposit box? And what were the chances they wouldn't just call the cops as soon as he handed it to them, anyway? His options were dwindling into one inevitable decision. He felt like he was on a cliff staring at the cold water far below. There was no turning back.

There was a neighborhood on the other side of the road behind him. He remembered seeing it on the map. There had to be a nook he could hide the box in. Without the box there was a chance he could avoid the police.

He turned off that part of the brain that said, *This is crazy,* dug his feet into the ground, and took off through the hedge—with screaming pleas trailing behind him like a jet stream.

CHAPTER **NINETEEN**

David Chance led the way up the rotting, wooden stairs of the food kitchen and opened the creaky door. "Hello?" he called.

The main room was clean with simple furnishings. There were several brown, fold out tables surrounded by basic kitchen chairs, a few food carts, a coffee station— and a half a dozen people who all looked in David's direction. Only one looked like a street person, the rest could easily be lower, middle class eating at McDonalds, by the look of them.

A plump man called out from behind the counter, "Come on in."

David and Karen stepped in and Karen closed the squeaky door behind them. They made their way to the counter.

"The line starts over there," the man said, pointing to a stack of plates and plastic containers of utensils.

"We're not here to eat, but thank you," said David, wondering how he would introduce the topic of him seeing messages, and that a message had sent him here to see about a care package he didn't need.

The man's round, bearded face turned up when he saw Karen. "Oh! I recognize you. You're with the news. Are you here to do a piece on us?"

Karen smiled and looked at David. "No. I'm sorry, we're not here to do a story. David is here to ask you some questions, and I'm here to watch."

David smiled back. *Way to throw me to the wolves,* he thought.

"Okay. Well, we'll do what we can."

David turned to him. "Do you have something called a care package?"

"Yeah. Sure do. Mostly we make them up for the holidays, but we usually have some on hand."

"Do you have any right now?"

"I think we have a few left."

"Could we see one?" asked David.

"Ah, sure." The man wiped his hands on his apron. "Things are slow at the moment, so I'll go take a look." He disappeared behind the wall.

Karen leaned in. "Maybe there's more to the message. You should try looking around in here."

He turned and surveyed the room. The operators of the soup kitchen were not big on decor; the focus was clearly on functionality. Most of the walls were barren, except for an occasional information card. There was a sign that listed kitchen hours, another that said, "Place dirty dishes here." And there was a schedule for a Bible teaching. He bounced his eyes off a couple of words, but nothing clicked. "I don't see anything," he said.

"Do you think this place is connected to the case somehow?" she whispered.

"I don't know," he whispered back.

The man appeared from the back room and placed a cardboard box on the counter. "Here we go." He smiled. "We had one left."

"What's in it?" David asked.

"Well, during the holidays it can have a whole turkey, mashed potato mix, canned cranberry, that sort of thing. But this one is more of a generic pack. It's got ravioli, beans, beets, some bread, juice boxes and waters, stuff like that."

Karen leaned in and spoke in a low voice. "Are you getting anything?"

"I'm hoping I will soon," he said, placing his hands on the sides of the box and looking at the man. "May I look?"

He gave them an odd look. "Sure."

The food was packed tightly inside a plain cardboard box with the words Care Package in black marker on the side. He scanned the items inside the box—until it became uncomfortable for everyone.

Karen took a step back. "Ah... Maybe we should look somewhere else."

"What are you looking for?" asked the man.

She gave David expectant eyes, once again happy to throw him under the bus.

He pushed the box away. "We're sorry to have wasted your time, sir."

The friendly man's brows lifted. "You're not wasting my time. Take it with you, if you like."

"No, that's okay."

But before David could turn away, his eyes landed on a sign on the counter. It said: "Deposit dishes in tub. Put food in trash. Place returnables in box." His eyes bounced from *Put* to *in,* and up to a sign on the wall that said: "Help us keep a safe environment," where he grabbed the word *safe.* There was nothing else close enough to jump to, so he dropped back to the sign on the counter and bounced his eyes off of *deposit* and *box.*

Put in safe deposit box, he repeated in his mind. Put *what* in a safe deposit box? The food?

Karen had a pleased look on her face, obviously picking up on his behavior. It was too bad the look would soon be replaced with disappointment.

David put a hand on the box. "Um, yeah, I guess I will

110

take it. How much is it?"

The man looked confused. "We don't sell them," he said, "we give them to people in need."

Karen jumped in. "David's been beating around the bush. The truth is, things haven't been so good for him lately. He's just an intern at our television station." She shook her head apologetically. "It's lousy pay."

Seriously, Karen?! This was how she wanted to play it? He squirmed as she spoke her half-truth.

"Money is tight for his family and he's been stressing about whether or not to get another job. We'd like to keep him around, but he needs a little something to get through. Could we arrange for him to get a few boxes? I would be happy to do a piece on the food kitchen."

The man's eyes shifted to David. "Is this true?"

David choked on the words. "I really need this care package."

"You have a funny way of beating around the bush."

Karen put a hand on David's shoulder. "He's a proud man."

"You don't have to feel bad about this. Look, it happens to the best of us." As he talked, he stuffed napkins, paper plates, plastic wear and even a small, steel can opener into the box. "We're happy to help. If you need more boxes, stop by any time, or bring your family down and have a meal with us."

David clutched the box. "Thanks."

Fake compassion beamed from Karen's eyes. "It happens to the best of us, David." She pressed her lips and patted him on the arm. But it was the slight cocking of her head that bugged him the most. "Don't worry," she crooned. "We'll get through this together."

CHAPTER **TWENTY**

After running for what felt like forever, Jon found himself between a warped, wooden fence and someone's garage, hoping desperately that they didn't have a dog. Around him lay cinderblocks, a broken window in a frame, a rusted lawnmower, and a variety of wood, from particle board to two-by-fours. The owner of the house looked to be a pack rat, or a slob. Jon couldn't decide which. But if he left the safe deposit box laying out in plain sight in the middle of the yard, the authorities would be hard-pressed to find it. He chose to hide it, for extra precaution. He tucked it behind some sheets of wood and slid a cinderblock up against it.

There had been no sirens. Jon's best guess was that vandalism held a lower priority than murder, which was working to his advantage. All he had to do was stay low and wait for them to write up their report, do a cursory drive through the neighborhood, and be on their way to more important endeavors—like hunting down assassins bold enough to kill someone in broad daylight.

As he peeked around the corner to find cover for his escape, a voice spoke. Actually, it was more of a thought, but once again, not his own thought. "She's not home, go in," it said.

Then came another. "I'm Maddy. I'll be your waitress today."

"Key's in the troll."

"Okay to hide."

He pressed his back against the garage and continued to listen to the random thoughts pushing out of his subconscious.

"Yeah, I'm *sure,*" said a slightly clearer voice.

"She'll want to know," said a deep, man's voice.

Then a static voice: "Caller said he saw a suspicious boy running through his back yard..."

Jon rushed back to consciousness. As his eyes snapped open, he caught the tail end of a police cruiser through a missing slat in the warped, wooden fence. He slid out of the opening and beelined toward the house. If the voices said go inside, he was not about to argue.

The key was in the mouth of a yard troll next to the stairs leading up to the back door of the house. He snatched it and bolted up the stairs. The back screen door swung open with a creak he was pretty sure everyone in the neighborhood could hear, but he fought the urge to crouch. If someone did see him entering, he wanted to look natural. He didn't need any more heroes calling the police with updated information on his whereabouts.

The key slid into the door, and the door opened easily. But it took every ounce of his will power to push through. He wanted to look around to see if the neighbors or the police were watching, but he couldn't afford to look suspicious. He wanted to peek into the window to see if the house was really empty, but, again, that might catch someone's eye and raise suspicion. Instead he pushed through as if he owned the place, deciding to deal with whatever consequences lay on the other side.

Immediately he was hit with the smell of flowers and cooked sausage, but thankfully nothing else. There was no attack dog baring a set of razor-sharp teeth, no screeching woman or old man with a shot gun; just a dirty kitchen and a mixture of smells he wasn't sure smelled good or bad.

"He*llo?*" he called out, moderately loud.

He searched the small, cluttered house, pulling shades and drawing curtains as he went. The bottom floor was mostly kitchen and living room, with a walk-in storage closet full to the windows with items one might find on eBay.

On the second floor there were two bedrooms (though only one was used as such), a closet, and a bathroom. Judging from the dozens of towels, hanging and littering the floor, and the sweet smell of flowers, he guessed the home was owned by a woman. Was it the woman whose voice he had heard? Was it Maddy?

The answering machine would be a good place to find out. He went back down and into the kitchen. No answering machine was immediately visible in the piles of junk, but on an envelope, balanced on a stack of letters next to the kitchen table, was a name: Madelyn Stein. Jon sank down into a kitchen chair and stared. Maddy was short for Madelyn.

He wasn't surprised to find it was true, but he couldn't help but be overwhelmed. Somehow he had tapped into her conversation. What could *do* that? What could allow him to hear police scanners and conversations going on around him?! Could it be some kind of psychic power? The voices used to be random; he was sure of it, but now they had become something more tangible. It seemed that some were talking to him—no—directing him. Were there others with the same power? Watching him? Guiding him? Were they watching him now? Could they see what he was seeing? He felt exposed and embarrassed as his mind started to drift back to private things he had done recently, things he would never tell anyone about. But he stopped himself. If they could read his thoughts, then they would know for sure the things he'd rather keep secret. It was possible his secrets were still his, and possibly his dignity as well.

He sank down into a kitchen chair. So, now what? Attempt to get the money from the Norfolk County Savings and Loan and flee the country? Track down the man who had turned his life into a living hell? Or both? He could do both. With the money, he would have the resources to avoid the police and search for answers. There was a chance he could get his life back. Then he wouldn't have to leave the country.

"You could do it," whispered his thoughts. "You can stop this."

He put his elbows on the table and rested his head in his hands. *But I couldn't go into the bank. They would recognize me.*

"We'll show you," they whispered again.

Show me what?

"It can if you want it to," said one.

"Is someone in here?" said another.

"We know who knows."

He was beginning to get a sense for what was real and what was random. The real messages felt different, less like room noise, and more directed toward him.

A voice burst forth with an Italian bounce. "Never you mind-a." He immediately disregarded it.

"The bank people don't know you," whispered his mind.

"One does," it whispered again.

"I'm not feeling well. Can Davis take my shift?" said a female voice, way off in the distance.

Jon reached out into his mind. *Who are you?* He could almost sense the spot where the voices came from. It felt like vibrating energy, but there was no rhythm to the vibration. It undulated like waves in an ocean. As it destabilized, another phrase emerged.

"I count three cats," it said.

What?

It undulated again. "I'm an astronaut, JIM!"

More random phrases.

Then it buzzed. "We protect you." It was distinctly different, not so much in the way it sounded, but in the way it came to life inside his head.

It buzzed again. "Go- to- the bank."

Would they protect him? Did they know?

"She's home but don't go," it buzzed again.

His body went rigid as the front door opened, and footsteps moved through the living room. He sat frozen, staring at the doorway, his heart pounding in his chest. Was it Maddy? Wasn't she at work?

He heard the sound of fluttering paper, then something clunked. The footsteps approached the kitchen. Before Jon could make a run for it, a teenage girl was standing in the doorway. She let out an ear-piercing screech.

His hands shot out. "This is not what it looks like!"

"Jon?" she panted, with a hand on her chest.

His hands slowly sank down into his lap.

"Jon Blake?" she gathered herself. "You scared me half to death!"

Did he know her? He didn't recognize the wavy, blond hair and perfect cheekbones, or the round red lips and blue eyes. If not for her baggy clothing, he would have taken her for a cheerleader, or one of the popular girls at his school, which meant she was *definitely* not someone he hung out with.

"Does my mom know you're here?" She stared at him with unsettling intensity.

"Ah... no, isn't she's at work?"

"Did Jakson send you?" she said, her beautiful sapphire

irises floating in her wide eyes.

He shifted in his chair. "Um—are you sure you have the right Jon Blake?"

Her face soured. "I've been tracking you since you were ten, I'm pretty sure I know who you are."

He stood up. "What is this, the Twilight Zone?"

"No. The Twilight Zone is hearing voices in your head—voices that know things."

He pointed at her. "Okay. Stop. Just stop. I am seriously getting freaked out here!"

Her shoulders slouched. "Jakson was supposed to bring you up to speed. It wasn't supposed to be like this."

"Is this some kind of government experiment or something?" His eyes scanned the tops of the cabinets for cameras. "Are you messing with my head?"

She stepped toward him, grabbed his hands, and stared intently into his eyes. "I'm not good with people. You're the only friend I've ever had, and we've never even spoken."

Only friend she'd ever had? His brain was reeling. The fabric of his reality was splitting. How did this girl know him? Why was she watching him? And how on *earth* did he just *happen* to wind up at her house?!

"My mother doesn't know about what I do; her life would be in danger if she did. I'm begging you. Go. Jakson will explain everything." He could see the emotion welling in the corners of her eyes, but the last thing he wanted to do was let go of her warm hands or stop looking at her beautiful face.

"Can I come back—some other time—maybe?" he said, unable to mask his desperation.

"I'll call you on your iPad." She drew away from him. "I'll call, even if he doesn't. Please, just go."

Jon took the iPad from the table, and froze. "What

about the police?"

"The police?"

"They're looking for me because I took a box from the cemetery. They're here, in the neighborhood." He looked out the window, reflexively.

"What kind of box?"

"I thought you were watching me."

"I- am." She stumbled with her words. "I- I mean, I was. My mom left for work, and I snuck out to get a snack at the store. She doesn't like me eating sugar. I thought you would be safe with Pete."

She knew Pete too? How much did she know? Obviously not everything, otherwise, she would have known that Pete was murdered. He didn't bother sugar coating it. "Pete's dead."

Her eyes got wide then slowly turned down toward the floor. Her mouth gaped open.

"A blue car with tinted windows pulled up in front of the 7-Eleven. I couldn't see who did it but someone shot him dead."

Her eyes snapped back up. "Do you know who killed him?"

"What?" He shook his head. "I- no, I couldn't see anyone. The windows were tinted," he said, matter-of-factly

Her face scrunched. "Windows?"

"The windows in the car," he cocked his head, "you know, in front of the 7-Eleven."

He studied her face. There didn't seem to be any deception. Was she genuinely confused?

"They shot him," he said. "All I heard were the gun shots. I didn't see them. They drove up to the 7-Eleven and just killed him."

"In front of everyone?" Fear washed across her face.

"This is not good. They're getting bold."

"Who? Who's they?"

"The government."

"*Our* government?"

"Jakson should have told you all this."

"You keep saying Jakson. I don't even know who that *is!*"

She studied his face, looking even more perplexed. "Then—how did you find my house?"

He stared at her. "I have no idea! But the voices told me to come in. They showed me that your mother was at work and that I could hide here."

"Did they say how long she'd be gone?"

He shook his head. "All I know is she was serving people at a restaurant."

"How long ago?"

"Maybe twenty minutes."

"Will they tell you if she's heading home?"

"I don't know. I'm only starting to figure out which voices are real and which ones are my imagination." He let out a puff of air. "I can't even believe I'm telling you this. It's like I've stepped behind the curtain in OZ. Everything I thought I understood has been flipped on its ear."

"I know this must be weird for you. This wasn't how we were supposed to meet. Jakson said he would make contact with you." Her eyes continued to train on his face. "He said he would bring you in like he brought me in. His agency recruits people like us, people with talents."

Jon studied the girl's soft, beautiful face as her eyes searched for what to say next. "He found me when I was eight, right after I broke into the Pentagon mainframe. He had to go slowly with me. He was afraid I might tell someone or let something slip because I was so young, and he didn't want anything bad to happen to my mom."

He rewound her words in his mind, and came to an abrupt stop. "You broke into the *Pentagon* when you were *eight?*"

She stomped her foot. "This is so awkward! I'm so bad at this." Though she was clearly his age or older, she gave the momentary appearance of a child. "I don't know what to say first, or what not to say. I'm trying to say that I can't imagine what you're going through. It must be scary, and I'm sorry."

He didn't know how to respond. There seemed to be no end to the questions swirling in his head.

"I'm sorry all this is happening to you, Jonny, and I wish I had time to explain, but you have to go."

He opened his mouth to speak, but she cut him off.

"I need you to understand one thing, my mother and I have only each other. The man behind all this... He killed..." she choked back her emotion. "...he killed my father."

"Wait. So you know who's doing this to me?" The room seemed to shrink. Had the voices led him straight to the one person in the world who was both willing and able to give him all the answers?

"Let me finish, Jon." Her response was sharp and lacking in social tact. "His name is Elliot James, he is a high-powered business man with deep connections in the government. Eight years ago my father stumbled onto something terrible, something Elliot James had been planning for years. A week later he was dead."

More questions flooded his mind, but Jon reined them back. He didn't want to scare her into silence; he desperately needed her to continue.

"After the funeral Jakson contacted me, well, more like recruited me. No one knows about this, not even my mother. If Elliot and his people find out what I've been doing for the last eight years, they won't just kill her, they'll torture her in ways you can't imagine." Her voice broke. "She can't know who you are or why you're here. You can never tell her."

"I won't. I promise," he said, defensively.

She stepped in close. He could feel the heat of her body as her crystal eyes studied every crease of his face. "I believe you," she said, with a tear threatening to break the corner ridge of her eye. "I knew I could trust you. I've truly believed it for some time. Is that weird?"

He had no idea what she was talking about, but he was willing to say yes; he was willing to say anything if she would keep looking at him like that. To be trusted by someone so beautiful was surprisingly intoxicating. It set all his fears and questions in retreat.

"I've wanted to speak to you, but I was so afraid."

"Of what?" he said. "Of me?"

"Afraid to let anyone know my secret, and yet here you are, brought to me by your voices, as if they are saying it's okay for me to give into the feelings I have had for some time."

Was it possible anyone so beautiful could love him? If it was a mistake, he certainly had no desire to clear up the misunderstanding. He was happy to allow her to continue to think whatever it was that made her look at him with such rapt intensity, but a nagging question pushed its way to his lips and came out without his consent. "How do you track me?"

She pulled back slightly, and a blush rose up in her cheeks. "I've watched you." She stopped abruptly. "But never inappropriately. I swear, I never invaded your privacy."

"How? Is there a camera in my house or something?" The thought caused immediate alarm, not out of offense, but out of embarrassment.

"I sent a letter to your father through your mother's email. I told him I was sending you an iPad for your birthday. He, of course, assumed it was from your mom."

Jon looked down at the iPad in his grip. His father never told him it was from his mother. What else had he hidden about his mom? Had she tried to contact him in other ways over the years? His father had always painted her as a miscreant, but Jon still held out hope that she was not all the horrible things he had called her.

"I wrote a piece of code that lets me see where your iPad is, through GPS, and I can access all of its features."

"Like—the camera?" He said, returning from his introspection.

Her cheeks flushed again.

He pulled back, unsure how he felt about his privacy being invaded. It helped that she was beautiful, and that whatever she had seen had not caused her to look on him with revulsion. But there were things about him he didn't want anyone to see. Had she seen? Did she know the full extent of his sickness?

"I know what you're thinking, and you don't have to think that way. You don't have to be embarrassed."

Her words were hitting too close to home now. He took another step back.

She pulled her sleeves up violently, exposing both forearms. There were several pink scars stacked on each arm, and a new wound that had recently scabbed over.

His eyes snapped up to hers, and her expression spoke volumes. This was what bonded them. This was why she looked at him with such fondness. They shared the same affliction.

She inched in toward him and reached for his shirt. He allowed her in close to his body, even though his emotions were screaming to withdraw. Her thin lovely fingers curled around the hem of his t-shirt and pulled upward, revealing his lean tight abs. He spent most of his time doing push ups and crunches to burn off his frustration, but when that fell short, which it often did, he resorted to greater measures to relieve his emotional torment.

She slid her hand across the scars on his side where he had dug at himself with whatever was available. He didn't understand why, but the physical pain had a way of driving away the emotional pain. He guessed it had something to do with endorphins. They acted as an emotional anesthetic.

"We are the same, you and I." She left her soft, warm hand on the scars and looked up into his eyes. "We care too deeply."

He had never heard anyone put it that way. When anyone else had ever referred to his personality quirk, his caring too much, which was the source of his torture, it was always in terms of words like: petty, juvenile, or selfish. Everyone in his life, at some time or other, had felt the need to tell him to let go. They didn't understand. He couldn't flick a switch and turn his emotions off.

How could they understand the deep feeling of worthlessness he felt when his mother left? His own mother abandoned him to a drunk, and he was expected to just let it go? They said he needed to let go of his bitterness when he quietly held the secret that his father laid in bed with a hangover every morning while he made his own breakfast, got ready for school, and walked to the bus stop, at the age of seven. Unlike his father, he cared to save what family he had left, even though it barely resembled one.

She was right. He did care deeply, and it was his curse. Life would have been so much easier if he could care less.

123

He studied her perfect face as she studied his. How could someone so intelligent and flawless have any troubles at all? What would drive such a beautiful girl to cut herself?

"Why?" he said, unable to keep the question internal.

Her face tightened. "Why what?"

"I can understand why I do it, but why you? You're so beautiful."

She pulled away and stared at him.

"I'm sorry. Did I say something wrong?"

She slid her sleeves down and looked at him with an emotion he couldn't decipher. "You want to know why I cut myself? Because men prey on pretty girls, and sick men don't care how young they are."

Suddenly the living room flickered with a brilliant, white light, and the doorbell sounded. *What the...?* He jumped back.

The girl ran into the living room, and he inched over to look in. She peered through a crack in the front curtains and whatever she saw made her snap back out of view. She stooped and ran back to him.

"Who is it?"

Her eyes glowed with terror. "It's the police."

CHAPTER TWENTY-ONE

David sat in the passenger seat of the news car, the box of food heavy in his lap, and the image of the soup kitchen diners staring at him with looks of pity heavy on his mind. He didn't deserve this. He had worked hard to turn his life around. He'd done his time at college, studying his craft and working a part time-job to support his family. Though Karen's over-dramatic comments were simply a ruse, they'd managed to tap a raw nerve.

How did he get to this place of such dire economic duress? More importantly, why had God allowed it? Didn't he do his part? Hadn't he been a good little human? Would it kill God to throw a couple of winning lottery tickets his way, or how about a lead on a full-paying job? That was a message he wouldn't mind getting. But no, God's plan was to have him run all over the countryside, chasing after bread crumbs (tiny morsels of the larger picture), from one uncomfortable situation to the next without any concern for his happiness. Of all the people on this hunk of rock who deserved a break, he had to at least be in the top five. Was it too much to ask for some kind of reward for his efforts?

Karen hopped in the driver's seat. "Okay, spill it. I know you got something at the end there."

There was no masking his sour mood, "I'm not a charity case, you know."

Her face lit up. "Really? You're sore about that? I was just having fun."

He gave her the cold shoulder.

"Now, David." She fluttered her eyes and spoke to him as a mother might talk to her child. "I'm sorry. I didn't mean to step on your delicate man feelings."

"Oh, that's real mature," he said.

"You're the one acting like a baby."

"I'm just saying I don't appreciate you making me look like a charity case."

She laughed. "This is really eating you up, isn't it? Were you on welfare as a kid or something?"

He squirmed. "No. I wasn't on welfare."

"So what's with the mood?"

"It's just—getting to me, that's all."

"The messages, or your finances?"

"Both! It just sucks. I do all the work and what do I get for it? It's like God doesn't care how miserable I am."

"Well, I'm not the best one to talk to about God. I haven't exactly been a model church attendant. But I know this, when you get these messages, something miraculous happens—something few people ever get to see. You see a glimpse of something beyond all this. There isn't a person in this city who wouldn't want to be you."

He seriously doubted that, especially if they had spent an afternoon following the messages. But she was right; his financial woes and the fear of being thrown into another life-threatening situation were skewing his perception. His whole life he had yearned to know if God existed, and God had answered that question, quite definitively. Now it was simply a matter of getting to know him. Funny, his years of laboring over the question of God's existence seemed trivial now, compared to this greater question of whether or not he could trust him.

Karen cocked her head. "You still with me?"

"Yes," he said. He heaved a sigh. "You're right. I'm fine.

126

Let's just drop it."

"You sure, because I can get you some warm milk and a blanky."

"I get it! You made your point."

"Good. Now, spill the beans. What did you get in there? I saw that dopey look you get when you see something."

The message flashed in his mind. *Put in safe deposit box.* Was it literal? Was he supposed to store the contents of the care package in a safe deposit box? If so, how did that have anything to do with clearing the name of a young man accused of murder? "It's stupid," he muttered. "It is so stupid."

"Just tell me!"

"I'm supposed to put this stuff," he plucked out a can of beets, "in a safe deposit box."

She didn't even blink. "Okay, which bank?"

"Really?" he said, tossing the can back in. "You're cool with that? That doesn't seem odd to you?"

"Sure, I'd prefer a message like: The smoking gun is in a green trash bag on a dump truck marked 352, but we have to work with what we've got. Maybe there's someone at the bank who's involved in all this." She put her key in the ignition. "What bank?"

"I have no earthly idea," he said.

"Will it work if we go to a random bank?"

"I don't even know if we're supposed to go to a bank! It just said, 'Put in safe deposit box.' That's all I have."

She turned the key and the car started up. "There's a bank in the center of town. Let's try that one."

"And do what? Walk in and say, 'We'd like to store some canned food in your safe?'"

"You don't have to tell them what you're putting in there. It's confidential."

His frustration boiled over again. "I'm holding a box of

food! You don't think they'll ask me why I'm holding a box of food?!"

"We'll get you a backpack or something. Besides, who cares what they think. If you want to put food in a safe deposit box, what does it matter to them?"

He reached in the box and took out a can of creamed asparagus. "It's just *weird.*" He held it out to her.

"Come on." She swiped it away. "Let's get you a backpack and go from there. I think I saw a sporting goods store on the way through town. I'll swing over there. Who knows, maybe you'll get something while we're at the store." She put the car into gear and pulled out into traffic—a woman on a mission.

"It doesn't bother you that this has nothing to do with that young man who is suspected of killing his father's girlfriend?"

"We don't know that. I've been tracking clues for years, and most of the time it's just like this. You get a lead and you follow it, even if the lead doesn't make sense."

"How is it you're cooler with all this than I am?"

She laughed. "Who says I'm cool with it?"

"Look at you, you're like a giddy school girl." It was true. He had never seen her so lively.

Her face beamed. "I just married the man of my dreams and nailed the job of my dreams. Not to mention, I'm untethered from any real responsibility for the first time in my life. And, I'm doing what I love, chasing a mystery. Why wouldn't I be giddy. I'm having fun."

He sneered. "Yeah, this is a real blast."

"You need to stop taking this so ser..." The sound of her phone filled the cab of the news car, and she responded reflexively by pulling it out and checking the caller ID. "Speaking of responsibility," she said, stabbing the talk button with her manicured nail. *"Hello?"*

David sat in awkward stasis, waiting for Karen's attention to return. It was an all-too-familiar state, one that quickly reminded him of his station in life. Karen Knight had everything going for her. He, on the other hand, was nothing more than a side-show act.

She flipped the phone shut. "That was Coldfield." He set up an appointment for me to meet with Ross Blake at the jail. He wants me to get a statement."

"Are we still going to the bank?"

"Yes. I have time to get you that backpack and drop you off, but you'll have to do the safe deposit thing without me."

"What about when I'm done?"

"I'll give you money for a cab back to the station."

"What if I get a message to go somewhere else?"

"We'll play it by ear. You have a phone. Call me, and we'll figure something out."

He preferred to have his own car but as the thought came into his head he realized, with the state of disrepair his car was in, his chances of walking were about the same whether he had his car or not. He was better off to go with the cab money.

CHAPTER TWENTY-TWO

After a furious whispered debate, the results of which displeased the girl with the wavy, blond hair, it was decided that Jon would hide in the kitchen. It was too dangerous for him to sneak out the back. If someone saw him enter the house, they were probably watching the back yard still. His only chance was to find out what the police knew and hope they didn't have a warrant to search the house.

"Afternoon, miss," was all the officer said. Then there was silence. Jon strained to listen. Why was it so quiet? Was she giving him away? His heart began to throb. She wouldn't do that, would she?

"I'm sorry, miss," said the officer, with a strange enunciation. "We're looking for a young white male. A neighbor of yours heard on his scanner that we are looking for him, and he said he saw him run into your back yard. Have you seen anything?"

There was silence, for a long time.

"No. We don't think he's dangerous," said the officer. "He stole something from the cemetery—a metal box. If you see anything, can you contact us?

Why wasn't she talking back to the officer? Why the silence? The urge to peek was driving him nuts, but he didn't dare to chance it.

"Thank you, miss."

It sounded like she had given them what they wanted. The door sealed shut with a thump, and Jon watched the doorway with nervous apprehension, half expecting one of the officers to appear in it.

A few moments later the girl stepped into view, alone. He let out a breath.

"They're gone," she said, somewhat sullen.

A black tablet with chalked words dangled from her right hand. Jon's eyes flashed back up to her face. Suddenly it all made sense, her not catching some of what he'd said, the flickering, white light in the living room, the almost indistinguishable speech impediment.

"Are you, ah, not able to hear?" he said.

She made a reactive attempt to hide the tablet.

"I'm sorry," he put his hands up in defense. "I didn't mean to make you feel bad."

"It's okay," she said, "I know it's weird, but for some reason I wanted you to think I was normal. I didn't want you to see me like everyone else sees me, as handicapped."

"Um. Okay."

"No one knows I can speak, not even my mother."

He stared at her, not understanding. "Wh- why? Why would you keep that from her? You speak perfectly. I couldn't even tell."

"Because I have to be here. I don't have time for school, and classes, and people. I have to be watching."

"Watching what?"

"Everything!" She walked over to the kitchen table and plopped down on a chair with a squelch.

He waited till she looked up at his face. "Is this all because of your father?"

Her chin tightened and she looked away.

He sat across from her and waited again for her to look in his direction. "Are you okay?"

"It's been so hard, pretending to be this person, but

131

I don't know how to escape this life—these lies. I just want to hide from it all, but I can't leave my mom. I have to protect her. And I can't stop my work. We're so close, Jonny, and yet things are falling apart. Something has changed, and Jakson won't tell me what it is. The organization he works for has become desperate—even resorting to killing." She looked at him with desperate eyes. "We've never killed anyone before! They must really be afraid."

Jon tried desperately to unravel what she was talking about. "Afraid of what?"

"Despite our best efforts, Elliot James is almost finished. And if he does finish, there won't be any place for my mother and me to hide."

"What's he finishing?"

"It's a secret, a secret apparently Elliot would kill to protect."

"Did Sandra uncover the secret?" Jon said, almost to himself. "Is that why this is happening to me?"

The girl studied his mouth. She nodded slowly. "Indirectly, yes. Sandra's sister is Kathleen Peltz."

Sandra had never mentioned having a sister, but where had he heard that name before?

She must have read the question on his face. "She's been all over the news because of her research into Parkinson's Disease. She's the country's leading specialist in stem cell research. I intercepted an email between Kathleen and Sandra a week ago. It sounded like Kathleen had a falling-out with Elliot James and intended to go into hiding, and she was afraid for her sister. But Sandra never got the email. It was routed through an unknown socket and deleted."

Jon tried desperately to understand. "Someone— intercepted it?"

"This thing is big, Jonny, bigger than you can ever imagine. We've done everything possible to stop it, but it's like it's destined to happen, like it's happened before and we are cursed to repeat our mistakes. You're the only one who can stop this."

He looked at her, stunned. *"Me?!* What can *I* do?"

A buzzing noise from under the table caused her to dig for something in her pocket. She pulled out a smart phone and read a message on its face. Her eyes bounced back to his, her look was intense. "You have to go."

"Why? What's going on?"

"It's a text from my mother. She hurt herself at work and they're sending her home." She grew rigid. "You have to go. You have to go, now!"

"But I have so many questions."

She got up and clutched him by the arm. "I'll talk to you on your iPad. Don't worry, your questions will be answered."

"What about the police?"

"Ask the voices to guide you," she said, tugging him toward the back door. "And if you meet a man named David Chance, trust him. He'll help you."

He hardly heard what she said, all he could think of was being with her and fighting this battle at her side. The thought of not being with her caused a surge of panic. He turned to her as they got to the door. "Will I see you again?"

"I hope so," she said, running a hand down the front of his t-shirt. She opened the door and pushed him out.

"Wait," he said, holding the door open. "I don't even know your name."

Her eyes darted left and right, then settled on his face. "Canary," she said. "My name is Canary."

CHAPTER TWENTY-THREE

Karen pored over the police report and ran through the facts in her head as she sat in the waiting room of the police station. There was something more than a simple murder investigation here. Probably not something on the scale of a presidential assassination, but definitely more than a man killing his girlfriend and blaming it on his son.

The report said the father eventually confessed to having blacked out during the event, after he was questioned about the blood he had attempted to wash off in the sink. This meant they were holding him for more than questioning even before David found the fragment of burnt cloth in the kitchen wood stove. So what happened? Did the father give in to a fit of rage, black out, and kill his girlfriend? Then, upon awaking, realize his son saw the whole thing? That seemed to be the direction the police were taking with the investigation. But until they were able to produce a murder weapon, no court in the land would arrest the son or the father. There was no record of physical abuse, and no incidents of domestic disturbances. Both were squeaky clean.

A buzzer cut through the air, and Karen's heart jumped. It had been a while since she'd confronted a suspected killer, and the first time without a sheet of Plexiglass to protect her.

The man who entered looked like a criminal, or at the very least a biker with an attitude. He had a thick mustache and stubble for a beard, a strong muscular build with tattoos on his forearms, and a military haircut. His expression was flat and his eyes looked dead.

A police officer came in behind him, said something she couldn't hear, and closed the door. Blake crossed the room of mostly-empty cafeteria tables, and the officer took a seat next to the door.

Blake towered over her. "Karen Watson?" he said. It seemed everyone knew her from her recent bomb scare coverage.

"Knight," she corrected, waving an open palm toward the chair across from her.

"Don't you news people have enough misery to broadcast?"

"I'm not here about the story," she said. "Have a seat."

He slid the chair out and sat down. "Not here about the story?" There was a generous amount of cynicism in his voice.

"No. I've come here to talk to you about your son."

"Why do you care about my son?" he growled.

"It's complicated," she dodged.

"I bet it is." The corner of his mouth turned up in distaste.

She looked at the scribbled notes on her yellow pad. "The story you told the police is that your son shot your girlfriend Sandra, then ran into his room and jumped out the window. You later added that you experienced a loss of time. Can you tell me about that?"

"What's there to know? I was drunk."

"Can you describe what happened?"

"I've already given my statement to my lawyer and the police."

He was digging in. His self-preservation instincts were telling him, the less said the better, but she had not gotten

135

to the top of the news barrel without having learned the artful skill of information extraction. It was a simple matter of understanding one's prey. This was not a cold-blooded killer, even if he looked like one, this was a man who had made a mistake and acted out of panic to cover his mistakes. When pressed, he would break. "You claim your son shot your girlfriend, but you didn't actually see it happen. Is that correct?"

He turned a hard cheek toward her.

"Are you aware that forensics place the shot near the front door of the house? Where were you standing before you blacked out?"

His brow ridge dropped. "I already told you, I have nothing further to say."

"Okay," she said taking up an attack position. "Then you just listen, and I'll tell you what I think. You came home from the bar and you were angry about something. Words got heated, and you told your girlfriend to shut up, but she wouldn't. You grabbed your gun and you shot her dead."

"I don't have to listen to this."

"What happened next, Ross? Did you hear your son escaping out the window so you pursued him? Did you chase him to silence him, only to have him slip through your fingers?"

"You don't know what you're talking about."

"You want to know what I know? I know your son is innocent, and that you're a liar."

The bomb was planted. She expected him to explode into a fit of indignation, to which she intended to respond with an accusation he could have no answer for. If his son did shoot his girlfriend, why did he chase him out into the darkness, unarmed?

But the explosive rage never came. Instead, Ross Blake

sat with something that looked like shock on his face.

"Mr. Blake," she said.

His eyes lifted to meet hers. "You know my son is innocent?"

Did she detect relief in his voice? Was it possible that he truly believed his son had done it? Had she completely misread the entire situation?

"Beyond a shadow of a doubt," she continued. "But what surprises me is that you don't."

"I blacked out," he said. "I don't know what happened."

"You killed your girlfriend, that's what happened."

"I couldn't. I could never do something like that."

"Then you need to help me," she said, "because the police have everything they need to lock you away for life. You need to level with me and tell me what happened that night."

His eyes shifted erratically as he pieced things together in his head.

"Run down through what happened, and let me help you."

His eyes focused on her.

"Please," she said, "I can help."

"I was having a fight with Sandra," he said, "because my best friend said he was sleeping with her. I know it sounds bad, but I was just gonna throw her out of the house, not kill her."

"I believe you. What happened next? Did you go for the gun?"

"*No,*" he growled. "We were arguing. I got mad, and I knocked some of her things off the top of the television. I was so angry, but the worst I could think to do to her was break her stuff. Then," he said, allowing his mind to go back to that place, "I looked at the broken things on the floor and I wished I could just die. I didn't want to be hurt again. Losing Jonny's mother was the worst pain I've ever felt in my life. I didn't want to feel that again. And I think that's when I just let the alcohol take over."

"What do you mean, take over?"

He looked disgusted. "Not like that. I didn't turn into some kind of drunk monster. I just stopped fighting that drunk feeling. I gave into it, thinking I'd puke or pass out, it didn't matter to me which. I just wanted to disappear."

"Did you pass out?"

"I don't think so. I don't remember passing out. The next thing I remember I was standing over Sandra's body. I remember falling down on my knees and touching her shirt where the blood was and feeling for a pulse. She was dead." He fought back the emotion of it. "That's when I heard a noise in Jonny's room. I went in and saw him outside the window and I chased him."

"You chased your armed son out into the night?"

"I was in shock! And drunk! I don't know what I was thinking! I just wanted to know what happened."

"So what made you think your son killed your girlfriend?"

"Who else could have done it? There was no one else in the house." He looked down at the table. "I thought maybe I blocked it out. Maybe the image of him killing Sandra was so horrible, my mind hid it from me. I didn't want to believe he did it, I didn't want to believe my son was a murderer." His eyes connected with hers again. "What did you find? How do you know for sure he's innocent?"

She wasn't quite ready to show her hand. "What about the shirt? Why did you burn your shirt?"

"Her blood was on it, and her blood was on my hands."

"What about the gun?"

He shut down.

"Do you love your son?"

138

"Of course I love my son!"

"Prove it! This is your chance to save him. What happened to the gun? Did you find it? Did you hide it?"

His face hardened. "I think it's time you tell me how you know he's innocent."

She was losing him, and it would only get worse if she told him it was a psychic who told her Jon was innocent. "Your son came to me," she lied, "and he told me you shot her."

He pushed back from the table with a squelch. "That's your evidence? My son told you?"

"There's more," she said, knowing definitively there wasn't. What evidence could she make up to clear the boy of the crime? Her window of opportunity was shutting fast. "He filmed it!" The words flew from her lips before she could fully consider the ramifications.

"He wha-? How?" he said.

That was a very good question, one she had absolutely no idea how to answer. To her great relief, he was quick to answer it for her.

"Did he fake something on that iPad of his?"

She pushed forward with mock confidence. "It was grainy, but there is absolutely no doubt you shot her."

There was no indignation, no look of denial, only complete and utter shock, as though, in his mind, there had been a seed of doubt the whole time. Of course there would be. There had to be. He came home drunk, angry that his girlfriend had betrayed him in the worst possible way, and then blacked out.

"Where's the gun, Ross? Where did you hide it?" she pressed.

The big burly man melted before her eyes. "It was in my hand. I thought I had picked it up. I thought he shot her, and I had picked it up. How could I have killed her?

139

I'm not a killer." His shoulders sank.

"Where did you hide it, Ross?"

He hung his head in defeat. "In the garage," he said in a weak voice. "I hid it behind the tool rack in the garage. I knew how it looked. I knew they would think I did it. I don't understand how this could happen. I couldn't..." his voice broke off.

Once again, she found her understanding of Ross Blake shifting. A guilty man would never have confessed to hiding the weapon. This was not the confession of a murderer. This was a man coming to grips with the horrifying possibility that he might be a killer. But was he? What if he was framed? What if someone drugged his drink, followed him home, and murdered Sandra after he passed out? The evidence all pointed to Ross as the killer, but what if he wasn't? She couldn't let him continue to believe that there was video evidence of the murder, not if there was a possibility that he was innocent.

"You didn't do it," she said, surprising both of them.

He looked up. "What?"

"You didn't kill her. At least—I don't think you did.

He tried to process her words.

"I lied," she said holding up her hands, "Not about your son being innocent, but I lied about the video. There's no video."

"You *lied!*" he snarled.

"I had to know."

"Know what?!"

"That you're both innocent."

His face twisted in rage. "We can't *both* be innocent!"

"I didn't think so either, until just now."

He sat glaring at her, then slammed a fist on the table. "Then *WHO* did it?"

"I think maybe you should see a psychiatrist and find

out. You've obviously repressed the identity of the killer."

"But we were alone in the house!"

"Maybe someone followed you home."

"This is crazy! Who would do this? We don't know anyone who could do something like this!"

"Are you sure?"

He gripped the table. "I trusted you. I laid my soul bare. How do you know my son is innocent? What evidence did you find?" The words sounded like a growl.

"We're done," she said, standing abruptly.

He reached out to snag her arm, but she anticipated his move and spun out of the way. The officer near the door was on his feet.

"You said you have proof. What's your proof?!" His face was red with rage.

"Step back and put your hands on the table!" said the guard.

There was a wild look in his eyes, and it looked like he might pounce. Karen shifted her weight and prepared to pivot if he decided to launch himself at her.

"I should have known!" he spat. "I can't believe I trusted you."

The officer stepped in between them. "Hands on the table, Mr. Blake!"

Karen's heart jumped as he slammed both hands down hard. "I never should have trusted you," he said. "You reporters are all the same."

The officer tore Ross's hands back one at a time, cuffed them behind his back, and spun him around. There was spit on his chin and fire in his eyes.

Karen squared off with him. "Whether you believe me or not, it doesn't matter. I'm going to do my best to prove both of you innocent. You have my word."

His face boiled as he tugged on the officer's grip. "Your

word doesn't mean jack to me."

She lifted her chin defiantly. "My word is all you've got."

CHAPTER **TWENTY-FOUR**

Canary? What kind of name was Canary? Was it her given name? Was it a nickname? Perhaps it was a code name. She was definitely a spy of some kind, so of course she would have a code name. Whatever it was, it only made him more curious about her.

He crouched in Canary's back yard, staring at her house for the better part of an hour, only hiding himself once when he heard her mother's car pull into the driveway. It felt weird lingering and watching her house like a peeping Tom, but how could he go anywhere? All his answers were here, and nothing but police and jail-time awaited him beyond the warped, wooden fence of the back yard. No. That wasn't quite right. He reached in his pocket and felt the envelope and the key. There was also the matter of a possible fortune hidden in a safe deposit box at Norfolk County Savings and Loan. It was where the voices were leading him next, and they hadn't steered him wrong yet. They wanted him to see Canary to get some answers, and he did, but this had become a dead end. He looked around. The prospect of spending any more time with Canary before late night seemed unlikely. Besides, his legs were starting to cramp up.

He adjusted the computer tablet in his lap. Would she contact him? Would the black screen suddenly light up with a message telling him what to do next, or would it remain as it was, dark and sorely unhelpful? Canary wasn't thinking about him, she was most likely occupied with her mother's ordeal. If he wanted answers, he would need to look somewhere else.

He emptied his mind and tuned into that place where the voices lived. Energy danced in the back of his mind, undulating with endless possible word combinations. With each attempt it was growing easier to tap into this secret place. It was simply a matter of letting go of his will and allowing the voices to exert theirs. His mind produced random gibberish from his own subconscious, like some kind of dream. But if he gave himself completely and waited expectantly, there was less interference. It was like riding a bike, eventually he would perfect it, then there would be nothing stopping him from being connected to the voices continually.

A phrase materialized. "By the end of the whirly one," it said. That was definitely random.

"That's how I roll," said another.

Then the buzz produced a third. "The cabbie doesn't know."

Cabbie?

"That's what I'm talkin' 'bout," said another random voice.

Then a buzz. "225 Third Street."

He repeated the address in his mind, but he could feel the effort bringing him up out of that empty place where the voices played. He attempted to hold onto the address lightly, and continued to listen.

"Act normal," said another much weaker voice.

If he kept emptying his mind and listening to the voices, he would lose the address. He decided to write it down, then he'd be free to go deeper and get a more substantial message. His eyes flicked open. Though he had only spent seconds in meditation, his lids felt heavy. Sleeping on the lumpy mattress in his friend's basement probably had something to do with it.

He entered the address into his iPad and flicked it back off. It would be nice if he could tap into the voices without having to be half asleep to do it.

His legs were screaming for blood supply, so he got up and paced behind the garage, careful not to kick any of the clutter and give himself away. Over the fence, and beyond some bushes, a yellow cab was parked on the side of the road. His mind whispered: *The cabbie doesn't know.*

Did the voices want him to take a cab to the bank? Why else would they say that? But what about Canary? What about his answers? He decided they could wait. It wouldn't take him long to get to the bank and back, and it beat crouching behind Canary's garage till nightfall.

He went to the corner of the yard behind the garage where he had originally entered through a large warp in the wooden fence, and squeezed through.

"Hello?" said Jon, tapping on the driver's window.

The cabbie pulled his sandwich from his mouth and opened the window. "Yeah," he said, peering up.

"I'm sorry. I didn't realize you were eating."

The cabbie started packing the sandwich into its white paper packaging. "It's okay. You need a ride, kid?"

"Yeah. I need to go to the bank, 225 Third Street."

"Which bank is that?" he said.

"The Norfolk County Savings and Loan."

"That's not on Third. That's downtown on Westwood Boulevard."

"What's at 225 Third Street?"

"I don't know," he said, wiping his mouth, "Do you need a ride to the bank, or what?"

"Yes. Please."

"All right. Hop in."

Jon pulled the door handle and slid into the back seat.

The cab reeked of onion and salami. At least he hoped it was onion. It wasn't exactly the most hygienic vehicle he had ever been in; there was a great chance the smell was body odor.

The seat cushion was torn in several places with yellowish foam pushing out through the tears, and the carpet had a few items stuck to it that would probably require a putty knife to remove. It was decidedly less than ideal—but he would travel to the bank in the back of a garbage truck if it meant a chance at a new life.

He desperately longed for a new life.

CHAPTER **TWENTY-FIVE**

Karen checked the break room of the police station for a cup of tea. Her run-in with Ross Blake had frazzled her nerves; she needed some soothing. The small room was cluttered, but reasonably sanitary. A twenty-year-old coffee and tea dispenser was tucked in a corner next to the door. As she fished in her pocket for change, a familiar voice caught her ear. It was Agent Collins'. She was sure of it.

"They just finished questioning the driver of the blue car," he said.

Was he talking about the blue car involved in the murder this morning? She leaned her shoulder into the wall and listened through the open door.

"We have a confirmation," said Collins.

"Lost time?" said another voice Karen recognized but couldn't place.

"He said the last thing he remembers is being in his house last night."

Lost time? Karen thought. Like what Ross Blake had experienced? Two killers, both experiencing blackouts? What were the odds on that?

"That's longer than the others."

"Yeah, a lot longer, but not the longest we've seen," said Collins.

The other man's voice dropped low. "Do you think this is connected to the others?"

"I don't know, Coop, but it's the fourth one in this state

147

in less than two weeks. It's reasonable to think they're connected."

Four murders connected to attackers who experienced lost time? That was the story of a lifetime! Why had she not heard about this before?

"Dr. Tanner is going to regress them both to see if it's what we suspect."

"You couldn't pay me to do that guy's job."

"I'm going to go grab a bite while we wait for the results. You want anything?" said Collins, moving closer to the break room door. Karen drew away and stood awkwardly by the coffee machine.

"What are you getting?"

"A sub or something."

Both men sounded as if they were walking past the break room. Karen attempted to look natural, but was sure she wasn't doing a very good job of it.

"Karen Watson?" said Collins suddenly.

She swung around and looked in his direction. "Oh, you scared me," she said.

"What are you doing lurking in the coffee room?"

"Lurking? I'm not lurking."

He threw a glance at Agent Cooper. "I'll catch up with you in a minute."

She could see the suspicion in Cooper's eyes, but also the resignation. It was clear that Collins held the higher rank; Cooper was forced to take his leave, however reluctantly.

"I'll be in the lobby," said Cooper, with casualness she was sure he didn't feel.

Collins filled the doorway of the break room. "So, you still looking for a scoop, or are you here on David's behalf?"

She considered her words carefully. There was a

greater chance he would release information if he saw her as an ally. "Just helping a friend," she said. "My desk at the station is cleared off, and I'm already working on leads in New York."

"Are you now?" he said with a slightly playful grin. You're just innocently eavesdropping on our conversation from the break room?"

"Eavesdropping? You think a little too highly of yourself. I was getting tea." She indicated the machine with a Price Is Right wave of her hand.

The humor left his face; his look was unexpectedly cold. "Stay away from this story, Karen."

"What story?"

"Powerful people do not want this to get out; you might find your job in New York suddenly filled by another."

"Are you threatening me?"

"Consider it advice from a friend. Go to New York and start your new life. There's nothing to see here."

She leveled her eyes at him. "And how could I possibly do that now that you've dangled the carrot in front of my nose?"

He stepped into the break room, and she leaned back on her heels. "Take it from someone who knows. Following this junk only produces one thing, humiliation. Before you know it, even The Enquirer won't hire you and you'll be working at some local news station in the backwoods of North Dakota doing corporate-sponsored pieces and community-service promos."

She grinned. "That's impressive. Did you work that one out on your own or is that in your field manual?"

By his expression she could tell he realized he wasn't getting anywhere with her. "Can't say I didn't try," he said, backing toward the door. "I guess I'll be seeing you around then."

"Before you go," she said, pursuing him slightly. "I don't imagine you'll tell me how far-reaching this blackout condition is, or how it causes innocent men to become killers?" She let the statement hang in the air, relishing in the uncomfortable way it choked the oxygen from the room.

The right corner of his mouth crept up. "There is a strong possibility," he said, leaning in close, "that it's extraterrestrial. But you didn't hear it from me."

CHAPTER TWENTY-SIX

The cab driver talked the entire way to the bank, but Jon responded with short answers, never making eye contact in the rear-view mirror. He trusted the voices when they said the cab driver would not recognize him, but there was no sense giving him a good look now.

"Here we are," said the cabbie. He slapped the meter and called over his shoulder, "$26.54."

Jon slid $27 through the opening. "Keep the change."

There was no response from the cabbie, who probably expected more.

Jon opened the door and climbed out onto the moderately busy sidewalk in front of the Norfolk County Savings and Loan. It felt larger than he remembered it, but perhaps it was the daunting fear that made it so. With eyes toward the ground, he walked up to the wall of glass doors and, without a glance to either side, entered the lobby.

There were many more people than he had imagined: tellers, loan officers, receptionists, and almost a dozen customers—so many eyes, not to mention the cameras. It was statistically impossible for none of them to have seen his face plastered on the news. And even if no one had seen him, he would likely draw attention anyway with his spiky hair, gauge plugs and black fingernails. His nerves wavered as he came to a stop in the center of the lobby.

A faint voice in his head said, "Be calm."

Another sounded. "They don't know."

He wanted to scream at the voices. *How could they ALL not know?!* Someone had to have seen the news! There were dozens of people on the first floor of the bank. This was a bad idea, a very bad idea.

He took a breath, stole a peek at one of the security cameras, and forced himself forward into one of the teller lines. No one appeared to pay any attention to him, though he felt like his sweat glands were squirting sweat straight out. He rubbed his hands and concentrated on his rate of breathing.

"You're safe," said a warm female voice.

He slid his hand into his pocket and felt for the key. All he needed to do was hand the key to the teller and say, "I'd like to open my safe deposit box, please." No one would ask questions. It would be okay. He would be in and out in no time.

The line inched forward, and Jon continued to stare at the floor, ignoring the man in the line next to him who seemed to keep looking in his direction, and ignoring the man in front of him who didn't seem to want to stay facing forward. Every time he turned casually to look back toward the entrance of the bank, Jon's body tightened. Why did some people have to be so nosey?

Finally the nosey man took his turn at the teller window, and as Jon moved to the front of the line, he felt fully exposed again. He kept his eyes on the nosey man's back and focused all his effort on keeping his face and chest from trembling.

Finally it was his turn. The teller waved him forward. "How may I help you?" she said as he approached the counter.

Fully aware that he was sweating, and possibly trembling, he attempted to play it off. He coughed into his sleeve. "Sorry, I'm fighting something, but hopefully it will pass." He took the key out and looked down at the number. "I'd like to get something from my safe deposit box, please."

"Sure thing," she said. "What's the number?"

"2362," he mumbled.

"I'm sorry, what was the number?"

"2362," he said, louder.

Her fingers made their clickty-click sounds on the computer keyboard. Her eyes studied the screen. "Name please?" she said, looking up at him.

Name? They needed a *name?!* His chest gave an involuntary quiver. What would it be under? Jon tried to remember the signature on the letter, but even that wouldn't come to him.

"Sir, I need the name on the account or the account number."

"Finch," he blurted.

She gave him a blank stare.

Finch? Was he out of his mind?! Why would the man who wrote the letter use his friend's name on the account? He would have used his own name, or an alias. Jon began to squirm.

The teller looked at him expectantly and said, "First name?"

Jon took in a breath and exhaled the only name he figured it could be. "Donnie," he said. Then he corrected. "Donald Finch."

She looked at the computer, and back at him. "You're Donald Finch?" she said.

Jon straightened up. "No. He's my grandfather."

She slid away from her computer. "One moment."

One moment for what? One moment while she went to get security? One moment while she went to get the box—which had the potential of being equally disastrous?

153

He gripped himself internally. *Be cool!*

He watched her walk behind the other tellers and pass through the divider wall into the lobby to where two men in suits stood talking. One was a handsome, middle-aged man with black hair that was graying on the sides. The other was a lean man with Coke bottle glasses.

Jon's mind whispered, "Hide your face."

Hide? From who? Had one of the men seen his face on the news? The voices had promised no one in the bank would know him. Jon turned and put his back to them, pretending to look at something on the other side of the room.

"He hasn't ssseen you," said a voice, elongating the s sound.

Where were you a couple of minutes ago when I needed a name for that key you gave me?

Another phrase formed. It had a masculine tone to it. "The young man with his back to us?" it said.

Was that one of the men with the teller? He could feel their eyes burrowing into the back of his thin neck.

"I'm sorry, Mr. James. I'll be up in a minute," said the same voice.

Jon's body shivered as fear snaked through his ribcage. Could it be *Elliot* James? Betrayal gripped his heart. How could the voices tell him it was safe and then lead him straight to Elliot James? Was it purposeful, or simply a miscalculation? If it was a mistake, what other things did the voices not know?

"Excuse me? Sir?"

Jon spun toward the teller window. The tall, lean man with thick glasses stood there, staring at him. Jon couldn't help but snap a glance toward where he had been standing a minute before. The middle-aged man was gone. His eyes snapped back to the name plate on the

154

man's chest. It said, Wellington. Jon felt a wave of tension release in his gut.

"I'm the bank manager. I can assist you with your box. If you'll follow me, please," he said, directing Jon to the end of the teller line. Jon walked parallel with him, past two teller stations to where a waist-high door opened up to allow him access. "This way, please." He led him past a thick, oak door and down a wide set of finely carpeted stairs deep into the bowels of the bank.

Halfway down, Jon said, "Who was that man you were talking to upstairs?" in as casual a tone as he could muster.

"Why do you ask?" said the manager.

"Just curious," said Jon, noting the suspicion in the manager's tone. He regretted he had said anything.

"That was Elliot James, president of the bank."

It *was* him! It *was* their conversation he had overheard! But—how was that possible? He hadn't heard the manager's voice, another man's voice had spoken his words, Jon was sure of it. Something, or some*one* had relayed them to him.

The man stopped and sized him up and down, then looked up at the cameras on the wall. "You really don't know who he is, do you?"

Jon shrugged. "Am I supposed to?"

His face looked briefly puzzled, then shifted to something unrecognizable. "You probably recognize him from television. He ran a ton of ads in the last election cycle when he ran for the Senate."

As he mentioned it, Jon did remember seeing some of those ads. "So I take it he didn't win," he said, continuing to make it sound like he was only mildly interested.

"He dropped out of the race."

"Why?"

The man looked irritated. "There were allegations of bank fraud—not by Mr. James, but by others who work in the bank, which have been proven false. Mr. James, being the man of integrity that he is, chose to table his campaign and put all of his resources toward clearing the bank of the baseless charges. He helped us restore our good name, a name we have all worked hard to uphold."

The intense look on the manager's face caused Jon to take a subtle step back. "I wasn't implying anything."

"In the end, all anyone has is their reputation. I can't imagine anything being more important." There was intent in the man's words, and a fire in his eyes.

All Jon could think to say was: "I agree." And he left it at that. There was obviously something going on here, and the last thing he wanted to do was get in the middle of it.

The man straightened himself and continued down to a set of double doors at the bottom of the stairs. He swiped his security card, and a loud click filled the stairwell. The doors swung open to reveal a large steel room with a bank vault at the far end, two curtained booths to the right, and a security guard at a desk. The enormous, stainless steel vault door behind the guard stood open. Jon could see the safe deposit boxes within. He could only imagine what untold riches were stored in that magnificent, shiny tomb.

"May I have your key, please?" said the manager, his hand extended.

Jon placed it in his palm.

"Follow me, please." He led him in and retrieved a box from one of a thousand shiny, silver doors in the wall. When he handed it over, the weight of it cut into Jon's forearms. The manager locked the door and placed the key on top of the box. "If you will follow me," he said, "I will show you to your booth." He led him out and over to the booths. One was occupied by a man in black, scuffed dress shoes, the kind his father had in the back of his closet—exactly the same kind. His father wasn't the dress-shoe type, so the shoes were always a curiosity to Jon. How odd that this man would be wearing the same shoes. The manager slid the next curtain aside. "Please let me know if I may assist you further."

Jon entered the cramped booth, set the box on a waist-high shelf, and closed the curtain. This was it. The moment of truth, the point in time when his whole life could change. It hardly looked large enough to contain a fortune, but stacked to the brim with hundred dollar bills... What were the chances, though? Even if the man who wrote that letter was smart enough to rob a bank for that kind of money—which he doubted—how could he ever possibly give it up?

There was no point in debating the topic with himself, the answer was in front of him. He reached out and grasped the lid with his finger tips, but froze as the curtain for the booth next to him slid open.

"Um," said a voice just outside his own curtain, "could I get a larger box? This one's not going to work."

"I'm afraid that's the largest we have," said the manager.

A larger box? What was he storing in the bank that he needed that large of a box? It must have been exceedingly valuable.

"Then could I get a second box?"

"Certainly. It is an additional $325 annually, uninsured. If this suits your needs, I'll bring another."

"Sure. What's another $325?" The man's voice dripped with sarcasm. "Because apparently I'm made of money."

The manager responded in a monotone. "One moment, I'll retrieve a second box for you."

157

Odd. Why would someone so concerned about their lack of finances want to store two large safe deposit boxes full of valuables in a bank? Maybe he was rich because he was a tight wad. It didn't matter. Jon turned back toward his own box, but couldn't help but overhear the man mumbling in the next stall. He probably thought the walls were thicker.

"Maybe I could sell a kidney," he said quietly to the air, "or cut back on this week's groceries, because everyone knows having a full belly is overrated."

What a curious man. He was clearly not wealthy, and yet someone had forced him to come to the bank and store something against his will. Jon couldn't imagine the man's predicament, but he appreciated his cynicism. It even brought a smile to his face. In some small way, it made him feel a little better about his own situation. But not much.

His face returned to its solemn position, and his hands again found the lid of the box. Enough messing around. It was time to tear aside the veil of mystery and see what the future held.

He flipped the metal cover up, and all the breath left his body. Sitting before him, fit as tightly as physically possible, was exactly what he had imagined: stacks and stacks of used, one hundred dollar bills. More money than he had ever seen in his entire life! There had to be millions! He began ripping stacks out of the box and setting them to the side. How far did it go down? Did they reach all the way to the back? He pulled and stacked until there was a tunnel deep enough that there could be no doubt. The entire metal box was filled to the brim with hundred dollar bills! He took a step back and looked at the piles on the shelf and in the box. Adrenaline surged, then disappointment.

He had nothing to carry it in!

He stood there, eyes wide, taking shallow breaths. He hadn't actually believed that he would find anything. Nothing like this ever happened to him. His big dreams were always crushed. Always. And now, without thinking, he had set himself up for yet another defeat. There was no way he could ever get back into this bank with all the news agencies running his face at the top of every hour. This was it, his only chance. He turned back toward the curtain, and took a deep breath. Maybe the manager had a container he could borrow or purchase. No, that would be suspicious! Who comes to the bank and unexpectedly realizes they need a large container? His fists squeezed; where his nails dug in, the skin burned.

Why didn't you tell me?! he screamed inwardly.

No answer emerged from the recesses of his mind. The voices had set him up for failure. They could have told him. They could have prepared him. Even now, they could speak, but they chose to be silent. Well—he wasn't about to let this slip through his fingers. He slipped out the curtain, leaving it closed. The manager was standing with the bank guard. "Excuse me," said Jon, lifting a hand.

Instantly a voice ripped free from some deep, dark place inside, as though it had been held captive. *"Return to the booth!"*

"Yes? Can I help you, sir?" said the manager turning his way.

"No," said Jon, leaping back to the booth. "Sorry, no, I'm all set." He pushed in through the curtain and fixed it behind him.

"Are you sure?" said the manager, outside the booth.

"Yes. I'm sure." Jon attempted to keep his voice from shrilling. "I was mistaken."

WHAT WAS THAT ALL ABOUT! screamed Jon into the

void of his subconscious.

This time a voice responded, but it was clearly labored. *"He* knows."

Jon's heart raced. *The manager knows who I am?!*

"David," said another voice.

David? Who's David?!

"We didn't know."

"You knew."

"It was hidden from us."

What was hidden? Who's David? How do I get this money out of the bank?! Jon was beginning to freak out. *Why didn't you tell me I needed something to carry the money in?!*

"You don't."

I can't just walk out of here with stacks of money stuffed in my shirt!

"Give it to Wellington," they whispered together.

The manager? Are you crazy?

"Wellington," they repeated.

His body shook. *It's stolen money!*

"He knows."

He knows it's stolen? How? Were they waiting to see if he would take the money? Had the voices set him up?

"Is there a problem, Mr. Finch?" called the manager through the curtain.

Jon backed into the shelf like a caged animal. "N- no. No problem."

There was a click on the hard floor outside the curtain, followed by a sliding sound. A briefcase slid into view.

"Will you be needing your briefcase?" said the manager.

What was going on? Jon stood there, frozen.

"Take it," whispered a distant voice.

"Ah—yes," said Jon, picking it up, "Thank you."

Please, please, please tell me what is going on, he begged

160

the voices.

"Charlie Wellington had a son," they whispered.

Charlie? From the note?

The sound of a curtain sliding caused Jon to spin around, but it was not his curtain.

"Two boxes," said a voice just outside.

"Very good, sir," said Wellington. "If you wouldn't mind, sir, could you bring the other?"

"Sure," said the man who had occupied the booth next to his.

Jon heard two sets of feet walking away. He opened the briefcase and quickly began transferring the money. All but three stacks fit neatly into the case. He tried to stuff them in his pants, but the bulge was prominent in his skinny jeans. Even if he broke it down into small wads, it would have been hard to conceal in his pockets. He held the bending stacks in his hands and looked around. Sitting on the floor, next to the divider post between the booths, was a red backpack with the zipper open. Jon peered into the empty compartment. It was deep and dark enough to hide the wad of bills. He doubted the man would realize it was there until long after he left the bank.

He stuffed the three stacks deep into the hole.

Immediately a voice screamed in his head. "What are you *doing?!*"

"No!" screamed another.

A third chimed in. "He's the *enemy!*"

Jon stared at the dark hole. *Why didn't you say something before I threw it in?!*

"We don't read minds." He could hear the sarcasm dripping from the words.

What? You've been reading my mind for the last ten minutes!

"Not reading," said a distant voice.

161

"Listening," said another.

Listening? Reading? What's the difference? He hovered over the bag. Would they see him shove his hand in?

"Thanks for putting up with me," said the voice of the bag's owner. Jon's hovering hand retreated.

"Is there anything else we may assist you with?" The manager's voice sounded close.

"No. I'll be on my way."

It sounded like the man was leaving without his bag. Jon pressed his hands against the sides of his booth and exhaled.

"Sir," said the manager, his voice filling the hollow room. "You forgot your bag."

Jon watched in horror as the bag slid from view. He had no idea what he had done, but it felt bad. Very bad. Who was this enemy the voices apparently feared? He didn't sound threatening. He sounded disgruntled, and broke. Did the voices want him to stay broke? How much had he given him? Probably thirty thousand dollars anyway. That was a lot of money.

The door to the vault room opened and closed, and his enemy was gone, for the moment. Jon closed the briefcase, closed the lid on the safe deposit box, and exited the booth.

The manager turned to him. "Did the case meet your needs?"

"Yes," said Jon, gripping the handle. "It did." Jon studied the man's face, as if for the first time. He looked noticeably nervous. Why? There appeared to be no end to the questions—Jon's head was starting to hurt. He just wanted it all to be over with.

The manager moved past him and retrieved the safe deposit box from the shelf. "If you'll follow me, please." He carried the box back into the vault with Jon on his heels. When he saw that Jon was in position to watch him secure the box, he slid it into its socket, and locked it in with the key.

"Your key," he said.

Jon took it.

"Now, if you have no objection, I'll accompany you to the lobby."

He had a ton of objections, but he shook his head no.

They climbed the stairs slower than Jon would have liked, then strolled through the double doors at the top. Jon kept his head down as they passed through the lobby—and past the front door...

Jon looked around. "Where are we going?"

"There is one more formality," said the man.

Formality? The formality of them slapping cuffs on him and throwing him into the jail cell next to his father?

The manager disappeared into an office with an enormous oak door, and Jon's courage began to fail again. If he made a run for it, could he make it out of the bank before they took him down? There were at least three security guards, and one was standing right next to the door.

"Is there a problem, Mr. Finch?" said the manager, coming back into view.

Jon wiped his forehead. "No. No problem."

"Then please, have a seat. This will only take a moment, then you can get on with your day."

It took every ounce of willpower for Jon to push himself over the threshold into that office but, once inside, seeing that there were no authorities waiting to arrest him, the adrenaline released.

"Are you okay, Mr. Finch? You seem nervous."

He swallowed. "No. Ah, I just have a touch of something."

The manager flashed his crooked teeth. "We'll make this quick then. Please, have a seat." He closed the door with a thud, circled the desk, and sat down in his plush chair. "I have to say, I knew someone would come for the money eventually, but I'm surprised it is someone so young."

Well, there it was. He knew it was too good to be true. It was the inevitable certainty of his life. Nothing this awesome could ever happen to him.

The manager leaned back in his chair. "At first I thought you might be a young, undercover cop straight out of the detective academy looking to make a huge score." He laughed a squeaky laugh. "And then those questions about Elliot James... I didn't know what to think." He paused, then sat forward. "You obviously didn't come prepared to take any money out, that's why I thought you were a cop. But then when you came out of your booth, I knew you had stumbled onto this."

Jon lifted his chin. "I don't know what you're talking about."

The man's thin lips stretched, and his crooked, slightly yellow teeth popped out again. "You're not with the police, and you're not a treasure hunter. I think you stumbled onto something which led you to the key."

The temperature in the room climbed ten degrees as the man leaned over his desk looking like the Grinch who stole Christmas. Jon braced himself for what would come next.

"Was it all there? All 2.6 million?"

2.6 mil...? Was there really that much?! Jon's eyes fixed on those of the manager's. There didn't seem much point in trying to hide the truth any longer. "I don't know how much there is," he said, "but it's a lot."

"My father said he never spent a dime of the money. He

164

said he put it back where it belonged. So when I stumbled upon that safe deposit box with Donald Finch's name on it, I knew it was in there. I just knew it!"

"And now you want it back," Jon blurted.

The manager stared at Jon, an odd expression on his face. "I don't want that money," he said, his voice intense. "It's nothing but a blight. Because of that money, I have worked my whole *life* to restore our family's name."

"Ah... O-*kay*." Jon tried to grasp what he was hearing. "So you're—going to give it to the police?" It had to be something like that.

"If I had had the key, that money would have been burned in a pit years ago. The last thing I want is a media circus with our family name being dragged through the mud, yet again. I'm glad to see it go. I don't care who you are, so long as you're not the police or a reporter. Take it! You have my blessing. But I do expect one thing in return."

Jon sat frozen. Was it really his? Once again, cynicism kept him from savoring the thought. There was always a catch.

The manager wrote something on a piece of paper and slid it across the desk. "Take one million and give it to this retirement village. My mother has suffered ten lifetimes for money she never saw a dime of. Do this, and you're free to walk away with the rest."

Jon couldn't say the words fast enough. "You have a deal." He looked down at the paper sitting on the desk. It said: "Pleasant Oaks Retirement Village, 225 Third Street."

"And, Mr. Finch," the manager said sarcastically, "I don't *ever* want to see you in this bank again."

CHAPTER **TWENTY-SEVEN**

David stood on the sidewalk in front of the bank with only one thought in his head. *My wife is going to kill me.* $650 a year for two safe deposit boxes? Who was going to pay for that? He certainly didn't have that kind of money.

He looked up at the sky. I hope you have a plan, because when that credit card bill comes in, Sharon's going to divorce me. Unless that's your plan! There was no response, of course. There never was. All he had was the messages, and those were only interested in steering him through some new gauntlet of terror. It didn't seem to matter to God if he was happy about it or not. Apparently, there was some grand, divine plan being shaped, and, for some reason, God wanted *him* to make it happen. Did he not care that he had lost his best friend? Did he not care that his wife and children were terrorized? Was he so focused on the big picture that he had lost the ability to feel the pain of those fighting this battle for him?

As he stood, clutching the red backpack in his hand and grinding his teeth, his eyes landed on a sign across the street. The raging sea of anger became as smooth glass. In bold letters, on a sign that had to be twelve feet long, were the words: *EYE CARE.*

David's response was immediate and visceral. *Then why don't you throw me a bone! Haven't I given enough? Am I not doing enough?* His eyes brushed across the store fronts on the other side of the street and bounced on three more words hidden amongst the noise. *Eye Gave*

Everything.

He took a step back as the familiar feeling of truth washed over him. That deep part of him that allowed him to recognize which words were messages, and which were not, was revealing something to him. It wasn't simply the idea that the earth and everything in it came from God, there was something more. With this message, there was a sense of deep, personal loss, as though God had given to humanity what was most precious to him. David could feel the emotion weeping from each word on a level he could never fully comprehend. Yet he understood one thing. God wasn't asking David to do anything he hadn't already done, or to give anything he hadn't already given. God had given everything.

He let the words trail off—and a sense of embarrassment washed over him as he became aware that he was standing in the middle of the sidewalk with tears streaming down his cheeks. He quickly brushed an arm across his face and looked down at the empty, red backpack in his hand. His other hand dug into his pocket and pulled out his cell phone. With a few clicks, the phone dialed Karen Knight.

"Hello?"

"Karen, this is David. How are things going there?"

He could hear the smile in her words. "You'll never guess who I ran into at the police station."

"Jonathan Blake?"

"That's a good one, but no. I ran into Agent Collins and Cooper, and check this out. You remember when Collins made that comment about the supernatural?"

"Yeah."

"Well, the plot thickens. Apparently Ross Blake and the killer in the blue car both experienced a blackout during the time of the murders."

"I'm sorry, what blue car?"

He could hear a puff of air escape her lips. "Why are you in the news business again? Don't you ever check the AP on your phone?"

"The Associated Press? They have an app for that?"

"Okay. I'm going to pretend that you're not completely useless and continue on as if this is going really well. In the last two weeks, here in Massachusetts, there have been four cases where suspected murderers have confessed to a loss of time during the time of the murder."

"So they're copycats."

"Copycats? How do you imagine that? Have you heard anything about murderers experiencing blackouts in the news lately?"

"No."

"That's because they aren't being reported. You can't copy something if you don't know about it."

"They have to be reported somewhere. How does something like this just slip by the media?"

"Investigative journalism is dead, David. Most news agencies just get the police report, slap it on the teleprompter, and call it a day. No one is digging anymore, for the same reason soda doesn't come in a glass bottle and everyone buys formica furniture at Walmart. Doing something right takes time, and time is money. But don't get me started." She sucked in a breath and rolled on. "This isn't an isolated thing either, Collins let it slip that there were other cases outside of Massachusetts, maybe nationwide."

"Okay, that's just weird."

"Something really strange is going on here. And after talking to Ross Blake, I was sure he was innocent."

"Really?"

"I mean, he's not the most even-tempered man I've ever

met, but you should have seen him. He was absolutely convinced his son committed the murder, as if he could not imagine himself capable of such a thing. He had me convinced. But if these blackout events are happening all over the place, it might be that he *did* do it, but there was coercion involved."

"Like hypnosis or something?"

"Maybe the government is working on some kind of weaponized psychotropic drug, and Collins and his department are playing damage control."

"That's creepy."

"Creepy doesn't even begin to describe it." He could hear the shiver in her voice. "So, anyway. Have you come up with anything else?"

"Nothing more yet. I deposited the food and I'm outside the bank."

"Okay. Well, get a cab and come to the police station. I'll hover around Collins and Cooper and see if I can glean any more useful tidbits."

"I'll see you in a few, then."

"Okay, see you soon." The phone went dead.

David slid it in his pocket and lifted his head. The traffic on the downtown street was moderate, but there was no sign of a taxi. A shiny, black Porsche approached, slowed to a crawl, then pulled into a parking space in front of him. The man in the driver's side climbed out, circled to the back, and opened the trunk. Within seconds four suitcases sat on the road behind the parked sports car. David stepped back to give the man room to put his bags up on the sidewalk.

"Can I help you with those," he said, noticing the frantic look on the man's face.

The man looked up from under a sweat-covered brow. "I'm sorry, what?"

"Can I help you with your bags?"

The finely dressed man shot a look up the street, gripped two bags, and said, "Yes. Thank you. Yes."

David swung the backpack on his shoulder, grabbed the remaining two suitcases and followed behind the man. "Where are you going?"

"Just to the corner," he said.

"No. I mean, where are you headed? Are you going on vacation?"

"Yeah, sure," he said, laughing. "I'm going on vacation."

A bus lumbered by and came to a stop at the corner in front of a local Greyhound station. The man checked his watch and walked faster.

"Are you taking the bus?"

"Yeah," said the man brusquely. It was clear he had no desire to discuss the details of his trip, if it even was a trip. David had seen an expression like his before, the many times his mother had fled a broken marriage.

"I didn't mean to pry."

The man's face lost its hard determination. "I'm sorry. I'm a little preoccupied. I really appreciate the help." He came to a stop at the side of the bus.

David popped to the side to avoid running into him. "I'm glad to help."

The man looked down the street and then back at David as if seeing him for the first time. "People like you are a dying breed," he said, almost sorrowfully. "Wolves eat the sheep. I'm so tired of being a wolf." His countenance was labored.

David didn't know how to respond.

"Here," said the man, holding out his car keys. "I'm not coming back, so why not give it to you?"

David blinked at the keys, then slowly lowered the suitcases to the ground.

170

"She's paid for," he said, forcing the Porsche keys into David's hand. "Title's in the glovebox. I intended to give it to my son, but he's too busy to care." His lips pressed. "It's not easy doing the right thing. The wrong thing never gets hard. You just hop on and before you know it, you can't imagine how you got so far from what you know is right." He tilted his head as though working the thought out for the first time. "What's your name?" he said, suddenly.

"David."

"Don't take the easy path, David. Do what's hard. It's so easy to cut corners when building a house. Don't be lazy. If you put the effort in to build the house right, you won't have to spend the rest of your life fixing it."

Again. David stood, speechless. He didn't dare ask the man a question. Whatever crisis had caused him to flee his life and his possessions had temporarily impaired the man's ability to control his own emotional state.

David tightened his grip on the keys. "Are you—sure about this?"

"I signed the title for my son but in the last sixty seconds you did more for me than my son has done in the last six years. Keep it."

"Sir? Ticket please." said a tall, round-bellied bus driver.

The man turned and held a ticket toward him.

"How many bags?"

"Four."

"Thank you, sir. You may board. We leave in five minutes."

The man put his hand out to David, and David shook it.

"In your whole life you might never get another reward for doing good. Let this be the reward for them all." He gripped David's hand and pulled him in slightly.

If the eyes truly are the window to a man's soul, there could be no doubt that this man's soul was boiling in the

171

torment of regret.

He let go of David's hand. David looked down at the key and back at the man. "I don't know what to say."

"Don't say anything."

David gave silent acknowledgment to the man's request.

The man chuckled again at a private thought. "You know, it's ironic," he said, "I spent my whole life giving people the one thing I can't give myself."

"What is that?" David studied the deep lines in the man's tired face.

He looked off into space and gave a short inward laugh. "Life," he said. And with that, he backed away, turned on his heel, and disappeared into the bus.

David watched as the last of the passengers boarded. He watched as the baggage doors were closed, and he watched as the bus pulled away. But he didn't see the man again. That was when he decided to believe that the most incredible thing that had ever happened to him, was actually happening.

He turned and walked up the sidewalk to where the black Porsche sat gleaming in the afternoon sun. The style suggested that the car could be as little as four years old, which meant it could easily be worth more than fifty thousand dollars. Was this really happening?

On the curb, behind a newspaper vending machine, David spied a trash can. He looked down at the red backpack, which reminded him of the soup kitchen, and strode over to the trash can. He stuffed the backpack into it then practically skipped his way around the Porsche to the driver's door. But before he could open it, his attention was drawn to a word fluttering on a flag above a store front. His mind went into auto pilot, and soon his eyes had bounced their way to the end of a new message.

His heart began to pound, and the breath left his body. He squeezed the keychain in his hand, tilted his head back, and screamed into the sky. "YOU'VE GOT TO BE KIDDING ME!"

CHAPTER TWENTY-EIGHT

Jon squinted at the afternoon sun and turned his face from it as he rushed down the sidewalk, putting as much distance as humanly possible between himself and that bank. He was only too happy to comply with the manager's wishes. The last place on earth he ever wanted to set foot in again was Norfolk County Savings and Loan. As far as he was concerned, Elliot James could rot in that building with the weird bank manager and the stranger from the booth next to him. He now had the resources to leave all this behind and go live on an island somewhere near the Bahamas.

"Fun, wasn't it?" interrupted a voice in his head.

"He's having fun," said another.

Not exactly fun, said Jon, inwardly, as he slowed his pace on the sidewalk, his head bowed to hide his face from stray pedestrians.

"We'll have more fun now," said a woman's voice.

Jon came to a stop. *Who are you?* he thought.

There was silence for a moment.

"Show him," said the voice that had spoken first.

Had the voices always had the ability to speak to him while he was fully awake, or had they strengthened in power? There had been a few isolated incidents, but nothing like this; the voices were definitely getting stronger.

"See the black Porsche?" said a new voice, boldly.

He did. It was parked on the side of the road, three cars

174

up.

"Under the bumper, under the plate," said the new voice.

Jon gave a paranoid look up and down the sidewalk. No one paid him any attention. There was no pursuit from the bank, no suspicious blue cars waiting to gun him down. But still, he felt as if they were there, hunting him.

"The doctor won't be back," they said. "Go ahead."

Steal it?

"Borrow," they said, "not steal."

Why? I have money now.

"Just do it."

He waited for a gray-haired lady with a dog to pass by, then skirted over to the Porsche. His fingers groped under the bumper and found something hard. With one motion, he gripped it, pulled it free, and stood. It was a magnetized Hide-A-Key box. He pressed his thumb on the cover and slid it open. Inside was a gold key with a red Porsche logo.

His head snapped back up, eyes scanning the road and the windows on the buildings to each side. No one was watching.

"We can give you anything you want," said a scratchy voice.

I have the money to buy a Porsche, why do you want me to borrow one?

"Why should the rich get good things?" said a deep voice, "while you wallow in your muck?"

"We can change your fate," whispered another.

How many of you are there?

"Do you feel it, Jon? The shackles of your pathetic fate loosed from your soul?"

The feeling *was* there, unmistakably. He had always felt bound, bound to poverty, bound to misery, unable to claw

175

his way out of his wretched circumstances. But holding the briefcase full of money and staring at the sweetest ride he had ever seen filled him with a satisfaction he had never known. He didn't have to follow the rules anymore. What had the rules ever done for him, anyway? His life, if you could call it a life, was nothing but a prison. But now the prison door was creaking open. Why not? Why shouldn't he?

"You deserve better than the hand you were dealt, Jon."

"Everything can change today."

"There is nothing we cannot give you."

"And no one to stop you."

He stepped around the car and slipped the key in under the door handle. The faint sound of suction could be heard as the door seal broke. It was the sound of quality craftsmanship, something Jon had been denied his whole life.

Why is it that one person is born into money, and another is forced to live in squalor? Why should one person be born smart and another barely able to get a GED? he thought. But—were they his thoughts? It was getting hard to tell his own thoughts from the voices.

This is where you change your destiny. Reclaim your life. You can have it all. You don't have to live in shackles.

What would he be giving up? His life had no meaning, no value. It was hard and full of the destruction of other people's choices. He didn't deserve the life he'd been given, but what was this new life opening up before him? Was it criminal? Was it even real? What if he was experiencing a psychotic break (which he strongly suspected).

What difference did it make? It felt real. Whatever this was, it was far better than what he had before. He slid into the car, placed the briefcase and iPad on the seat next to him, and closed the door with a warm thump.

The interior was brown leather with black trimming. The console and controls infused him with a sense of power. He attempted to slide the key in, but there was a cap on the ignition. A sliver of a hole on the side of the cap was just large enough so he could pry it off. He slid the key in, twisted, and the engine roared to life. The dash glimmered with the golden light of a hundred letters and symbols; it was the most beautiful thing he had ever seen. He was sure that driving this car for ten minutes would be worth a lifetime in prison.

He checked and adjusted the mirrors, shoved the automatic stick shift in gear, and pulled out into traffic. The responsiveness of the steering took his breath away. The only two vehicles he had ever driven were his father's truck and the fifteen-year-old Chevy Dart he had owned for five months, both of which steered like a sailboat.

This little Porsche moved like it knew what he was thinking. He turned left, and the tires gave a short squeak as they gripped the road. He turned right, and his body pressed into the firm, leather door cushion.

His mind whispered, "Go faster."

But prudence gripped him in its all-too-familiar clutch. He was driving a stolen car with a briefcase full of stolen money—not to mention the fact that he was wanted for murder. The car slowed, and the engine shifted down as his body reacted to the thought. *Get a grip, Jon! You're not out of the woods yet!*

You are in command of your destiny, his mind whispered. You don't have to live in fear anymore.

I'm wanted for murder! his mind screamed, as though at itself.

"We can fix that," a voice said.

How?

"We can lead you to the murder weapon."

You can what?

BEEEEEEEP.

He swerved back into his own lane.

But how can I get to it? The police are guarding my house.

"It's not at your house."

Then where is it?

"At the police station."

Well good. Right? I'll just wait for them to check the prints, and I'm set.

"It's hidden," said another voice.

What? Why would it be... Before he could finish the thought, he realized the implication of the statement. Could someone at the police department be working for Elliot James? Did that mean his father was innocent? Was his father supposed to shoot Sandra and lose his nerve?

Whose prints are on the gun?

"We will guide you," they said.

I'm supposed to trust you now? Where were you when I was floundering at the bank? How do I know you won't do that to me again?

"We didn't know you were the one."

"Now we know."

Don't blow this, Jon, his mind chastised him. Do you want to go back to who you were? A loser? A nobody?

He gripped the steering wheel. *What do you want me to do?*

"Go to the murder weapon, your name will be cleared."

You won't have to run from the police any more, his thoughts whispered. You will be free to live your life, to spend your money. You won't have to run anymore.

But to drive right into the belly of the beast in a stolen car with a case full of bank robber's loot? That was crazy!

Did he possess the strength to do that?

We are strong, said his mind.

He downshifted and the engine roared. The wheels bit into the road as he did a U-turn and headed back through town to the police station. He had to be out of his mind, or perhaps in his right mind for the first time in his life.

What would your life be like right now if you had taken charge? If you hadn't been so weak, you would have made a name for yourself. You would have fought back against the bullies who pantsed you in gym class just because you're different. You would have stood up to those stupid teachers who couldn't teach to save their lives and made you look like the stupid one. If you had taken charge, you would have made them respect you. When they hear about this, it's gonna blow their minds.

Jon found a spot in front of the police station and pulled in. His eyes rested on the three police cruisers sitting in a small parking lot on the side of the building. It was all he could do to not imagine officers inside them, watching him, waiting for him to exit the stolen vehicle so they could take him down. It took a few minutes for him to build his courage, but finally his hand shot out and pulled the handle. The door swung open, and he climbed out onto the tar.

The building was a towering monster. Every window was an eye taking note of his arrival. He imagined officers scrambling inside. Arming themselves. Preparing to take him into custody. This was the worst idea of all time.

His hand reached for the driver's door handle, and froze.

"Go to the rear of the car," said a very clear voice.

"Yes, we need him."

Who? he thought.

"Go to the rear..."

Jon shimmied along the side of the car, keeping it between him and the police station.

"Pound on it."

On what? The trunk?

"Pound it! Pound it hard!"

He clapped his hand down on the trunk.

"One more will be glorious!" said another voice.

He made a fist and struck the trunk three time as hard as he dared to.

"Open it. Open it up!"

He did as ordered. The trunk flipped up and Jon's body reacted to what was inside. He leaped backward and stifled a scream.

An arm shot up out of the trunk. "Don't shoot me, I'm unarmed!"

Jon clutched his chest and took a step backward. He stood staring, ready to sprint.

The man in the trunk sat up, blinking into the afternoon sun. He looked at Jon.

"We need him," a voice spoke low in Jon's mind. "Do not be afraid."

"Wh- who are you?"

The man blinked, shielding the sun with his hand, "David Chance."

David Chance? Canary had spoken the name. She'd said he could trust him. "Wh- what are you doing in my trunk?"

"*Your* trunk?"

Jon recoiled slightly. Did the car belong to this man? Had he stolen a car with the *owner* in the trunk?

"It's your car. Don't listen to him," said a voice.

He puffed his chest out, "Yeah, my trunk."

This had a noticeable effect on David. "Are you the son?"

180

"Yes, the doctor's son," a voice whispered low.

"Yes, the doctor's son," he parroted.

David lay back down in the trunk and balled his fists. *I knew it! I knew it was too good to be true! Nobody gives away a Porsche.*

"He is so easily moved," Jon's mind whispered. Jon sensed an intense hatred in the thought. Was the hatred for this man? He stepped closer to the car. "What are you doing in there?" he asked again.

David squirmed. "Does it matter? Just shoot me. Shoot me and get it over with."

Jon studied the man a moment, trying to figure why his voice sounded so familiar. He was sure he'd never seen the man before. "Why on earth would I shoot you? I just want you out of my trunk!"

David rolled onto his belly and pushed a leg out. With a few grunts and a whole lot of complaining, he was finally on the sidewalk, brushing himself off.

Jon slammed the trunk. "What were you doing in there?"

David looked up, and his eyes widened, like he was seeing a ghost. "Wait a min... You're not... You're Jon Blake!" he said, aghast.

And there it was. He hadn't even gotten into the police station before someone recognized him. But a voice suppressed the thought. "You know where the murder weapon is."

"I know where the murder weapon is!" he blurted.

It was clear from David's expression that he was attempting to figure out why Jon had blurted something so random.

"That's why I'm here," said Jon, "the murder weapon."

"Here?" David looked up at the building for the first time, then back at Jon. "The police station? The weapon is

181

here?"

"Yeah."

"That's weird," David said to himself. "Karen didn't say they found the weapon."

"They didn't. Well, someone did, but it's hidden."

David's face went slack. "At the *police* station?"

"Yeah."

David's eyebrows scrunched as he let this new information sink in. "Wh- What are you planning to do? You can't just waltz in there and accuse them of hiding evidence and expect them to bring you to it." His body flailed. "How do you even know it's in there?!"

"He is supposed to help."

"You're supposed to help," Jon parroted.

Yet again, David's brain was processing. *"How?"*

"Locker 2881."

"It's in locker 2881."

David started to pace. "Let me get this right. God told me to climb into the trunk of a car, which gets stolen, but then I end up at the police station, which is where I wanted to go in the first place, and then..."

"God told you?" Jon interrupted. This day was getting weirder by the minute.

"Yes. That's my thing. God shows me messages, and like an idiot I follow them. Don't you watch the news?"

"Okay. I get it. You're nuts," Jon said, backing up.

David puffed up. "Yeah. I'm the crazy one! You showed up at a police station in a stolen vehicle to tell them one of them is hiding evidence, and you think they're gonna let you walk in there and show 'em where it is?"

"Tell him he's going to do it," said a clear voice.

"No, you're going to do it," he said, unable to keep his face from revealing his complete shock.

"And that!" said David, pointing. "How do you know

182

that!"

Things were beginning to spiral out of control. This was not going at all the way he had imagined. He thought the voices would guide him into the police station and lead him to the location of the weapon, maybe by announcing where the police were standing and which way they were facing, like something out of a movie. Not this! This was insanity.

"Come to think of it," said David, "Why did you pound on the trunk like you knew I was inside, but then you leaped back when you opened it?" His head tilted. "You didn't know I was in there."

Jon inched backward.

"And now you say *I'm* going to go into the police station and point them to the evidence like you know this for certain. You don't even know me!"

Jon's fight or flight instinct drove him back around toward the driver's door.

David pursued him. "If you want my help, you need to tell me something. Are you getting messages too?"

"Yes. Tell him yes!"

"Yes," he said.

David's mouth hung open.

"I'm just like you. Following messages," said a voice.

Was it true? Did this David guy hear voices too? "I'm following messages too," Jon said.

David deflated. "I thought I was the only one."

"So did I," Jon said. It was true. He thought it was just some weird thing his mind was doing. But if the voices were coming from outside of him, what was the source? He patently rejected the idea that God was speaking to him. Beyond the fact that he considered religion a fairy tale, it was absurd to think that God would speak to him in a hundred different voices. But, if it wasn't God, then

183

what was it?

Guardian angels, his mind said.

Ridiculous! Was his response to the thought he was sure was not his own.

David's voice fought for his attention. "I can't believe this. We're not alone—I wonder how many of us there are?"

"Look," said Jon, getting exasperated, "this is great and all, but I'm a little preoccupied right now. I'm not really looking at the big picture. Are you going to help me or not?"

"Yeah," said David, snapping out of his reverie. "So, I'll—ask them to check the locker?"

"I guess."

"What about you?"

"I'll just wait in the car," he said, looking around to see if their exchange had caught anyone's attention.

It had. An officer was standing just inside the glass doors of the police station, looking out at them. He was joined by two more officers and the three started talking.

"I have to go!" Jon bolted for the driver's door.

"What? You can't go."

"I have to go." He fumbled with the door handle. "They know I'm here!"

"Then I'll go with you," said David.

You don't have to run anymore, Jon's mind whispered. He locked up.

"Come on!" said David, running around the car.

"No," said Jon, watching in horror as the three officers exited the building and headed straight for them.

CHAPTER TWENTY-NINE

David looked over the smoked glass moonroof of the Porsche at Jon's look of horror. "Get in! Let's go!"

"No. I have to stay," said Jon, though he looked like he wanted to run.

Had he seen a message? Was it telling him to stay? David understood all too well the young man's discomfort.

"Jon Blake!" called one of the officers. "Put your hands where we can see them and place them on the roof of the car."

David twisted around. All three officers had drawn their revolvers and were creeping in.

"Don't shoot!" he screamed. "He's turning himself in."

"Hands on the car!"

Did they mean David as well? His hands shot up. "Okay! Okay!"

"Hands on the car!"

David spun and slapped his hands on the roof. Jon had done the same. David saw intense fear in the boy's eyes and wondered if he would bolt. "It's okay, Jon," he spoke low. "You can trust the messages. They're never wrong." He felt an officer come in behind him, and soon both of his hands were locked in cold hard steel.

They did the same to Jon, then led them up to the police station where two more officers were waiting. They were ushered through the doors and into the lobby where even more people were standing, including Karen Knight and

185

Agent Collins.

"That's David Chance! He's with me!" said Karen over the commotion. "He brought Jon Blake in!"

The sergeant turned to her. "We need to process him and get his statement. He's not under arrest."

"Then why is he cuffed?"

The men shuffled around. Jon was taken from the room, and David was released from the cuffs.

The sergeant spoke over his shoulder. "I'll give you a minute, but then we need to get a statement. Do you understand?"

David nodded. Karen leaped toward him. He thought for a moment she might hug him. "Are you all right?"

"Yeah," he said, rubbing his wrists.

"This is unexpected. Not only did you find him, you brought him in."

"Actually, he brought himself in." *And me,* David thought.

Collins stepped in beside Karen, and gave David a silent greeting.

"Well still," she said, "here you are. This is amazing. So what's next?" She rubbed her hands together, clearly having fun. "Did the messages tell you how we're going to help clear Jon and his father of these charges?"

"You think they're both innocent?" interrupted Collins with a lift of his brow.

"You tell me," she said, with a glare.

David noticed the tension between them. "Is there— something I should know about?"

Collins turned a cool face toward him. "Karen has a theory that there might be extraterrestrials involved in this case."

She laughed his comment off. "Agent Collins thinks he can cover up his agency's secret research into weapons-grade psychotropics with charming subterfuge."

Air puffed from Agent Collins' mouth. "Is that your new theory?" he said, sarcastically. "I like it. It has headline flare. Not necessarily broadcast news headline flare, but definitely tabloid flare."

She gave a snide tilt to her head. "Oh I see how it is. Well, we'll see how smug you are when they seal you in your cell at Fort Leavenworth and flush the key down a toilet."

David interjected. "You two need a room?"

"No," said Karen. "We're just working out a few diplomacy bugs. We're all set."

Collins looked almost like he was enjoying himself.

"So," said Karen, looking at David expectantly, "what's next?"

Could he come right out and say it? Would the police give him access to the locker room, or would they attempt to search it on their own? For all he knew, the mole was already heading to the locker to move the evidence. "I know where the murder weapon is," he said loudly. The room quieted. "It's here, in the police station."

Karen immediately caught the implication. "Someone tampered with the evidence?"

David addressed the room. "Someone in this station took the weapon from the crime scene and hid it here." He hoped for a noticeable reaction, or, even better, a guilty departure, but there was none. Everyone just stared.

He addressed the sergeant who was waiting to get his statement. "I need immediate access to your locker room. He looked around at the puzzled faces. "And I need witnesses. The mole could be anyone in this room."

"A mole?" The sergeant looked doubtful. "What is your source for these allegations?"

"I'm not at liberty to reveal my source."

"You said in the locker room? Where? Inside a locker?"

"Yes."

"Do you have a locker number?"

"Yes."

"What is it?"

"I can't give you that. I have to show you."

The sergeant considered the volatile nature of the situation, and finally turned and addressed the officer behind the counter. "Call the captain."

"He's on his way," he said.

Within seconds Captain Jackson pushed through a set of doors on the right side of the lobby with a suited man following on his heels. "Bring me up to speed, Sergeant," he said, assessing the occupants of the room.

"This man works with Karen Watson." The sergeant indicated David with his hand. "He says someone removed evidence from the crime scene and hid it here, in our locker room."

"Does he, now?" said the captain, leveling his eyes on David. "And how would you know *that,* Mr. Chance?"

"I'm not at liberty to say."

"Are we going to be host to more of your party tricks?" His lip curled under his burly mustache.

"I came here with Jon Blake. I think I've more than proven myself."

"Young man, you haven't even begun to prove yourself to me."

David stuck his chest out slightly. "Are you afraid of what we'll find in that locker?"

The captain's face was devoid of humor. "It is a matter of protocol. We don't make it a habit to allow civilians into our locker area. And it is a matter of security. You need evidence or a source to back up your claim. But I'm guessing all you have are weird psychic readings to share."

David was inclined to continue pressing the captain, but there was a chance the captain would shut him down out of spite. So he kept his peace.

Captain Jackson let out a sigh. "I want you to know, I don't take the invasion of my officers' personal space lightly. If we don't find what you claim is there, things are going to get very uncomfortable for you."

David gave a less-than-confident nod.

"What locker do you claim this evidence is being hidden in?"

"I'll show you when we get there."

"I'd like to have the officer in question present at the inspection."

It seemed like a reasonable course; having the guilty man in the room would keep him from fleeing. David leaned in and said, "2881."

The Captain walked over to the desk. "Call up the record on 2881."

After a long and painful pause, the desk officer said, "Sergeant Gram."

The name immediately sent David back to his run-in with Sergeant Gram at the crime scene. It made sense. He had acted suspicious the whole time.

"Where is Sergeant Gram right now?"

"In with Jon Blake."

The Captain waved David to follow, and picked up two officers on his way to the holding room. Karen and Agent Collins trailed behind. Through a one-way glass, they could see the tall, muscular Sergeant Gram sitting across from Jon Blake with a note pad. The Captain leaned into the room. "Would you come with me for a moment, Sergeant."

David could see the sergeant's expression. He was stoic,

yet curious. He slid back from the table and came out of the room.

"Follow me, please," said the captain.

An officer stepped in between David and the sergeant, but the sergeant caught a glimpse of David over the officer's shoulder. "What's *he* doing here?!"

"This way," said the captain.

The officer behind the sergeant gave him a nudge, and they continued down the long, thin hallway to another hallway, and then around a corner to the locker room.

"Take a position by your locker, Sergeant."

"What's all this about?" he protested.

"It's probably nothing, but I need to do a quick inspection of your locker to avoid a media backlash. We'll keep it private." He stood in front of the locker and looked back at the doorway where David and the rest were standing. "You all keep back."

The sergeant's eyes became wild. "This is an invasion of privacy!"

"No," said the captain, slipping on a pair of medical exam gloves, "this is a routine inspection between you, me, and Officer Walsh here. If the locker is clean, you're free to go." The Captain slid the master key into the center of the combination dial and twisted.

Sergeant Gram craned his neck to see. The motion was curious, like Gram himself was wondering what was in the locker. It was hardly the action of a man who had been caught red-handed.

With a squeak the door opened, and the Captain's hands disappeared inside the cavity of the locker. Sergeant Gram and Officer Walsh both attempted to catch a glimpse inside. There was something that sounded like sliding hangers, followed by a shifting of materials at the bottom of the locker.

The captain pulled his gloved hand out, revealing a plastic evidence bag containing a hand gun. He turned to the sergeant, whose face was in a frenzy. "Officer Walsh, take Sergeant Gram into the next room and read him his rights."

"My *rights!*" said the sergeant, struggling against Officer Walsh.

"I'm sorry, Tom," said the captain, placing the bag back in the locker.

The sergeant pulled away, and Officer Walsh lurched forward. There was spittle in Gram's mouth. "You're sorry?!" His voice rose. "YOU'RE *SORRY?!*"

The Captain's hands slammed into the sergeant's chest and held him back as two other officers ran in to help subdue the large man.

Gram's right hand pulled free and swung at the captain. *"You're sorry!"* The fist missed its mark as the captain leaped back against the locker.

Officers piled on top of Gram, but he continued to stand. "You did this for *him?*" There was an eerie sound in the sergeant's voice, an anguish David could not have imagined in his worst nightmares. "We did what you said, and you betrayed us for *him?!*"

One of the officers managed to get his billy club out and struck the sergeant just above the knee. Gram shifted his weight and threw the officer back five feet, using only one free arm. David danced out of the way and crouched near the corner.

"Get more men in here!" screamed the captain.

Collins, who had moved in to assist the officers, ran back and hollered out the door. "We need more men in here!"

"Betrayer!" screeched Gram through spit-covered lips, his eyes like a wild animal's. "We were *promised!*"

The interwoven mass of officers undulated like a mound of blue snakes slithering around Gram, as he continued to bash them against the walls. Several billy club strikes hit their mark, but the sergeant remained standing. Three more officers filed into the room and joined the snake pile, filling the locker room aisle.

A blood-curdling scream filled the air and reverberated off the hard, metal locker room walls. One of the officers fell back, gripping his arm. There was blood on it, and blood on the sergeant's mouth. Another man screamed, and a spray of blood splattered across the locker wall.

David scurried toward the door. Collins had his handgun out and stood in front of Karen, protectively. He aimed the weapon at the sprawl of men. *Is he going to shoot him?!* thought David. Collins' eyes sighted down the barrel, and there was a loud *crack!* It wasn't the sound of a bullet. Perhaps a dart? There were two more cracks, and the heap of men collapsed to the ground. One by one they climbed off the pile, revealing the body of Sergeant Gram, lying still on the tiled floor.

"What was *that?*" said one of the men, clearly shaken.

"Get him into holding," said the captain.

"I've never seen anything like that," said another officer.

They cuffed him, and three of the men, who hadn't been bitten, dragged Gram from the room.

Karen pushed out from behind Collins. "You care to tell me what that was?"

Collins sheathed his weapon. "Looks like drugs to me, maybe bath salts."

"Bath salts?" she said incredulously. "An on-duty police officer on bath salts?"

"Well, it was some kind of adrenaline enhancing agent. We'll know more when they do a toxicology report."

Karen's eyes flared. "And you just *happen* to carry a

tranquilizer gun?"

David's eyes flicked down to the agent's holster, and up again. That was a good point! Why was Agent Collins carrying a tranquilizer gun? Was this sort of thing common for him? If so, he hoped Karen would pry the truth from him. If anyone could do it, she could.

He gave her a serious look. "We don't carry firearms. Our mandate is to take the extraterrestrials alive."

"Extraterrestrials." she said, clearly disgusted by the absurdity of his answer.

"It's a good thing, too. If there were bullets in this thing, that junkie would have tore this room, and everyone in it, apart."

The Captain left the two wounded men and came over to them. He was carrying the plastic bag with the handgun. "Whatever's going on, we're going to get to the bottom of it. Here," he said, handing the gun to an officer. "Take this to the lab and get me some prints."

David watched as the officer passed by with the bag dangling from his grip—and a single question formed in his mind. If Sergeant Gram took the weapon to hide the identity of the killer, then why did he put it in a plastic bag to preserve the fingerprints?

CHAPTER **THIRTY**

Jon Blake didn't have to imagine what was happening down the hall from the holding room; the voices wouldn't shut up about it. There was a level of hysteria in his head which had ended with one voice repeating over and over, "Deepest darkest, deepest reaches, sacred trust abandoned us." Jon sat listening to it for several minutes, repeating its loop, until eventually he built up the nerve to pose an inward question. *Who abandoned you?*

"Not us. Them," said a strong voice.

The chanting voice ceased its lament.

Who was abandoned?

"They don't listen. They don't understand."

Who!

"They know the rules. They cannot be broken."

Jon's hands squeezed into fists. *"Who?!"* he said out loud.

There was a long pause—which made Jon very uncomfortable.

"It is unlawful for us," said the strong voice.

What is?

"Flesh and blood, and mortal breath," it said.

"But he is different," said another. "He is open."

"True. He is for us. But flesh and blood and mortal breath."

"He wants to know. What can we tell?"

There was dissension among the voices? This was a new thought for Jon. But why not? There were many of them. Why wouldn't they have different opinions and personalities? He had imagined they were a concoction of his own subconscious, and therefore all uniquely him. But now he was seriously beginning to question that hypothesis.

"Things of earth," said the strong voice.

"Tell him his life was slated for misery, and we have been allowed to rescue him."

"This is acceptable."

"Tell him that, even now, Elliot James is hunting him."

Jon interjected his own thought. *Here? In the station?*

"He tracked you to his thorn."

Tracked me to what?

"He doesn't know you are drawn to her."

Canary? He realized as the name leaped into his mind, unrestrained, that he was, indeed, very drawn to her. She was beautiful, and seemed smart. And even though she had watched him for years, she still liked him, maybe even more-than-liked him—though that was probably just wishful thinking. Regardless, there was no denying that he was drawn to her.

Is she in danger? he thought.

"We are moving to protect her, but Elliot James has many operatives."

Talk to her. Warn her!

"We cannot."

Why not?! You talk to me!

"You are different."

What about the sergeant, or the captain, you talk to...

"Do not explain!" interrupted the strong voice.

"But he needs to know," said the softer.

"He will know what to do when the time comes. We will guide him."

Will she be hurt? thought Jon.

"We don't know," said a new voice.

Please don't let her be hurt.

"The police will let you go soon. It's up to you, but we will help."

CHAPTER **THIRTY-ONE**

To say Karen Knight was unhappy would have been a gross understatement. One would have had to blatantly ignore the tight folding of her arms, the unmistakable clenching of her jaw, and the incessant clipping of her high heels on the concrete floor of the janitorial room. One would also have had to ignore the incessant muttering and occasional outburst of, "Collins can't keep us here!" By David's estimation, she was well past unhappy and barking on the heels of livid.

He sighed. "He said he'd be back in a second."

She chewed her lip. "He's up to something, probably covering things up. There's something in that locker room he doesn't want me to see." She tried the doorknob again. It was still locked. Funny that.

"It doesn't help anything to get all worked up about it."

She shot him a look like a prowling animal. "He locked us in a janitor's closet!"

"It's hardly a closet."

"I should scream bloody murder and bring the whole police department down here."

David picked up the receiver of the phone sitting on the desk behind him. "Or you could call them."

"I'd prefer to scream," she said, irritated with his assumption that she was unaware that the room contained a phone.

He had seen Karen in just about every emotional state possible, but this was a new one. It wasn't simply irritation or frustration, there was a hint of something else. Was it fear?

"You ah... You gonna be okay, Karen?"

"No, I'm not okay!" she snapped.

He rephrased. "There's something bothering you and it isn't just Agent Collins."

She continued to pace, and offered no response.

"Are you claustrophobic?"

"No," she said, disgusted.

"Well you're worried about something."

She twisted around. "Aren't *you?*"

"What?"

"Worried?" she said.

"About what?"

"About whatever made that sergeant lose his mind in that locker room?"

"Well, since I'm not currently taking bath salts..."

"*Bath* salts." The words spit from her lips. "You believe that garbage?!"

"Only slightly more than the extraterrestrial thing."

"The government is doing something creepy, David, and this guy, Collins, is their clean-up guy. I have a very bad feeling about this." Her eyes scanned the room.

"You think Collins is going to kill us?"

She clip clopped over to the window and looked through the blinds. "I don't fear death, but whatever happened to Sergeant Gram is worse than death, like some kind of zombie lobotomy."

The thought of being injected with a lobotomizing drug caused a reaction in David's gut, but it was immediately suppressed as the words *Eye Care* flashed in his mind. It was true. He knew it. God did care. As hard as it was for him to cling to that understanding intellectually, he knew the message was true. He could feel the emotion behind the words, like those emotions were his own. God cared for him. He would protect them. "I don't know, Karen. I think if we were about to be lobotomized, God would have given me the heads up. I really don't think there is anything to worry about."

She turned and studied him. "Maybe he did. Maybe you missed the message."

"Trust me, he doesn't let me miss them."

"Maybe he..." She froze in mid sentence as the door knob began to jiggle. She moved briskly to the desk and sat on the edge, near the phone.

Agent Collins came in and put his finger to his lips. He shut the door and pulled an electronic wand from the inside pocket of his suit coat. Slowly, he circled the room, waving it high and low as they watched, speechless. The way Agent Collins manipulated the wand was mesmerizing, so much so that even Karen was unable to interrupt.

"It's clear," he said, at last, sliding the device back into his pocket. "We can speak freely."

"Who do you think is listening to us?" said Karen, clearly not buying the performance.

"Extraterrestrials," he said, with no hint of humor on his face.

Karen slid off the desk. "Are you *kidding* me?! It never ends with you."

Collins stood like a grim statue.

"How about we talk about what is *really* going on here? How about we talk about what kind of drug can make a human gain the strength of ten men."

"How about you relax and let me explain," he said. His voice was commanding and even-tempered.

Her eyes stayed locked on his, and a silence descended upon the room. Collins stood, stone faced, waiting. Finally,

Karen backed down. "I swear," she said, "if you throw that extraterrestrial line at me one more time..." Her stiff finger floated in front of his face.

He pulled a black device from his pocket. It had an illuminated screen with an image of a man's face. "Do you see this man?" he said, showing it to Karen.

She peered at it. "Oliver Cloverfield," she read from one of the lines of text below the image.

"Oliver Cloverfield," said Collins, "born 1953 to Charles and Thelma Cloverfield. He lived a normal, low-profile life until one day he was found dragging the body of his dead mother through the woods in back of his house. He told authorities he had blacked out, and when he woke he was standing over his mother's dead body." He flipped to another photo. "This is Elizabeth Carter. She was a school teacher until she showed up at the police station covered in the blood of her neighbor. She claimed that she had no memory of what had happened." He flipped again. "This is Gordon Singleton. He was a scout leader until he pushed a U.S. Senator off a mountain ledge." He dropped his hand and locked his eyes on Karen's. "He said he lost five minutes of time. He didn't remember even meeting the Senator."

"All of them blacked out?" she said, dumbfounded.

"I have fifty-seven cases, if you would like to see them."

Karen's aggressive stance melted.

"Those are just the cases where murder was involved. We've tracked over four hundred cases of amnesia-related crimes worldwide, but nothing we've seen compares to what's going on here in Massachusetts. And that's saying something, since the most violent and news-worthy cases seem to be coming out of Colorado."

Collins read the questioning look on Karen's face. "Do you remember the man who opened fire in the shopping center, killing eight?" He lifted the device and showed his picture. "He has two things in common with Ross Blake. He doesn't remember the event, and he has no remorse for committing murder."

"Ross Blake has plenty of remorse," she said.

"Don't confuse regret with remorse. That man doesn't care that his girlfriend is dead. He's not sorry he killed her, he's just sorry he had no control over how it happened."

"I don't believe Ross Blake would kill anyone," she said.

"Only for fear of the repercussions, but if something were to numb that fear and remove his inhibitions, I assure you, he is a cold-blooded killer."

As Karen struggled to unravel what Collins was implying, David took the opportunity to interject. "Are you saying there's a drug that suppresses a person's natural inhibitions to do the evil they are capable of?"

"I wish it were that simple, David. If all we had to go on were the incidents we've all seen in the media, I would say yes, but there's more to this than I'm allowed to say."

Karen's chin lifted. "Then why tell us anything at all? Why the sudden partial honesty?"

"We need the help of David's messages."

Karen shifted to a more poised posture. "Then you'll have to give a full disclosure. David won't go into this thing blind. You need to be straight with us. How is all of this connected?"

A loud pounding startled them all. Collins peeked out the shade on the door, his hand slipped inside his jacket and pulled out the dart pistol. He held it down by his leg as he opened the door. Captain Jackson's face appeared in the opening.

"What are you three doing in my janitor's office?"

"Having a private conversation," said Collins, evenly.

"Well do it somewhere else; this area is off limits."

"We won't be long," said Collins.

"I'm not going to ask you again, Agent. You do not have jurisdiction here. If you don't get yourself back up to the lobby, this is going to turn into something your superiors will find most uncomfortable."

"I imagine it will," said Collins, slipping his pistol under his suit coat into the back of his pants. "Well, we don't want to have an incident, do we?"

David wasn't sure if he was imagining it or not, but the captain's voice seemed to take on a deeper, darker quality. "Not if one can be avoided," he said, "But the days of avoiding conflict are almost at an end."

CHAPTER **THIRTY-TWO**

David sat down on the marble stairs in front of the police station and watched as Collins spoke with a group of serious-looking men standing at the bottom of the stairs. Based on their suited attire, tight haircuts and all-business demeanor, his guess was that these men were from Collins' agency. Over his shoulder he could see Karen, still pacing, and five officers standing in front of the police station with hands clasped on the buckles of their utility belts. Had something dangerous just been averted? The group in front of the stairs began to disperse, and Collins strolled up to where David was sitting.

Karen stopped pacing and faced off for another round. "What was that all about?" she said, locking her hands onto her waist.

David lifted a hand. "Karen, back off." His voice sounded weak, even in his own ears.

"I need you two to come with me, please," said Collins, discreetly, "where we can speak privately." He didn't wait for a response, but pivoted and started down the steps. Karen looked weary, but she followed, and David picked up the rear.

They followed Collins down to one of the black SUVs on the curb. He opened the door and motioned for them to climb in. Karen looked less than pleased with the idea of going anywhere with Collins or his men, but he was quick to address her unspoken concern. "If we intended to kidnap you, Mrs. Knight, I assure you, you wouldn't see it coming." His expression made his unwavering confidence apparent.

Karen acknowledged his dig, stooped down, and climbed in.

The back of the SUV felt more like a limousine with its plush seats facing toward each other. Collins sat in the rear. David and Karen sat with their backs to the driver in the three piece suit. The door made a hollow thump.

Before Collins could get a word out, Karen started right in. "Do you mind telling us why Captain Jackson went all Invasion of the Body Snatchers down there in the janitor's office? That voice was *not* normal.

"Karen, we've already been down this road. You don't want to hear my answer."

"Not if it has to do with little green men from space."

"We don't know what color they are," he said, without the slightest hint of humor.

That set Karen off. "Seriously? Why are we bothering with you?" She clutched David's wrist. "Come on, David. This was a bad idea. We'll get more information out of Captain Jackson."

He resisted her grip. "I'd like to hear what Agent Collins has to say."

Collins and Karen locked eyes. Both were unflinching.

"I have an idea," said David. "Why don't we just agree to disagree."

"How about this," said Collins, "we stick to the facts and let the truth reveal itself."

Karen gave a suspicious glower. "What *facts?* All you've given us so far is misdirection."

He looked at David. "As Karen has demonstrated so candidly, the general public is not ready to hear our position on these strange occurrences, so, at the very least, we would like to keep imaginations from running wild. That is why my superiors believe it is in our best interest to have someone in the media see what we are doing from behind the scenes in order to play damage control. But, clearly, this will have to be handled delicately."

He could tell Karen wanted to say something, but instead chose to hear him out.

"How about I lay out the facts as we know them, and you make your own assumptions as to what you think they mean?

She folded her arms. "Fair enough."

"All right, here's what we have. Ross Blake killed his live-in girlfriend Sandra Pinkerton, whose sister happens to be award-winning chemist, Kathleen Peltz. He says he doesn't remember doing this. We also have an amnesia-related incident at the lab of Dr. Peltz, as well as three more blackout victims related to the Blake case. One was taken into custody this morning near the 7-Eleven just after he shot Ross's long-time friend Peter Hargrove. His name is Adam Gordon. Gordon was seen at the bowling alley last night during the time Ross Blake and Peter Hargrove had the conversation that caused Blake to go home and execute his girlfriend. Gordon, like the others, claims he has no memory of shooting Peter Hargrove. Then we have Sergeant Gram going crazy in the locker room, and now Captain Jackson is showing signs of contamination." Collins paused.

Karen couldn't help herself. "Contaminated with what?"

Collins chose his words carefully. "We don't know. It isn't a drug; we're sure of that much, because we've run toxicology tests on several victims and found no traces of any substance that would cause this. There have been many cases where illegal substances were found, but there is no correlation between victims. Our tests have also shown no evidence of a physical parasite."

"So—something is controlling these people—but you don't know what it is."

Once again, Collins was careful to direct the conversation back to the empirical. "What we've learned has been from the mouths of the victims themselves and cannot be trusted."

"How many cases are there, total?"

"Dozens, over the course of the last forty years."

"Forty years?" said David.

Karen's lip curled. "This has been going on for *forty* years?"

"I don't know why you're surprised. These stories are all over the news, look them up yourself. We aren't hiding anything. They're in the newspapers, the tabloids, on the Internet."

"I've never heard of anyone talking about an epidemic of crime where all the criminals claim to have amnesia."

"That's not because of us. These are closed-off individuals who don't understand what is happening to them. Most of them aren't willing, or maybe aren't able, to explain their actions, and the ones who are usually won't admit they can't remember. The few that do speak up get ridiculed by the press and the public. The last thing anyone wants to hear is that a murderer claims they can't remember. They want justice to be served. They want people to be held accountable for their actions."

"So what you're saying is that this is happening right under our noses?"

David shifted in his seat. "Hold on a second. If something is controlling these people, how does a prominent police captain like Jackson walk around like a puppet without anyone noticing?"

"It is apparent that he is only being controlled for short moments of time. Most of the victims we've tracked experience short disorienting events where they get turned around or lose only a couple of minutes. I doubt the captain has lost enough time to even realize that anything is happening. And if the controlling force is discreet, no one around him will be the wiser."

A dark thought began to creep in from the cracks in the vehicle and soak into David's veins. Could they control *him?* Could they make him do something horrible without his consent? His pulse started a soft pound in his neck and his fingers began to tingle with fear.

No. Collins said that none of these people ever did anything they weren't predisposed to do. Whatever this was, it couldn't control him unless he let it. Right? The thought comforted him, but the question still found its way to his lips. "They can't control us, can they?"

"That's an unsettling thought, isn't it? But no. As I said before, these perpetrators aren't doing anything they weren't already considering. So if you're not thinking about blowing up The Federal Building, they can't make you."

"But do they influence us?"

"We don't know what they are capable of."

Karen shook her head. "When you say 'they,' you believe it's extraterrestrials."

There was no noticeable ruffle in the agent's feathers. "We agreed to stick to the facts, and the fact is, we have an enemy, and that enemy is controlling these people."

"Why?" said David. "Do you know what they're planning?"

"Not yet, but we believe Jon Blake is important to them. He is being herded toward something, but we don't have a target yet." His strong eyes connected with David's. "We were hoping you would help us find that target."

CHAPTER THIRTY-THREE

Jon Blake sat in the midst of a sea of desks, waiting for the officer who'd been taking care of his out-processing to return from whatever errand he had been given on the phone. The room was busy with activity, but mostly on the far end toward the front of the station. No one was paying any attention to him.

Now what? he thought.

"Wait," they said.

A tall, black police officer walked by. He gave Jon a friendly smile, but Jon did not reciprocate.

Are they going to hurt Canary? he thought.

"Wait," they whispered.

"How am I supposed to help her if you won't tell me what to do?"

"See the keys?"

He saw a set of keys laying in a clump on the other side of the desk. *Yes. I see them.*

"You will have to be quick."

To do what?

"Grab them."

Why would I...

"GO!" said a voice that sounded like an old man.

The command caused him to stand, but he didn't go for the keys. *Someone will see me!* he thought, frantically, as he twisted around to see if anyone was looking.

"Quickly!" said a female voice.

There was an officer four desks away, but he had

209

turned his back. In the corner, two men stood talking, and a female officer was exiting out a side door. This was crazy! There were officers everywhere!

"Trust us," said a soothing female voice.

Jon pushed his fear into his belly, reached out and snatched the keys, and sank back into his chair, all in one motion. His heart was racing.

"Stay calm. You're safe," said another voice.

All he could think about was the processing officer returning and finding his keys missing. *What about the officer, where is he?*

"Badger, badger, two can play," said a crackly, southern voice.

His body jolted. *Seriously! Can we stay focused here?*

"Silver and round. Flip the keys. Silver and round."

He flipped the keys until the voices said, "Stop!"

The key, pinched between his finger and thumb, was round and silver.

"Get ready."

For what? What's going on?

"When they are distracted, be ready."

What are you talking...

"Now!" said a firm voice. "In the desk drawer. Grab it!"

Jon rose to his feet, but froze again. The back of the room was now clear, but there were dozens of officers toward the front. Then a loud noise erupted from outside, and every last officer went to the front doors to see what had caused it.

Jon walked backwards around the desk, keeping his eyes on the commotion, and crouched down in front of the desk drawer.

"Bottom drawer, quick!" said the voices.

There was no time for indecision. He obeyed without dissension. He slid the key in and twisted. Inside the drawer was a mess of things. On top of the mess was a handgun in a holster.

"Grab it. Keep it low. Take it. Keep it low," they said.

Are you kidding me? I'm in a police station!

"You need it. Take it!" He sensed the urgency in the voices. It was deeper than inflection or tone. He felt the concern they had; they were worried about him.

He snatched it from the drawer, closed the drawer and locked it, and put the keys back on the desk. Across the room an officer started to turn toward him. His body shivered, but he forced himself to stand slowly and move casually back toward his seat, keeping the gun low and behind his leg.

"You are safe. Hide it. Keep it," they said.

He turned, pulled his shirt up, and stuffed the small holstered gun into his pants. The metal clamp on the back of the holster was cold against his skin—and it seemed like every eye in the station had turned back toward him. It took every ounce of courage he had to sit calmly, but he managed.

There was no shout of alarm, no rushing of feet. His actions had gone unnoticed, just as the voices had promised. But why did he need a gun? Was his life in danger? Were Elliot's people inside the police station? Were they outside waiting to gun him down, like they did to Pete?

He put his arms in his lap, pressed his forearm against the hidden weapon, and sat, motionless. Listening. Watching. Ready to pull the weapon out when commanded. Ready to defend himself if an attack came. But it did not come, and slowly his body allowed itself to loosen.

"Okay," said a voice behind him. His ribs jumped.

"Sorry about that," the officer said, taking his seat at his desk and shuffling the papers in front of him.

Jon resisted the urge to look at the keys. They were clumped differently and no longer in the same spot the officer had left them. Would he notice? Would he check the drawer?

"You're safe," said the voices.

The officer's eyes flicked up. "Are you nervous?"

"What?" said Jon with a jilt. "No. Why?"

"I was called away by the captain because he thought you might be nervous."

"About what?"

"He read your statement and he is concerned for you."

Jon tried to unravel the officer's words, but his head was spinning with questions—and he felt like he might throw up.

"You said you believe your father was provoked into killing his girlfriend. Is that correct?"

Now it made sense. With Pete dead, it seemed unnecessary to hide what Elliot James and his people had done. Though he didn't mention Elliot by name, he had told them all about his conversation with Pete and the money he had been given to lie to his father. This was about that.

"Yes. That's what I was told, by Pete."

"You said you thought someone was chasing you?"

"I did."

The officer wrote something down and nodded his head. Then looked up. "Do you believe they are still chasing you?"

His mind whispered. "Yes."

"Yes," he said, clearing his throat. "I do believe they are."

"Who do you believe is chasing you?"

"I don't know," he said. "Dangerous people." A memory flashed; he heard the gun blast and saw the reactions on

212

the faces at the 7-Eleven. "Dangerous people, capable of killing someone in a public place."

The officer wrote something else, then set his pen down and looked up. "The captain believes the threat against you might be credible, but we don't have enough to put you in protective custody. He asked me to advise you on this matter so that you would be as safe as possible."

Jon swallowed. "Okay."

"He feels it would be safer for you if you were to slip out the parking garage discreetly, rather than leave out the front. We could call you a cab."

It sounded like a good idea, but what about the Porsche? What about the money?

"I don't think..." he started.

"Are you worried about the car?"

Jon groaned inside. There was no end to all the ways they could find reason to slap cuffs on him and throw him in a cell.

The officer gave an examining look. "Are you okay?"

"Yeah. It's just a lot to process, you know?"

"We ran the plates on that car and made a call to the owner."

Jon's gut rolled. This was it, the thread that would unravel the tapestry.

"If I was just given a Porsche, I'd feel the same way."

Wait, what? Why on earth had the owner of the car said he *gave* it to him? Jon stopped the impulse rushing to reveal his surprise in all the creases of his face.

"It won't be long. We'll tag it so it doesn't get towed, and you can pick it up tomorrow or the day after, whenever you feel it's safe." All Jon could do was nod as the officer smiled and looked back down at his paperwork. "All right. Just one more question. Do you want to see your father before we send him to county lockup?"

Even if he didn't have the officer's pistol stuffed in his pants, he wouldn't have wanted to see his father. He had no desire to hear his lies, or to fend off the attempts to apologize for his weakness. Whatever ties, or whatever obligation he had felt toward him, were now buried in a tomb of his father's own making. As far as he was concerned, his father was dead.

He shook his head. "No, sir. I don't want to see him."

"Okay then. I'll file this, and we'll call you a cab."

Immediately, Jon's mind went to the money in the briefcase. He couldn't leave it sitting there in the Porsche. He had to get it. He had to hide it. But what about Elliot's people?

"They won't hurt you," said a warm voice.

"Get it and go out the back," said a sultry woman's voice.

"Sir?" he said, lifting a hand.

The officer stopped shuffling papers.

"Can I grab something from the car first?"

His brows scrunched together for a moment, then loosened. "I'm sure you'll be safe in front of the station. I don't see why not." He scooped up his papers and stuffed them in a folder. "Come on. Let's get you signed out."

CHAPTER THIRTY-FOUR

"Me?" said David. He found it hard to believe that the FBI would want to hear what he had to bring to the table.

"Yes. We have several possible leads, and you could help us isolate our search."

"The federal government wants to know what the messages have to say about all this?"

"Yes. We'll give you whatever you need."

"I don't get it. Three months ago you didn't trust a word that came out of my mouth, now you're believers?"

"David, please understand, our people here on the ground don't have all the information, most of the evidence surrounding this case is classified. But my superiors in D.C. never doubted you, that's why they sent me, right now, they're convinced that you could be the key to averting this crisis."

David's eyes flared. "I don't even know what the crisis *is!* The last thing I knew we were chasing down evidence in a domestic violence case, but now the FBI is facing off against God only-knows-what inside that police station, and now you tell us something is controlling people's minds and controlling Jon Blake who is being herded toward some evil outcome." David took a breath. "It's a little overwhelming and quite frankly hard to believe!"

Agent Collins held his hands up in defense. "Look, this is what you need to understand. Last year, Congress passed a bill to prevent the research of a compound called X11 because of its highly controversial use of stem cells.

We have several cases that directly tie these encounters of mind control to the creation of that legislation, including the death threat on the president last fall."

"What?" David shook his head. "All this is connected?"

"Yes. The president survived the attack, but then lost the election. And now our new president has reversed all the previous rulings on stem cell research, so X11 is back on the research table with more funding than it had before. That means the enemy won that round. See, the team working on the research for X11 is headed by Dr. Kathleen Peltz, who I mentioned before. Their main facility is on the outskirts of Boston. The increase of these unexplained incidents in the Greater Boston Area leads us to believe that the enemy has shifted from a national agenda to a focused exploitation of this facility."

"Exploitation? How? And what's X11, some kind of virus?"

"No, a super virus, or at least it will be."

David had a vision of hazmat suits and city-wide riots.

"As with every scientific breakthrough, this virus can be used for good or for evil. Dr. Peltz and her team claim they are working on a cure for AIDS and they have considerable backing from Washington. But our enemy would like to see X11 used for more destructive ends."

"What are we talking about here," said Karen, moving to the front of her seat, "some kind of biological weapon?"

"Yes. In the form they are hoping to get it to, it will be easily weaponized. We believe someone on Peltz's team has been compromised..."

David felt a buzz in his pocket. He dug his phone out and looked at the caller ID.

Karen's face scrunched. "Seriously, David?"

"It's my wife," he said, flipping it open.

Karen's head rotated, and she gave Collins an

incredulous look.

David didn't bother with his usual greeting but leaped straight to the point of the matter. "Hi, honey. I'm in the middle of something, is this important?"

"Not terribly," she stammered. "I just need you to know that I got a ride home and you don't need to pick me up." The sound of her voice brought comfort to his soul, but the expectant look on Collins and Karen robbed him of its full effect.

"That's great. All right, I have to let you go."

"Will you be home for dinner?"

"I'm not sure."

"It's taco night."

"That's my favorite night."

"I hope they're not making you jump through a bunch of hoops."

"No, I'm fine."

"Call me if you're going to be late, okay?"

"I will, sweetheart. I love you."

"I love you, too."

"Okay. Gotta go."

"Call me."

"I will. Bye."

He flipped the phone closed and gave a sheepish look.

Karen's face lightened. "Only you would take a domestic phone call in the middle of a debriefing on a global, biological threat."

"Not quite global," corrected Collins. "At least, not yet. But they're getting close."

"Sorry," said David, shoving the phone back into his pocket. "Life doesn't stop for an almost-global, biological threat."

"And," said Collins, "as I was saying, we believe that someone within Dr. Peltz's team has been..." He stopped mid-sentence and held his hand up. A dark quiet filled the compartment. From his earbud a tiny indistinguishable tin voice could be heard. "Jon is on the move," said Collins, looking out the window.

David looked out and saw Jon Blake bobbing down the stairs in the direction of the Porsche, his eyes scanning the street and his expression revealing his curiosity at the line of black SUVs. It was hard to imagine that all of these trained, government agents were focused on this unassuming young man.

But it wasn't him they were interested in, was it?

He was just a pawn—a rat in a maze—leading them to the cheese. Did they know about his ability to see messages, or were they watching the sea of faces around him, waiting for the slightest hint of suspicious activity? It had to be maddening, not knowing who was being influenced. Even knowing, the challenge of dealing with someone infected had to be a slippery slope. One couldn't simply arrest the captain of a police station without evidence or motive. And how do you lock down a motive with something like this?

He looked at Collins in a new light. This was a man under tremendous pressure, yet his face appeared placid. Was it a mask placed there with self-determination and training or was he truly at peace in the midst of this storm?

"No," said Collins, "let him go. Let's see where he takes us."

David looked back out and spoke low against the surface of the glass. "May I ask a question?"

Collins kept his eyes on Jon. "Of course."

"Are you aware that Jon is receiving messages like I do?"

"We were not certain, but we had a hunch."

"So why do you need me?"

"Because whoever is sending messages to you is clearly on our side," he said, bluntly.

David pulled away from the window as a ripple of shock washed over him. "Are you saying Jon is receiving messages from…" He didn't want to finish the question.

"From-?" Collins said, still focused on Jon.

"The devil?"

Collins glanced at him, and then back out the window. "I thought we established that we would refrain from conjecture like that and stick to the facts."

"Well, the fact is, I'm getting messages from God, and…"

"No," said Collins, pulling away from the window. "The fact is: you're getting messages. And whoever is sending them to you wants to stop this crisis from happening, and that makes them our friend. Is it necessary to get into semantics about where the messages are coming from? We have a young man here who drove to the police station in a Porsche with a suitcase full of hundred dollar bills, and at least three people in one degree of separation have shown signs of possession. That places Jon at the center of this investigation and makes him highly suspect. You, on the other hand, have no incidents of influence and a track record for being in the right place at the right time. *That* is something we need. It seems less-than-productive to engage in conjecture on the origin of things we cannot possibly know."

His words weren't harsh or pointed, simply truthful, and David was satisfied with that. They didn't have to agree on the origin of the messages. What mattered was that they shared a common goal, to keep the people of Massachusetts safe. He still didn't fully understand the nature of the threat, but he felt confident of one thing; he could trust Collins.

"Just watch him," said Collins. "Don't take him yet." His eyes lifted to David's. "Jon has the case and is heading back inside."

David watched as the young man ascended the steps with the briefcase in hand. He paused halfway up and looked over his shoulder. For the briefest of moments, it looked like he knew they were watching him. A smile formed, and his chin rose slightly, as though he was acknowledging their presence. Then he turned and continued on into the station.

CHAPTER **THIRTY-FIVE**

"Take a right, here," said Jon.

"I thought you wanted to go to Cambridge Street?" said the Cabbie over his shoulder.

"I changed my mind. Turn right, here, please."

The cab shifted lanes, and Jon watched apprehensively out the window.

The driver's eyes studied him in the rear-view mirror. "Where are we going?" he said.

"The other side of town," said Jon, sliding a hundred dollar bill over the seat. "That won't be a problem, will it?"

"For a hundred bucks I'll help you hide a body!" said the man with a strong Mass accent.

After several minutes the cab passed by the cemetery where Jon had dug up the bank box, and another minute found them on the street parallel to Canary's. He didn't want to chance going directly to her house; it was too dangerous.

He looked down at the briefcase in his lap and regretted leaving his iPad behind. The voices had assured him that he wouldn't need it, but it still felt weird not having it.

"I need you to wait here," he said, slipping another hundred over the seat. "Can you do that?"

"Sir, I will pitch a tent for $200 dollars."

Jon climbed out and looked in through the open passenger window. "I won't be long."

The cabbie flicked a switch near the meter box and settled back in his seat.

Jon headed up the sidewalk, keeping a weary eye on the traffic passing by. As he got closer to where he intended to cross over to Canary's street, he noticed a burning smell. He looked up, above the houses and trees he could make out the top of a smoke plume. Something was burning, he picked up his pace. He came to a spot between two houses where he could see the flashing lights on top of a fire truck, and a sense of horror descended on him.

He ran across the lawn of a ranch-style house, through two back yards, and out onto Canary's street. There were emergency vehicles everywhere and a police officer directing traffic. Behind the noise, confusion, and flashing lights, two streams of water arched through the air in the direction of Canary's house.

He called to the voices. *What is this? What's going on? Did they take her, or is she in there?!*

"Elliot James," they whispered.

I know who did it! he screamed internally as he jogged down the sidewalk toward the fire perimeter. *Where is Canary?*

"Don't tell him," said a voice.

"He has to know," said another.

Know what?!

Through the sirens, shouts, and confusion, Jon's mind was eerily quiet.

I'm trusting you! he thought. *You have to be straight with me. What's going on?*

"Elliot James," they whispered.

Jon came up on the backside of a fire engine and saw a paramedic speaking with one of the firemen.

"Um- excuse me," he said, trying to control his voice.

"I'm a friend of the family."

They looked in his direction.

"Was anyone in the house? Are they okay?" he said with more desperation than he cared to show.

They looked at each other in silent communication, then the medic stepped toward him. "I'm so sorry to have to tell you this," he said with a somber face, "but they found two bodies burned in the fire."

Jon gripped his gut.

"I'm so sorry," said the medic. "I'm so sorry."

Jon stumbled backward as the world began to spin. "No. No. It's not right. Something isn't right." *How could this happen?* The voices wouldn't allow this. How could she be dead? "This is wrong!" he said, defiantly, as if speaking to the flood of tears threatening to overtake him. "This can't be right!"

The medic motioned toward the back of the ambulance. "You should sit down. We can talk this through."

Jon wiped a tear trickling down his cheek. Why did everything he ever loved get taken away from him? Why?! Was he cursed?

The medic tried to connect with him. "Did you know the young lady who lived here? Were you close?"

Jon gasped for air and began to pace. He yelled into the void of his own thoughts. *Why?! Why didn't you tell me?!*

"We did," said a female voice.

When?!

"At the station."

I thought I had time. I thought I could save her.

"There was no chance to save her."

But can't you see everything?

"Not everything," said a male voice.

"What's your name?" said the medic.

Jon waved his hands. "I can't do this. I just- I need to be

223

alone." He turned and started back down the sidewalk.

Why did you let me come here to see this?! Why didn't you tell me she was already dead?!

"Would it have stopped you from going to see for yourself?"

No. They were right. He would have gone anyway. He would have wanted to see, wanted to know for sure.

You could have told me there was no chance to save her. I was coming to rescue her. I didn't think she was... he couldn't finish the thought.

"You needed to see this," said the female voice. "Canary would have wanted you to see this."

Why? Why would she care? She's dead!

"You can do what she couldn't."

The pieces of the puzzle began to slide together. There was only one way out of this nightmare—a way the voices had probably known for some time. That was why they had led him to grab the gun at the station, and why they'd allowed him to come here to see this. They knew there was only one way he would ever be free, only one way he would ever be safe.

His thoughts rested on the beautiful, blond girl who shared his affliction—the only girl who had ever cared for him. And as regret gnawed at his bones, it became clear. He could do it for her. For her, he could kill Elliot James.

CHAPTER THIRTY-SIX

The door to the SUV opened, and Collins appeared in the opening. David caught a glimpse of Karen behind him on the sidewalk, still talking to Brad on her phone. He was at the airport waiting for his flight. In all of the excitement, she had missed her chance to say goodbye to him face to face.

"We found another one," said Collins, handing a book into the vehicle. "It's an S.O.P for vehicle maintenance. How's that?"

David took the heavy paperback into his hands. "Does it have words?"

"Whole pages of them."

"Then we've done our part. Now it's up to the messages to do theirs."

"I'll go see what else I can find. Let the driver know if you need anything."

"Sure." David set the book down on top of the others in his lap as Collins backed out and closed the door. What were the chances he would find anything in this book when there was nothing in the last three? The messages were not coming.

All right, David. Get a grip. Stressing out about it is not going to make them come any faster. The messages had always been there when he needed them. He simply had to have faith. He cracked the book open and began slowly turning pages, bouncing his eyes off words as he went. There were a few interesting combinations, but nothing spoke to him. The pages were cold dead things—until his eyes landed on the word *noise.* The familiar sense of confirmation washed over him. He hopped his eyes over to the word *growing* and then *shaking.* He turned the page and found the word *safety* then hopped three sentences down and grabbed *shines.* Noise growing shaking safety shines.

What the heck did that mean?

"Let's see what else we have." He paged to the middle and bounced off more words: *Take your new car.* With the words came the feeling. There was pleasure in it; the kind of pleasure one might have when they give a Christmas gift. But the next words felt like a dire warning. *Go alone.* He sensed that the consequences for not obeying this message had ramifications he would never be able to live with.

The final two words were *bank* and *booth* which were also connected to a feeling, like God was saying, "See, I didn't send you there for nothing." It was a point of reference, he knew now exactly where he had to be. He slid the books off his lap and climbed out of the vehicle.

Karen was still on the phone. "Yes. I took care of that weeks ago. Yes. What's your flight number? Okay..." she turned her back to David.

He looked up the row of Black SUVs. Two strong men in three-piece suits stood talking by one of them. Collins was not visible. He was probably off getting more books. David looked at the Porsche and his heart began to pound. Was this the right thing to do? The FBI had trusted him. Would they ever forgive him for ditching them? Would Karen forgive him? In a strange way, he was more worried about her than the FBI.

Her back was still to him, he had to move now. He reached in his pocket and felt for the keys. He pulled out his house keys, then the two keys for the safe deposit boxes. Where was the Porsche key? He dug into his other pocket and felt a wave of relief. All right, it was now or never. He casually walked down the sidewalk and in between the first SUV and the Porsche, out of sight of the two men. He turned casually and looked through the windshield of the SUV; it appeared to be empty. The element of surprise was definitely his. No one had any idea he had a key to the Porsche in his pocket, and by the time they did, he would be gone.

He surveyed the traffic as he walked briskly to the driver's door. It beeped lightly when he grabbed the handle. Karen was still turned away from him, and from his vantage point, the two men were hidden. He quickly pulled the door open, climbed in, put the key in the ignition, and let the door thump closed as he fired it up. His hand shot out with confidence and slapped the car in gear. It made a satisfying click as it locked into drive, and exhilaration caused his body to tingle.

He mapped out a route that would take him to the parking garage two streets over. By the time any of the black SUVs could follow him, he would be on the next street and turning into the alley that cut across.

A sudden bleep caught his attention and he looked over at the passenger seat. An iPad sat face up, and a tiny box in the center of the screen said, "Incoming message."

CHAPTER **THIRTY-SEVEN**

Terrence Peltz eyed the security guard next to terminal 47B but made no attempt to hide his nervousness. It was all a part of the plan, a plan only he could execute. If this was a movie, he would have been forever typecast, unable to find a part in anything else. It was truly the only role he was fit to play.

Fate had not given him good looks or social skills, but had chosen to make his frame thin and gangly—and his skin paler than the accepted norm. But this was their normal, not his. They wanted him to believe millions of years of evolution had spit out a reject, fit for only abuse or pity. But he would show them. They would see that they had underestimated him.

A voice broke him from his introspection.

"Are you sure?" said a man, standing with his wife and two children. The airline attendant swiped his boarding pass again, and a low buzz rang out.

"I am sorry, sir," said the attendant. "It's not in our system."

The man turned to his wife. "Let's try yours."

His wife handed him an envelope with the boarding pass on top. The attendant slid it off and ran it through the machine.

Bzzzz.

The man took in his surroundings. "This is the gate for flight 304, right?"

"Yes. I'm sorry, sir. You'll have to step over to the service counter. They can help you there."

His wife attempted to quiet their questioning children as the man made one last plea. "We have to be on this plane. My sister is getting married. She'll kill me if we miss it."

Terrence was disgusted by the amount of empathy on the attendant's face and the obvious regret in her voice. It wasn't manufactured emotion, like he was used to receiving. It was genuine. And why shouldn't it be? They were pretty people with pretty children and designer clothes and expensive carry-on bags, the kind of people everyone wants to know and be seen with. How sad that they should be inconvenienced in their perfect, little lives.

He might have gotten a similar expression from the attendant, but he wasn't the fool people took him for. Oh, people loved pretending like they cared; it made them feel good about themselves. But they were always relieved when they were finally rid of him. Their lives were so wonderful when they didn't have to be inconvenienced by his awkward presence. It didn't even matter that he avoided looking at them or that he attempted to speak only when he had something of interest to say. Most would never admit it, but they were uncomfortable just being around him.

"They should be able to help you," said the attendant. "There's still time." The man and his family left the line peaceably, and the line lurched forward.

Eventually, Terrence had his turn with the attendant. He didn't have to pretend to be nervous, his forehead felt noticeably flush, and his skin was slick with perspiration. The attendant swiped his ticket but did not take notice of his heightened level of duress or question him about his obviously labored breathing. What did he have to do, draw her a picture? Where did they get these people from?

He snatched his ticket from her pinched fingers and took comfort in the fact that his plan did not hinge upon this one incompetent attendant and her inability to properly screen passengers. He had accounted for the likelihood that the boarding attendant would do as everyone else did and consider him invisible. It didn't matter. She was only a pawn he had wished to capture. The game was far from over, and his strategy allowed for many failed variables.

He trudged forward through the reinforced, metal door and up the long, suffocating hallway that led to the side door of the passenger plane, following the line of living corpses, like cattle being herded to the slaughter. He never understood why anyone would want to climb into the hull of a plane; it was nothing more than an airtight Petri dish in the sky. Not to mention, the only thing keeping the almost two hundred tons of sheet metal airborne were two shaky wings, both of which were absolutely required to keep the cylinder of death from plummeting to the earth like a missile.

As he rounded the corner he craned his neck to see, over the people in front of him, the crew greeting people as they entered the plane. There was a male attendant and a female attendant, but she wasn't Joyce.

He fought the urge to second-guess whether or not she was even on the aircraft, and consoled himself with a reminder that even she was not necessary for the success of his plan. She was a happy coincidence. He'd been planning this long before she'd started dating his neighbor. It just made sense to add her the day he'd found out that she made the trip from Boston to Los Angeles on a weekly basis. She simply gave him one more chance at a perfect outcome.

He continued to watch for her as the passengers entered one at a time, but she never showed. No matter. He would simply have to trust that another attendant would take notice of his nervous and suspicious behavior. They couldn't all be buffoons. What were the chances? He gritted his teeth as an insidious thought attempted to root itself. Why would fate treat you any different than it has since your unfortunate birth? *Shut up!* he thought. *It doesn't matter!*

He had not given himself over entirely to fate. Most of the variables were well within his control, especially the critical details. Besides, fate had not abandoned him his entire life. It could be argued that she had made all this possible by giving him access to the substance that would ensure his name would be remembered long after the handsome man and his wretchedly pretty family were long forgotten. He preferred, however, to think of it more like: fate had underestimated him. She thought him incapable of inventing such a plan, and thus considered it safe to taunt him. Fate, like all the rest, imagined he would just take the hand he was given and give into the inevitability of his obscure and worthless life.

But fate was wrong, whispered his mind.

His cheek fluttered.

Fate couldn't have been more wrong.

CHAPTER THIRTY-EIGHT

Jon wasn't cold, but his body shivered. It came in uncontrollable trembles as he walked up to the front of the bank. In the glass he studied his disguise one last time. He looked like a plump Mexican. The bronze tanning spray and mustache made his features indistinguishable, and the pillow duct-taped to his mid section gave the appearance of added weight. The clothing he'd grabbed from the store beside the costume shop had a sports theme: baggy jeans, jersey, Red Sox cap, and high top sneakers to complete the look. His own father wouldn't have recognized him. But he was still terrified.

He pushed through the doors into the lobby. Two security guards were visible, one near the entrance, the other over by the loan department. In the center of the room, people funneled through a roped-in section to get their after-work banking done. He headed across the back of the lobby toward the bank manager's office. The door was open a crack, so he pushed through and closed it behind him. "Show me your hands or your mother is dead," he said, pulling the handgun from under his shirt.

"My mother...?"

"Hands up, or the man I hired to kill her will put a bullet in her head."

His hands shot up. "Okay. Okay."

A voice screamed in his head. "His foot! Back up! Back up! *The button!*"

"Back up!" he said forcefully.

"What?"

"Do you think I'm bluffing?! With the money I got from you I could have hired fifty assassins. Back away from the desk! You push that button with your foot, she's as good as dead!"

The man slid back with a look of shock. "Why are you doing..."

"*Shut up,* and listen to me closely. I want you to call Elliot James. Have him meet us here in your office. If I don't think you sound convincing, your mom is dead, you're dead, and everyone in this bank is dead. Do you understand what I am saying to you?"

The man held his composure and nodded. Jon envied him, and the training he must have gone through to acquire such resolve. Jon wished he shared his courage. His hand wouldn't stop shaking, and there was a chance he might vomit on the desk.

"I'm getting the phone," said the man calmly. Jon watched his body, making sure he stayed clear of the desk. Wellington picked up the phone and dialed an extension. "What if he's not there?" he said, setting his jaw.

Jon tightened his eyes. "You better hope he is."

CHAPTER **THIRTY-NINE**

David pushed through the lobby doors of the bank and scanned the room apprehensively. God only knew what was waiting for him here, quite literally. It was a big bank, and he had no earthly idea what he was supposed to do. There were some signs close by, so he strolled over and bounced his eyes off a few words, but nothing spoke to him. The security guard near the door looked him up and down. David offered a friendly smile and headed over to a table in the middle of the room where various bank slips and trifolds lay in shallow troughs.

Why was he back at this bank? Jon was at the police station, and Collins said the chemist had a lab on the outskirts of Boston. What was the significance of this bank? He bounced his eyes off of some trifolds and a sign laminated to the top of the desk. Still nothing.

Okay. I'm here. What next? What do you want me to do? It felt like the entire bank was watching him, standing there, aimlessly looking around, but he knew better. It was just his overactive imagination. He tried not to slip into that cynical place he always seemed to go to. It wouldn't do him any good to get frustrated. He had done his part, now God would do his. Right?

He grabbed a trifold about auto loans and opened it. His eyes bounced from the bold heading to the thinner line of words in the subheading then down into the body. A message formed. *Use the phone 6112561.* What was he supposed to say to whoever answered? He bounced his eyes around the trifold, but nothing else would come. That was the entire message. Call 611-2561.

He took a step back, looked around discreetly, and reached into his pocket for his cell phone, but his pocket was empty. *Where's my...?* It was in the SUV! He'd set it on the seat and left it. *Great!*

He considered asking the woman standing next to him, but as if on cue, her young son started groping at her purse. "Mama! You said I could have candy if I was good! Mama, I been good, gimme it! Mama!"

Just beyond the woman and the disagreeable child was a line of people waiting to be served by the tellers. The man at the back of the line was already on his phone, and he didn't look happy about it. The woman in front of him was busy with a stack of paper slips.

He turned and looked around the lobby and noticed a black phone sitting on the edge of the unattended receptionist's desk a few yards from where he stood. Maybe he was supposed to use that phone? His eyes flitted up to a sign for the loan department. It said, "We are in the business of saying yes." David's mind pulled the word yes from it, and the familiar feeling of confirmation settled on him. He *was* meant to use that phone. He didn't know why, but he was certain of it.

He strolled over to the unoccupied desk and made a casual scan for the receptionist. If he did this quickly and with confidence, he might be able to make the call without getting in too much trouble. He leaned in, grabbed the receiver, and started punching numbers. On the third number, the phone started to ring. His eyes caught a note next to the phone. It was upside down, but he could still read it. It said, "For internal calls dial 611."

A male voice picked up on the other end. "Security Desk."

David froze. Of all places, why had it sent him to the security desk? Could they see what phone he was calling from and find him on a security camera?

Calm down, David.

"Hello? Security Desk."

He ran through the message in his mind. Use the phone 6112561. "2561!" he blurted, unable to mask his anxiety.

"2561," said the voice. "Got it. Are there any special instructions?"

Instructions? Was 2561 a code for something? "No," he said, "no additional instructions."

"We will inform the authorities and start the evacuation."

Evacuation? What had he done?! He struggled to think of something to say, but it didn't matter. The phone went dead.

CHAPTER FORTY

Terrence Peltz gripped his bag in his lap and leaned out to see up the aisle of the 747. Where was she? The itinerary she'd left on the kitchen counter said she would be on this flight to Los Angeles. He wiped at the sweat stinging his brow and leaned out again. In the compartment between his cabin and first class, he could see the male flight attendant's back as he worked on something. Beyond him was the other attendant speaking with a man in a white shirt and black tie, probably one of the cockpit crew.

Terrence fumbled with the zipper on the front of his backpack and pulled the pocket open. The vial he had stolen from his mother's office sat tucked deep inside. Unbroken.

He swallowed, and took in a deep breath.

It looked so small and insignificant—not unlike him. In fact, the similarities between him and this unassuming sludge was what made his plan infinitely satisfying. He reveled in the irony. To look at the glop of slime, an ignorant observer would never realize the power it had to take life. Inhaled it could take a life in under two hours; applied to the skin, in less than one. All he had to do was smash it against the hull of the aircraft, and within minutes half the people on the plane would be infected— but he had grander plans for his pets. He pulled the vial from the bag and slid it into his pants' pocket.

"Terrence? Is that you?"

237

His body spasmed.

"I didn't mean to scare you." He felt a warm hand touch his shoulder.

His hand slithered out of his pocket and he snapped a glance up into the beautiful, brown eyes of Joyce Simpson, his next door neighbor's girlfriend. She must have been in the rear of the plane.

"Why didn't you tell me you were taking a flight to Los Angeles? I could have gotten you a discount."

He spoke softly into his lap. "I didn't think I had the nerve."

She crouched down beside his seat, suddenly aware of the state he was in. "Look at you. You're soaked."

"I don't like planes," he said into his lap.

"Is this your first time flying?"

He nodded.

"Would it help if I got you a cold soda?"

Her legs shifted as if she would get up, and his heart jumped. "No," he said, "I just don't like not knowing who the pilot is. It scares me because I don't know him."

They were so predictable, the soft ones—but it wasn't always the case. And it had taken him a long time to realize that the soft ones didn't really care. The strong ones were easy to understand, but hard to predict. They would tell him exactly what they thought of him, and, in a way, he appreciated this. But it was hard to get them to do anything in a predictable fashion. The soft ones, on the other hand, had a consistent and quantifiable pattern.

"Well," she said, "the pilot's name is Conrad, and he's been flying planes for years. He even used to fly jets in the Navy."

He looked up and stared into her eyes. "Could I just see him? Could I see his face?"

She took in a deep breath, taken aback by his

uncharacteristically long stare. "Ah, I don't imagine that would be a problem," she said, standing. "I'll ask."

He returned to staring at his lap.

Within a minute, she returned. He flicked her a sheepish look, and she smiled down at him. "He says he'd be happy to meet you. Come on." She gestured.

Terrence climbed out of his chair and followed her down the long, thin aisle, brushing against a couple of shoulders along the way. When they reached the bathroom between compartments, he suddenly spoke up. "Joyce?"

She turned and looked at him.

"I think I'm going to be sick."

Her eyes snapped to the vacancy dial on the restroom door. "There's no one in the bathroom. Go ahead."

He flicked the latch, slid the door open, and climbed inside. He looked at his zombie-like visage in the mirror. He hated it. He hated his sallow, sunken eyes, thin lips, and weak chin. Fate had given him the worst of everything. It was easy for Joyce to find happiness, she had it all from birth. Oh how happy her mother and father must have been to have such a pretty child. They must have loved holding her and kissing her. *It's easy to love the pretty ones,* he thought, *but there's no love for the ugly ones.* They must scrounge for the bread crumbs of love given by the pretty ones, a love given only so that they can feel even better about their beautiful selves.

He pulled the vial from his pocket and ripped the cork from the top. Without hesitation, he tapped the goo onto his palm and rubbed it in. There was no immediate reaction, and for that he was thankful. He pushed the metal trash door open and dropped the vial and cork into it. It was done. The gun was loaded. There was no turning back.

His hand flicked the latch and he slid the door open.

"You okay?" said Joyce, her eyes concerned.

"False alarm," he said, looking at the floor.

"You want to go back to your seat?"

"No. I'm okay."

"Okay, then, let's go meet Conrad." She turned and began walking again. Terrence followed.

As he walked along, he rubbed his hands on the seats of first class, grinning internally as he went, wondering what joy would be lost from the world this evening. Would the world mourn a great composer whose unwritten music would die with him? Would the world lament over a movie star heading back to their plush life of fame and fortune? Oh how sad that one of the gods or goddesses of Olympus should perish. But why should they be remembered throughout the ages simply because they could cry on cue?

You will be remembered, his mind whispered.

Up ahead, the other female flight attendants was speaking in a flurry with the pilot. "Are you sure you don't need me?" she said, spinning around. She had her uniform draped over her arm.

"Get out of here before I change my mind," said the pilot with a snarky grin.

"Thank you, thank you!" said the flight attendant, disappearing out the side of the plane.

"What's going on with Emily?" said Joyce, as she approached.

"Her sister's having the baby."

Joyce squealed.

"I figured we could get by without her."

There was a short pause, then Joyce moved to the side. "I'd like you to meet a friend of mine. He's a little nervous about flying with us today and he said he would feel better if he could meet the person flying the plane."

Terrence looked up sheepishly.

"Well, the plane does most of the work," he said with a wrinkly grin. "It's a pleasure to meet you, young man." The captain put his hand out, and Terrence fought his natural urge to shrink away. This was his moment, his chance to be strong. He reached out and gripped the captain's hand, staring into his eyes. "My name is Terrence Peltz."

The captain's hand slid from his grip. "It's a pleasure to meet you, Mr. Peltz."

"Who flies the plane if something happens to you?" he said, looking past the captain at the cockpit.

"Well, if anything happens to me, my second-in-command will take over."

"And what if something happens to him?" he said.

The captain laughed. "This plane can practically land itself, so I'm pretty sure we're going to be just fine. Now, if you'll excuse me, we have a flight schedule to meet. Let the flight attendants know if you need anything else, okay? They'll be happy to help."

Terrence gave a jerk of a nod. "Kay. Thanks."

"Come on," said Joyce. "Let's get you back to your seat."

Terrence could already feel the bug beginning to boil in his gut. It was only noticeable because he was keenly aware of its cancerous presence. But the pilot would just think it was gas until they were well in the air.

By then it would be too late.

CHAPTER FORTY-ONE

"I know you're busy, Mr. James, but could I have a word with you before you go?" said Wellington calmly into the phone.

Jon held the gun low and looked warily out the tall windows which offered a view of a brick wall and an alleyway. It would be a ten-foot fall, then a short run to a side street where the cabbie sat waiting to carry him out of the city. But to what future? Canary would still be dead, and he would still be the same luckless loser. Hate boiled in his belly. Hatred for Elliot James. Hatred for life. He clenched his teeth. It didn't matter if he lived through this or not, death would be a sweet release from the torment of a life bent on denying him anything he cared about.

"Yes, Mr. James," said Wellington, "It's about the Van Buren account. I'd rather talk to you in person about it."

Jon thought of Canary. She seemed to care about everything and everyone. She had built a prison for herself, pretending to be something pitiful so that she could stop her father's killer from hurting anyone else, even going so far as to keep the secret from her own mother to protect her. So much caring, so much self sacrifice. He, on the other hand, had stopped caring about anyone, except her. And now she was gone. How ironic that she should be killed and he left alive. Turmoil boiled in his chest. He couldn't bring her back, but he could do what she never could have done. He could put a bullet in Elliot James.

A heavy knock on the oak door caused Jon to jump. He shoved the pistol into his pants and flapped his shirt over it. Wellington looked up at him. He let a warning leak from his flared eyes, and whispered. "Handle this."

"Be calm, Jon, it's okay," said a warm voice.

The door creaked open, and a woman in business attire peeked in. She looked at Jon and offered a warm smile. He didn't dare to return it, for fear his mustache would lose its adhesion to his lip. Instead, he nodded.

"Thank you, sir, that sounds good. I'll see you in a few minutes." Wellington put the phone down and looked up. "Yes, Amy, can I help you?"

"I'm sorry to put you out like this, Mr. Wellington. Is this a bad time?"

"It depends on what you need," he said, in his refined manner.

"The IT department needs to get on your computer to install something. They said they sent you an email about it."

"Yes, I got it, but I can't do it right now. I'm with Mr..." he looked up at Jon and selected a suitable name. "Lopez."

Her eyes shifted to Jon, as if deciding on whether or not he looked like a Lopez. She must have decided that he did, because her eyes flitted back to the manager. "You could use my office, I'm not..."

An ear-piercing alarm split through the air, and Jon's eyes snapped to Wellington. He was still at the corner of the desk with both hands visible and no way of reaching under his desk with his foot. "It's the fire alarm," Wellington said, lifting his hands. "I had nothing to do with it."

Jon's frantic eyes shot back over to the doorway. The woman was no longer standing there. What would he do now?! Everything was ruined! He pulled the gun back out

243

and shoved the barrel at Wellington's horrified face. "Get Elliot on the phone." He spoke through gritted teeth. "Tell him to come here. Tell him it's urgent!" Wellington picked up the phone and punched in the number. Jon hid the gun from view of the doorway and looked over his shoulder at the chaos in the lobby.

"He's coming down the stairs," whispered a voice. "Catch him in the lobby."

He put the gun to the general manager's forehead. "If you breathe a word to anyone..." He gave the gun a thrust. "...she's dead. Do you understand?"

"Yes, yes! I understand!" he said, wincing. "I won't say anything!"

Jon pulled the gun away, shoved it in his pants, and ran for the door. A steady stream of people poured from the elevators and stairwells and snaked toward the front doors. Three security guards attempted to channel the chaos, while other employees battened down the hatches.

Where is he? Jon thought.

"The stairwell," said a voice, "next to the elevator."

Jon locked onto the opening and moved briskly across the lobby, dodging people as he went. The alarm pulsed in the air around him, and his heart joined in the rhythm. Every part of him moved with singleness of purpose, numb to the consequences of his actions. Suddenly Elliot James appeared in the flood. He filed out and stood next to the door, scanning the room, assessing the situation.

What now? Shoot him dead, here in the lobby? If he did shoot now, at least he wouldn't have to go to prison. Surely he would be shot down immediately.

Prison would not be so kind.

His hand went to the gun on his waist. Off to the right, a security guard emerged from the door that led down to the vault; Jon slowed slightly. He could take Elliot down

244

into the vault room and shoot him there. With all the noise no one would hear.

Kill him now in the confusion, he thought—but the thought felt foreign. It would be easy. Put the gun to his chest and squeeze the trigger. Jon pulled the gun out, rushed in on Elliot, and pressed it to his heart.

Elliot's face melted into horror as he realized what was happening.

Jon glared into his eyes. *You killed her!* his mind screamed. *You took her from me! How many have you killed? How many more lives will you destroy?* His finger tightened on the trigger, but his mind screamed, *NO! I will NOT go down with him!* "This way!" he said, savagely gripping Elliot by the arm.

"They will see you," a male voice resonated in his head. "And you will be dead before you get to the door. Elliot will live, you will die."

Then tell me if they see me! or is that beyond your ability?

"No," said a female voice. "We will watch."

He moved briskly to the door. "Open it!"

Elliot fumbled in his pocket and pulled out a key card. Within seconds the door was open. To avoid suspicion, he resisted the urge to look back over his shoulder. He forced Elliot down the stairs, and the door sealed behind them.

"You were seen," said a voice. "A guard is coming."

He stabbed Elliot with the pistol. "Does this lock from the inside?"

"N- no," Elliot stammered. "It's electronic."

Jon looked down the stairs. "What about that one."

"Yes," he said, "that one..."

Jon gripped him by his silk dress shirt and shoved him forward. "Go!"

Their feet stabbed like pistons as they retreated down

the stairs.

"You're not going to make it," said a voice. "Shoot him now."

Jon snapped a look back at the closed door at the top of the stairs. It was heavy. Even if the guard had already swiped his card, it would take him time to get it open, enough time for them to get into the vault room and close the heavy reinforced steel door.

"Faster!" he yelled.

They breached the entrance to the vault room. He shoved Elliot aside and grabbed the door, pushing as hard as he could. It swung around in a slow arch.

"Is this a safe within a safe?!" he screamed.

"Wh- what?" said Elliot.

"Will we suffocate if I seal this?!"

"N- no. It's- it's not air-tight."

Jon pushed with all his might, and the heavy door clicked into place. "LOCK IT!" he screamed.

Elliot scurried over and clicked the dead bolts into place.

Jon surveyed the room. It was empty, but the vault had been left open. The guard who had left; was he the one who had seen him? Had he intended to get someone to seal the vault? There was always something, some hidden variable that would make him fail—yet again. Why would this be any different from everything else in his life? Now his fate was as sealed as the vault to this metal tomb. There was no getting out of here alive, even if he changed his mind and decided to spare Elliot James, which was not going to happen. "Turn around!" he screamed.

"Why are you doing this?" said Elliot, in a fashion considerably less manly than Jon expected.

He ripped the cap and the mustache off. "Do you recognize me?"

Elliot's head shook side to side in a quick vibration.

"I'm the one whose life you've been making a living hell!"

Elliot's hands shot out. "I'm sorry. I- I don't understand. I promise, whatever I've done, I'll fix it!"

"You'll *fix* it?!" He felt his face burn with rage. "What are you going to do, bring them back from the dead?"

Elliot cowered as Jon pushed in with the handgun.

"Do you think pulling some strings and getting my father out of jail is going to *fix* what you've done?"

Elliot backed against the steel door. "I swear! I don't know what you're talking about!"

Was that the way he was going to play it? Pretend innocence? Jon placed the cold barrel against Elliot's cheek, and the man's face quivered with fear. "Please," he pleaded, "I- I don't, I don't know what you're talking about."

"Did you think you could sit in your high office playing God and that no one could touch you?" He ground the gun in. "Well you were wrong, Elliot." His anger leaked into his hand and his entire being waited expectantly for the explosion that would soon come. He hoped, in the dead vibration after the shock wave of sound had pushed its way through him, that he would have a moment of peace and satisfaction, as Elliot James' lifeless body slid to the floor. He hoped to savor it, to stew in it, for as long as he could, before the authorities burned their way into the vault room.

Suddenly, something hit him hard on the side of the head, and he stumbled to the side. He caught his balance and swung around with the pistol raised high.

David Chance stood over him with a look of apology on his face.

There was only enough time to scream one word.

"BACK!"

David lifted his hands in surrender. In one, he held a shoe.

Jon rubbed his head. "What are you doing here?! And did you just hit me with your *shoe?*"

"I had to stop you from making the biggest mistake of your life."

Jon stared at it, and a sense of familiarity hit him. It was the same scuffed shoe he had seen on the man in the booth next to his. That was where he had heard his voice before! They had both been in this room. This man was the one the voices had called his enemy. The realization caused him to climb to his feet, waving the gun back and forth between the two men. "You're in this together, aren't you?"

Elliot looked at David with a puzzled look.

Jon's body shook. "Don't even try that garbage on me!"

David locked his eyes on him, and the words that came next rattled Jon's every bone and joint. "Am I even talking to Jon Blake?"

Why did he say that? Was it the tanning spray? No, it was something deeper. He must have sensed the controlling tendrils burrowing into his mind, masking themselves as his own thoughts. But instead of repulsion, Jon felt oddly protective of them. "Who else would I be?" he spat at David.

"Jon, listen to me. You're being controlled."

"Don't listen to him, he's trying to get inside your head," a voice soothed.

The room began to dip and sway. Was it from the blow he took to the head? No, it was a ripple in his understanding. One question rose to the surface. Why had Canary told him he could trust David Chance while the voices called him his enemy?

248

"He is stalling," whispered a female voice.

"Waiting for help to come."

"There's no time!"

"You can fight this, Jon," urged David. "This isn't who you are. You're not a killer."

"The only way out is to kill them."

"Kill them both!"

Jon brought the gun to bear on David. "How do you know me?!"

"We're the same, Jon."

"I'm sorry, David," he said, "But that's where you're wrong!" His finger tightened, but before the trigger gave way, a sound caught his attention. It was like a massive, continual explosion. The ground shuddered.

The terror on David's face was like nothing he had ever seen before. "This is it!" David's voice sounded hollow above the increasing noise.

Jon looked around, frantic. "Is it an earthquake?"

The ground rattled, and the walls trembled.

"RUN!" David screamed. He clutched Elliot by the arm and pulled as the entire room began to vibrate.

Jon lost his footing and fell to his knees. "What's happening?!"

"Shoot them! They're getting away!" a voice screamed.

He scrambled to his feet and ran after them. "STOP! Or I'll shoot!" he screeched.

They kept running.

He lifted the gun but something hit him on the back, forcing him to the ground. The room started to dim as a wave of nausea overtook him. The last thing he saw was one black shoe and one stocking foot.

Then everything went black.

CHAPTER FORTY-TWO

Karen Knight studied Agent Collins' face. She wasn't sure if the expression was shock or fear, but she had never seen anything phase the man. She would have thought him incapable of fear.

"Yes. I understand. We'll get every available agent on it. Yes. Thank you, sir." He pulled the phone from his ear and held it in his loose hand, his eyes vacant.

"Agent Collins? Are you all right?"

"We tracked the Porsche to a parking lot downtown. Traffic cameras confirm that David Chance entered the Norfolk Country Savings and Loan."

"That's good news, right?"

His expression was controlled. "There has been an incident." He sat, silent.

"What? What happened? Is David all right?"

"An airliner just crashed into downtown Milford." As he said the words, she realized she could hear the wail of every siren in the city.

The breath left her body.

"The airliner went through three buildings, one of them was the Savings and Loan. I'm sorry, Karen. The dispatcher doesn't believe anyone could have survived that."

"We don't know he's dead," she said defiantly. "Maybe he got out before the blast."

"It's possible, but highly unlikely."

Karen's phone went off, and she pulled it out. The caller

ID said Channel Seven. "I have to take this," she said.

Collins looked over his shoulder, "Ken, get us near the blast area."

"Karen?" said a voice in her ear. It was Brad's camera man, Larry Turner.

"Yeah, Larry, I'm here."

"Have you heard about the plane crash?"

"Yes. Does Coldfield want me to go with you to cover it?"

"Karen, it's flight 304 to Los Angeles."

"I'm sorry, what?" she said, trying to register why he had just said the flight number for the plane Brad was on. Slowly, her mind and her heart allowed the information to penetrate. The plane that had crashed wasn't just any plane, it was his plane. It was Brad.

"That's Brad's flight, Karen."

"No. No, there's a mistake. This is about David. David's in the bank. He's..." Everything began to spin.

"Not David, Karen, Brad. Are you all right?"

She reached for the door handle. "I have to get out of here."

Collins gripped her arm. "The vehicle is moving."

"I have to get out of here!" she said, desperately. How could he be dead? How could it be his plane? This wasn't happening. This was *not* happening! There had to be a mistake. *"I have to get out of here!"* she screamed.

He called over his shoulder. "Ken, stop the car!"

The car slowed, and Karen burst out of the door. Traffic was bumper to bumper, and everyone on the street was staring in the same direction. She turned and found the object of their intense interest. A plume of smoke was coiling its way into the sky, and a dust cloud rolling between the buildings.

"Karen!" Agent Collins sounded miles away. "Get back

in the car, Karen!"

She stared at the dark, black smoke, ignoring the honks of irritated drivers. It wasn't possible. She could imagine him dying while covering a hurricane, or a conflict overseas, but a random plane crash?

She lifted her cellphone, cut the call with Larry, and speed-dialed Brad's number.

HOONNK!

She looked at the car and its screaming driver—and moved to the side. It squelched past, only to join the crawl of endless traffic six yards in front of it.

"You've reached Brad Knight," said the phone, "I'm not available at the moment, but your call is important to me. Leave a message."

"Brad. This is Karen." As she searched for the words to say, she felt the emotion surging up to overwhelm her. "I need you to call me."

I need you. The words had a strange effect on her. She simply meant that she wanted him to call, urgently, but there was so much more to it. She had never needed anyone. A silent wall had been built long ago—an impenetrable shield that allowed her to be an objective journalist, to keep her emotions in check. But she had allowed one person in, and once a pathway to her heart had been made, there was no way to undo the damage. She needed him. She couldn't live without him. How could she ever live without him?

Tears flooded her eyes as she pressed the phone harder against her ear. "I need you to call me, Brad. Do you hear me? You better call. And don't even think about playing some kind of trick on me with Larry..." She sniffed. "...because I swear you won't hear the end of it." She smeared the tears down her hard cheek. "It's too much for me to bear. Don't do this to me. Call me." She pressed the cancel button, drew in a deep breath, and let it out.

Collins stood silently with the door open.

She composed herself, wiped her face discreetly, and went back to the car.

CHAPTER FORTY-THREE

David felt for the collar of Jon's shirt and pulled it up over his mouth to protect his lungs from the dense dust cloud that filled the safe. He turned to peer into the pitch dark where he thought Elliot was laying. "Are you okay?"

"I think so," said a voice. "Is the boy okay?"

He felt down both of Jon's arms and found his hands. The gun wasn't in either one. That was a relief. It must have fallen when he dragged him to safety. He put his fingers on Jon's neck. There was a pulse. "Yeah. He's alive anyway."

"It's David, right?"

"Yeah. And you're Elliot?"

"Yes," said the voice from the darkness.

"Do you have a phone, Elliot?"

"Yes. Right here," he said with a cough. A dim light illuminated a thousand floating particles.

"Can you call for help, and let them know we're down here?"

The light dimmed as he turned it to read the display. "No signal."

"Okay," said David, sucking air through his shirt. "How's the battery on that thing?"

"I've been using it all day. It only has a fourth charge left."

"Then we should turn it off and conserve the battery for when the cell towers come back online, that's assuming it's the towers and not the tons of brick and steel on top of us."

Jon coughed and gasped. "What's going on?" he shrieked.

David gripped his shoulder. "It's okay, Jon. You're okay. Just breathe through your shirt."

"What- what happened?!"

"I don't know. It sounded like a bomb."

Jon coughed again and groaned in pain.

"I can't see where you're hurt. Is the pain bad?"

"Only when I cough," said Jon. "What hit me?"

"I think a chunk of mortar from the ceiling."

He coughed again. "Where's Elliot?"

"Here with us." He could feel Jon tighten up. "I don't know what you think he did, but he didn't do it. You're being controlled, Jon."

"What are you talking about?" he growled.

"The FBI is tracking cases of people who are being manipulated into doing horrible things because of some kind of mind control. Are you experiencing anything weird right now, like lost time or blackouts?"

The dead silence gave David his answer. There was something going on, and Jon didn't want to talk about it. But the topic had to be breached before Jeckel turned back into Hyde. It was bad enough being buried alive without having to fend off a killer as well.

It was time to tell Jon about his conversation with Canary. Hopefully, it wasn't too late. David cleared the dust from his throat. "Canary contacted me, Jon."

Jon was quiet a moment. *"What?"*

"Just before I got to the bank. She contacted me."

"That's impossible."

"It's the truth, Jon. We spoke through some kind of video chat on your iPad. She wanted me to give you a message."

"But- Wh- How did you get my iPad?! It's locked in the car."

"I had a key, Jon. Listen, I'm telling you the truth. Canary contacted me. She was trying to reach you, but said I could give you a message. She told me that you can't trust Jakson."

The darkness was still. No doubt Jon was trying to figure out whether or not he could believe what he was hearing.

"Do you know this man—Jakson?"

"She mentioned him," he said cynically.

"Canary said she found out that Jakson was moving against her, but that she and her mother got out okay. She's alive, Jon."

"What are you talking about?" Jon said through gritted teeth. "Elliot was the one moving against her. He's the one doing all this!"

"No, Jon. You're being lied to."

"Why are you doing this to me?" he groaned.

"Whatever is going on with you, you have to fight it. You're being manipulated."

"Canary and her mom are dead. They found two bodies in the fire. Elliot killed her."

Elliot's voice drifted across the blackness. "I could never do anything like that."

Jon's body tightened. "*Shut up!* Both of you shut up!"

David held a hand on Jon's chest. "Think about it, Jon. Work it through in your head. There had to be times when you questioned what was going on, something that sticks out in your mind as odd, or inconsistent. See if you can unravel the lies."

It was quiet for a long time, and finally he spoke. "Canary said I could trust you," his voice quivered with emotion, "but they said you were the enemy."

"Who said?"

"They said the security guards were chasing us down the stairs, but they never came. They were never there, were they?" His voice dripped hopelessness.

"Has someone been talking to you?"

"No. Stop it!" he said. "*Shut up!*"

David didn't press.

"Get out of my head! I don't *want* you here!"

Was he fighting them? Were they influencing him even now? He felt Jon's hand grip his arm.

"When did you speak with her?" Jon whimpered. "How long ago was it?"

"Not long ago," said David, stunned by the possibility that he was getting through. "It was just before I arrived here at the bank, maybe forty-five minutes ago."

The darkness settled again, and in it he could hear Jon crying. He let him work through the emotion and hoped it was enough to break the connection to whatever was controlling him. After a long while Jon spoke. It was only two words, but it was enough to convey the reason for his tears. "She's alive," he said.

It all makes sense, thought David. Canary was a beautiful young girl, the same age as Jon. The enemy knew he would fall in love with her. And then they made him believe that Elliot James had killed her, so Jon would kill Elliot. Was Elliot somehow connected to Kathleen Peltz?

"Elliot? Do you know a Dr. Kathleen Peltz?" he spoke into the darkness.

"Yes. I've been a contributor to her AIDS research for years. Why?"

"Are you aware of a virus called X11?"

"No. What is it?"

"My guess is that it is what Jakson wants Kathleen Peltz

to weaponize, and you are somehow a threat to that."

"Why? Because I'm withdrawing my money?"

And there it was, the motive behind it all.

"How much do you donate?"

"The withdrawal of my funds will close the doors on that facility for good. Is that what this is all about?"

"Seems like it."

"But—why send a boy to kill me? No offense, young man."

That was the million-dollar question. Why would an organization powerful enough to gather resources for a dirty bomb not just kill him themselves? Why make a teenager do it?"

Jon's voice sounded stronger as he moved in the dark. "So this was all to stop you from withdrawing your *money*?" He grunted, struggling to sit up. "What is this X11?"

"It's a virus," said David.

He growled from the dark.

"Are you okay?"

"They're trying to speak, but they're weaker now."

"Who?"

"The voices. They're on fire in my head."

"Voices from who?"

"I don't know, just voices."

"And you've been listening to these voices?"

"They saved me from my father. I thought they were helping me—it doesn't matter now. They got what they wanted."

"What do you mean, they got what they wanted?"

"We're all as good as dead. The entire city could be rubble for all we know. Radiation could be leaking down through the cracks as we speak."

Elliot's voice trembled. "A nuclear bomb?"

Could it be? Were they finally successful at setting off a nuclear bomb in Boston?

"No," said David. "That doesn't make sense. If they had the ability to set off a nuke they wouldn't have been playing this cat-and-mouse trip with you. They don't have that kind of power, they can't even kill the one man capable of shutting their lab down. We're going to get out of here. We just need to stay calm and wait for rescuers to come."

CHAPTER FORTY-FOUR

Karen tried Brad's number again, with the same results. The cell network was overloaded. The sterile message asked her to be patient and try again later. She hit cancel and gripped the phone to her chest.

"What if he didn't get on the flight?" said Collins. But his words did not comfort her.

"Can you take me back to the television station?" she said, stoically looking out the window at the police roadblocks and fury of blinking lights beyond. The plane had taken out an entire block of commercial buildings, and it seemed like every emergency vehicle in the state was flooding into Milford to help.

It was the largest news story in recent history—but she wanted to be as far away from it as possible.

"We're penned in, Karen, and headquarters will want us to be involved with the rescue efforts."

"I just can't do this."

"You're safe here in the vehicle, and I'll check on you. Okay?"

Her thoughts fell on David Chance. It was the first she had thought of him since getting the news about Brad. She'd been so caught up in her own loss that she had not considered how his family would be affected by this tragedy. His wife, Sharon, and his kids were sitting at home, waiting for him to return for a dinner he would never eat. Sharon would want to know. She deserved to know. Karen, more than anyone, understood this.

"May I use your satellite phone, Agent Collins?" she said in a flat, automated voice.

"Yeah, sure," he said, fishing it out.

"Thank you."

"I have to go," he said, "but I'll be back to check on you, all right?"

She nodded, then looked at her cell's contact list and punched David's number into the satellite phone. It rang on the other side as Collins climbed out.

Sharon's voice answered. "Hello?"

"Hi, Sharon. This is Karen Knight."

"Wow! Karen. Are you guys at the crash site? It's all over the news. We've been glued to it since it started."

"Yeah. It's pretty bad," she said weakly.

"I imagine you guys are scrambling like crazy. Don't worry about us, we understand, keep him as long as you need to."

"Sharon..." her voice broke off.

"Are you okay, Karen?"

A stillness filled the phone line.

"It's about David," she said, choosing her words carefully. "I thought you would want to here it from someone, who..."

Sharon must have heard the sadness in her slow words and measured tone, because she didn't wait for her to finish. "Oh. No. Please, no," she whimpered.

"I'm so sorry, Sharon."

"Wh- what happened?" Her voice cracked.

"David was in the bank when the plane came down."

The phone became like death in her hand, cold and silent.

"I have no words to express..."

She heard a sniff on the other side as Sharon tried to hold it together.

"If there is anything I can do. Anything."

Sharon's labored breaths broke her heart, like she was hearing her own grief reflecting off a canyon wall.

"Thank you," Sharon said at last. It was short and controlled. She took in a shuddered breath. "I know this must have been hard for you."

"I'm so sorry, Sharon."

"I can't," she said, sniffing.

"I wish there was something I could do—something I could say."

"It's okay. Thank you. I'm sorry. I have to go."

"I understand."

The phone went dead. Karen dropped her hand into her lap and looked out the window. The shell shock was protecting her from the intense pain that waited to stab her. So much had happened. How could she begin to process it? Two hours ago all she could think about was getting to the bottom of this mystery, and now—now it seemed trivial in light of the immeasurable loss.

She lifted the satellite phone and punched Brad's number in. The system was still down, but she found a strange comfort in the message that promised that this was only a temporary problem, and that she would soon be able to connect with the man she loved.

CHAPTER FORTY-FIVE

Cindy Coulter organized the papers on the news desk as she waited apprehensively for the camera light to signal the return from commercial. The teleprompter was cued on the next story, but it would have to wait as the room flurried with the news of another breaking story.

The voice of Karen Knight buzzed in her earbud. It was not the voice of the young, confident woman who had wowed station executives and captured the heart of the greater Boston area only a few short years ago. It sounded tired and beaten. Needless to say, the loss of her husband was weighing heavily on her, as it was everyone at News Channel Seven. They were all grieving over Brad and David—but no one more than Karen. Yet she felt the need to press on, to pretend to be objective and strong. She wasn't fooling anyone, though.

They had heard her crying in the bathroom, and could see the circles under her eyes. Her sorrow was evident in her inability to stay focused—and in the temper that erupted when anyone pointed this out to her. Cindy had never cared for Karen; she was far too overbearing and opinionated. But even she could not help feeling pity for her.

She glanced at the monitor where Karen stood in front of emergency vehicles parked outside of the perimeter of the crash site. It must have been so hard for her, to be so close to where Brad's life had been extinguished, yet her face remained stalwart. Cindy doubted she could have done it, stand there in front of the camera and report on the tragedy that had claimed her husband's life. She honestly didn't understand why the station manager had allowed her to cover the story in the first place. Maybe they felt she could handle it. Maybe, in some strange way, they thought it would help her to heal.

"We have enough to go with the story," said Karen. "We're waiting for them to bring the survivors out."

Jim Coldfield's voice buzzed in Cindy's earpiece. "We're coming back from commercial in ten. Get ready."

Cindy straightened in her chair and looked into the camera.

The cameraman gave the countdown, then pointed.

"Welcome back. I'm Cindy Coulter. When tragedy hit Milford, Massachusetts ten days ago, the ripples of it were felt even here at News Channel Seven. We lost two comrades that day. But from the ashes comes a story of hope. We've just received word of a miraculous turn of events at the crash site of flight 304 where rescue crews had recently given up searching for survivors. We now go live to Karen Knight on the outskirts of the site."

"Thank you, Cindy," said Karen, looking up from her notes. Her plastic face showed no emotion as she ran through the facts that had emerged. "Rescue crews had been working around the clock for seven days when they announced there was no hope anyone else would be found alive in the wreckage left in the wake of the tragedy of flight 304. But at 3:15 this afternoon, construction crews heard a clanking noise coming from deep in the heart of the rubble that once used to be the center of commerce for the city of Milford. I'm told that a few minutes ago three men were recovered from a bank vault underneath the Norfolk County Savings and Loan." Suddenly she paused, and a strange look twisted her features.

What is she doing? thought Cindy as Karen stood motionless. Would she finally break? Would she come unglued on live television? Cindy could sense the tension in the newsroom building around her as everyone—especially those who had gone to bat for Karen to allow her to cover the story—sat frozen with her, wondering if they had made the wrong call.

"Come on Karen," whispered Cindy.

Karen's eyes flicked up to the camera, and there was a quizzical look on her face.

Come on, Karen. You can do this.

Karen continued. "Rescuers are calling it a miracle." There was a noticeable release of tension in the newsroom as she seemed to recover from whatever emotion had taken hold of her. "Rescuers report," she said, with renewed energy, "that the three men are healthy and in good spirits after being entombed ten days beneath the rubble of downtown Milford. They say that fresh air had made it in through a network of tunnels that run under the city center, and that..." Her voice cracked and she stopped again.

"What is she doing?" said one of the techs next to Cindy.

Karen brought her hand to her mouth. It looked like she was crying.

Jim Coldfield's voice went out across the comm network. "Do you need a moment, Karen? You want us to go to commercial and let you regroup?"

Karen stiffened and looked back at the camera, wiping the tears on her cheeks with poise and dignity. "I'm sorry. I'm sorry." She took a breath. "We are being told that the three men could not possibly have survived if not for the fact that food and liquids had been left in the bank vault before the disaster occurred."

Cindy was baffled. Karen now looked elated.

Suddenly a voice bounced off every wall of the studio. "David did that!" it screamed. "That's David's food!"

Cindy turned to see who was shouting. Through the master control window she saw Nerd standing at his station with both bony fists clenched in excitement, his eyes looking as though they might burst from his head. "He's the one! He saved those people!"

From the monitor, a loud male voiced shouted, "Hey! Where are you going?!"

Cindy turned her eyes back to it.

Karen had left her spot and was now being chased by her cameraman, Larry. The camera shifted to the right and attempted to focus on a woman with curly blond hair who had breached the police line and was now being chased by two officers.

The studio with all it's cameras and lights seemed to vanish around Cindy Coulter as she stared at her flat panel monitor, forgetting her job and her role as news anchor of a major network affiliate. Without her knowledge or permission, she had been relegated to the role of viewer, unable to pull her eyes away from the drama unfolding in real time.

Karen twisted back toward the camera. "Are you getting this?"

Larry's southern drawl picked up on the mic. "Does a one-legged duck swim in circles, darlin'?"

The camera tracked the woman as best it could as Karen and Larry reached the perimeter. Suddenly the background sound tripled as the microphone input was switched from Karen's hand-held to the camera's boom mic. Every noise around the camera fought for attention. A police officer screamed, "Stop!" Next to the camera, Karen pleaded to be allowed over the line, and in the distance the woman's voice rose above it all. "DAVID!" she screamed. "DAVID!"

The camera jilted to the left, and a group of men could be seen escorting three dust-covered men with blankets draped over them.

"Please!" screamed Karen. "That's his wife! I know them! Let me through!"

There was flash of yellow, then Karen and Larry were on the move again. Cindy could hardly breath. The camera trained on the three men as the blond woman ran to the man in the middle and wrapped her arms around him. She wiped at his face and kissed him furiously as the group of rescue workers circled around. The camera came in close.

"I can't believe it," said the woman over and over again.

Cindy could now make out David through the dust and the grime, and emotion welled in her own heart. It was true. It was all true. How could it not be? The messages were real.

David hugged his wife, and the crowd hushed.

"I was so scared," whispered his wife.

David pulled back slightly and looked at her. His voice sounded hoarse and dry. "How did you..."

"How did I know to be here at exactly 2:15 at the corner of Westwood and Center?"

The tightening of his face made the crust of dirt crack. "Yeah."

She smiled. "You don't think you're the only one getting messages, do you?"

Books in the David Chance Series
MESSAGES
VOICES

~Authors Note~

Voices is a work of fiction. If you are hearing voices at night, it is probably due to a mental phenomena called hypnagogia, which occurs during threshold consciousness, when the sleeping mind attempts to exert its influence on the waking mind. If you are hearing voices while you are fully awake and walking around, well, that might be another thing altogether.

If you want to read some non-fiction accounts of how God interacts with us, try Miracles: 32 True Stories. My wife and editor, Joanie Hileman, has compiled these accounts of God's miraculous intervention.

If you would like more mind-bending fiction from yours truly, you might try my other novels. UNSEEN and VRIN: ten mortal gods

If you would like to know when my next book is coming out, you can email me at johnhileman@gmail.com and get on my reader friend list or visit my blog: http://mysterynovel-blogspot.com